I0672077

YES YES Y'ALL

BOOK 3

A Novel by

Latif Mercado

YES YES Y'ALL Book 3

Copyright 2015 Latif Mercado

All rights reserved. This book or any portion thereof may not be reproduced or used in any manner whatsoever without the express written permission of the publisher except for the use of brief quotations in a book review.

Printed in the United States of America

First Printing, 2020

ISBN 978-0-9993189-5-9

Cover illustration by June ArcaMay

La' Entertainment

Monroe, NC 28110

www.LatifMercado.com

Dedication

Book Three of Yes Yes Y'all is dedicated to my wife, Angel Louise Mercado. If I could give everyone just one gift, it would be a spouse like mine. God knew what he was doing when he placed her in my path, as he knew, no one would've been able to deal with my craziness.

When I lost my mother, my greatest cheerleader, I didn't know how I would continue to go after my dreams, and just as her name implies, God sent her to me.

Babe, I dedicated this book to you. I love you, and God bless you.

- Latif

Table of Contents

CHAPTER 1

The Cuban's Talent

I lay in bed, staring up at the ceiling, thinking about what happened today. What a bad situation it could've become. The people whom I was now associated with, worked with, hung out with, particularly Sal, and Quenepa in my honest opinion were both a bit nuts.

Sal, I figured out to be a very dangerous person. However, I trusted him, beyond words. I'd trust him not only with my life, but also that of Grams, and even Porky. As far as I knew, this was common, for celebrities to have around them people who would protect you by any means necessary.

Q on the other hand, was different. I've been forcing myself to trust him, psych myself into believing that he truly had my back. Like for instance, the fact that he found the guy who had stolen my song. Not only did he find him, he damn near tortured him, but was that for me, or was it for his own sick pleasure? Hunting someone down, hurting them while they were tied up. Did it made him feel good? Powerful? Tall?

Whereas I could justify Sal's actions, Q's I'd have to write off as just plain ol' nuts!

Unable to sleep, I got up and turned on the lamp beside my bed. I grabbed my jacket off the chair and pulled out the cassette tape I got from the Cuban. I read the label and again shook my head. I stepped over to my box and rewound it to the beginning.

At first, just the thought of this guy doing this to my music was enough for me to want to burn it. But before I did, I really wanted to take a listen, and try and figure out what it was he heard that made him want to do what he did.

The intro began with just a piano solo, and as much as I hate to admit it, it was actually quite beautiful.

I knew it was recorded live, I could tell by slight tempo changes, but for some reason, that made it special.

One of the first things I noticed when I stepped into his apartment was the grand piano that sat in the middle of his living room. Having seen that piano, made it easier for me to visualize the Cuban, sitting there playing my song sort of Liberace-like!

The next thing I heard were bongos, soft at first, and becoming more dominant as it played. I was pretty familiar with both Bongos and Congas, because Grams use to take me to Central Park in the summers where a crowd of people, most of them Puerto Rican would gather and play theirs. Those were great times, and made a huge impact on me growing up.

I knew these were played live too, as I remember seeing The Cuban's Bongos up on the coffee table.

It wasn't long before it sounded as though an entire orchestra had joined in. Maracas, Shakers, Trumpets, and of course the signature Cow Bell. It wasn't until each one entered the track that I remembered spotting them somewhere within his living room, including that gorgeous guitar he had hanging on his wall.

I was seriously trying to hate this shit, looking desperately for imperfections. I caught myself, tapping my foot, and tried to stop it. But it was no use. His shit was incredible, and totally sucked me in, when suddenly I heard what sounded like voices, almost angelic, Oohs and aahs that filled my room.

I closed my eyes and allowed it to pull me in some more, when I realized that those backgrounds were all just one voice, all singing in different keys. And that one voice was none other than, the Cuban.

My hairs stood on ends, and I got up and moved closer to my box to raise the volume.

Suddenly, in came the hook. None of the words were changed. Only the melody and he pronounced his Y's like J's. But it fuckin' worked! He repeated it over and over, each time in a different key. I noticed that the sounds were echoing between speakers and when I closed my eyes, the way he had mixed it sounded as if I was standing directly in front of a live band, with the backgrounds being sung to the far left, the lead just off center.

Every note from every instrument, including all the voices were mixed perfect, and I couldn't help my body from pulsating along to this incredible rhythm he created. This shit wasn't a rap anymore, it was a song, and though my pride would insist that it was corny as fuck, truth of the matter was, it was genius!

He hadn't changed a word, and still I felt sort of unworthy of receiving any type of credit.

I began to understand the concept behind true talent, and what it really was, realizing in fact, that not an ounce of it I possessed.

I even tried to rap on top of the Cuban's music, but it didn't work. In fact, I kept messing up on my original flow, and ending up singing his. It was like he hi-jacked my shit. It didn't belong to me anymore. It was his!

I stood there a bit longer, captivated by what he had created. Half of me wanted to slam my box up against the wall. The other half, wanted to just sing along.

I was able to grab hold of the melody, as if I had been singing it that way all along. I pictured myself on stage, with the Cuban behind me, conducting an entire orchestra. As strange as it truly was, it...

"Hi Rey?" Porky greeted suddenly appearing out of nowhere, and scaring the shit out of me.

"What the hell you doing sneaking up on me like that, yo?" Not meaning to lash out the way I did.

"I'm sorry, Rey!" He cried out, surprised at the way I spoke to him.

"I had to go pee and heard you were up. I wanted to make sure you were okay."

I suddenly understood what was meant by puppy dog

eyes, as his started to flood. I exhaled and placed my hand on Porky's shoulder.

"I'm sorry, man. It's just that you scared me bro." I said then laughed to lighten the moment. It worked, as Porky laughed so loud that I had to put my finger to my lips to quiet him down, and just as he simmered down, I added.

"Yeah, I thought you were a ghost!" Again, Porky laughed out loud, this time covering his mouth with both hands.

"Okay man, did you pee already?" Porky nodded. "Washed your hands?" he nodded again, but also raised his hands toward my face to smell them. I declined.

"That's okay, I believe you! Now go to bed, you have school in the morning."

"Okay Rey!" He said, then threw his arms around my waist and hugged me.

"Good night!" He said on his way out.

"Good night, man." I replied then closed my door. I walked back up to the box, and this time with the volume lowered, I pressed play.

CHAPTER 2

It's Okay

I woke and proceeded with my regular morning routine. Afterwards I stepped out into the kitchen area, and as expected the scene was the same as it was every day, except everyone wore different clothes. Sal sat at the table reading his paper and drinking his Bustelo, while Rosie prepared my breakfast. Grams and Porky had already eaten and were heading out the door.

"Good morning." I said as I entered.

"Good morning Rey!" Porky called out, excited as always to see me.

"Morning, Kid." Sal followed. However Grams and Rosie both gave me dirty looks.

"I'll be back." Grams told Rosie as Porky ran over to me and threw his arms around my waist. I hugged him back, and then knelt down and spoke quietly to him.

"I'm really sorry about last night." I whispered into his ear.

"It's okay Rey."

"Bye Sal, bye Rosie!" He yelled out as his short chubby legs scurried to the door. His thick winter coat and knapsack made him look fatter than he actually was. Sal and Rosie wished him a good day just before he and Grams left the apartment.

"Mr. D, wants you to listen to some new stuff today." Sal said, his eyes not once lifting from his paper.

"New stuff?" I asked, as I took a sip of my coffee.

"He said he doesn't want to wait till shit is dead before starting something new."

"But he told me that I was going to be able to write the next album."

"Don't shoot the messenger." Sal replied. I looked at him, his eyes glued to his paper.

Rosie came over and pushed my eggs on to my plate. I reached down and stroked her calve. She flinched and shook her head.

"What's wrong with you?" I asked, realizing from the moment I walked into the kitchen that her and Grams both had a bit of an attitude.

"You shouldn't have ever yelled at him that way!" She said, pointing the spatula at me as if it were a weapon.

"What are you talking about?" I asked. Sal finally looked up.

"Last night!" She went on. "He just went to check on you, and you yelled at him."

"Oh, so now I get it!"

"Good!" Rosie replied as she continued serving me.

"Look he didn't think it was a big deal, why should anyone else?"

"Not a big deal? He cried for nearly an hour in his room, Rey."

"He did?"

"Yes, we went in there, and he was hysterical."

"Well, I didn't know this."

"His own parents basically threw him away, why wouldn't he think you might do the same!"

"You know I wouldn't do that."

"I know you wouldn't. We all know you wouldn't. But he's just a little boy, who's been through things that many adults haven't been through. Just be patient with him, please."

"What the fuck did you do?" Sal asked.

"Man, I didn't do anything. He barged into my room around 3:00 a.m."

"And what, caught you jerking off?"

"No, I was listening to something and..."

"And you yelled at him!" Rosie reaffirmed. "Can we both just agree on that?" I gave in and nodded.

"Listening to something?" Sal asked.

"The tape I got from the Cuban."

"Okay, and?"

"Nothing, I just had a lot going through my head at that moment, you know, but I apologized, and he seemed cool with it."

"Whatever! Sal replied, waving off to the side. Just hurry up and eat, we gotta get out of here."

CHAPTER 3

I Don't Sing

I sat in the back of the limo while Sal drove to The Funky Junky. I couldn't resist myself and pulled the cassette from my jacket and popped it into the player over my head.

Sal's eyes went from the road to the review mirror.

"That's it?" He asked. I nodded. Sal looked back at the road. I leaned my head on the window and just stared out listening once again.

I don't know why, but each time I found myself searching for flaws and imperfections, anything to make me hate this shit. But even the off notes and time lags that were typical in this type of recording had something that made me like it even more. In fact, it seemed the more I listened to it, the more I liked it.

Musically it made a lot of sense, and I was having trouble digesting the fact that the talent behind it was this little old gay dude from Cuba.

The Cuban's way of recording was in real time, straight onto his Fostex 8-Track. A process many producers wouldn't dare attempt. I know for sure, Red wouldn't.

I wrote it as a Rap, but now I was convinced, I did IT all wrong. *This* was the way this song was supposed to be laid down.

The Cuban was an incredible musician, and each instrument he played as if it were an extension of his very soul.

His arrangements were like that of an orchestra, listening you would never believe that he played each of the instruments himself.

"Not bad." Sal said from the driver's seat, snapping me out of my own deep thought. "You should let Mr. D take a listen."

"He'll never go for it." I replied.

"You never know."

"Mr. D is stuck on Rap, he wouldn't touch it. Besides, I gotta make sure *my* career is solid, before I go and pull someone else in."

"I'm talking about you singing it." Sal replied. I laughed and assured him.

"I don't sing!"

"Have you ever tried?"

"Well, in the shower of course."

"How did you sound?"

I looked up and thought about it for a moment.

"Not bad. But then again, who *doesn't* sound bad in the shower?"

"You're right there. But I still think you should at least let Mr. D, check it out.

I removed the cassette from the player and sat back staring at it as I twirled it between my fingers.

Sal pulled up in front of the Funky Junky to let me out.

CHAPTER 4

It's Business

"King!" Roller Girl yelled out giving me a big hug as I entered.

"What's up?" I asked her as she looped her arm through mine and rolled beside me as I walked.

"Everything," she replied. Hear you're going overseas in the Spring."

"Overseas?"

"Yep, we have most of Asia already on lock. China, Japan, Korea, and India... so far."

I stopped and looked at her. "How long will I be gone?"

"Well, we're trying not to keep you on the road for more than six months."

"Six months?"

"Yeah, that's Asia!"

"I don't know if I could do that?"

"That's crazy! You know how much money you will

make from that tour, not to mention what it will do for your record sales?"

"Do they even know my music there?"

"Doesn't matter, they'll still rap every word without a clue of what they're saying."

"I don't know, my Grandmother's pretty old now, I can't leave her for that long."

Roller Girl looked at me as if she sensed trouble. She was extremely happy about telling me what they were planning, but now seemed devastated that it wasn't something I was interested in, at least not for that long.

"I gotta talk to Mr. D." I said and then began walking down the hall towards his office.

Roller Girl skated beside me trying her best to convince me.

"This tour will take your career to a whole other level, King, beyond what you could ever imagine." I stopped talking, and so she stopped following.

"Come in!" Mr. D yelled out when I knocked, and of course, he was on the phone. He ended his call and walked over to me with his typical friendly greeting which usually consisted of a hug.

"Can I get you something?" He asked as he walked back toward his desk. I followed.

"Roller Girl mentioned something about an overseas tour you're planning."

"Can't tell that girl nothing!" He replied with a laugh. "Well, I wanted to be the one to surprise you. So far we have on lock, China, Japan, Hong Kong, Korea, India, and that was Dave on the phone, he just locked up the Philippines and…"

"…I can't do that!" I interrupted. Mr. D went silent. At first he didn't say anything, and seemed to be analyzing what I just told him. He looked me in the eyes, and they confirmed what I just said.

"Sit down, King." He said, gesturing to the big purple bean bag.

"I really don't want to sit, Mr. D." He looked away and then began pacing his office, looking now toward the floor. It took a while before he finally stopped and looked at me.

"King, you do understand that it's just business right?"

"Yeah, of course," I replied.

"This is the way I do business, whether it's for a soft drink, clothing line, or even, an artist. I invest money, with the expectation, not hope, the expectation of a considerable return!

My deal with you was, I will make you rich and famous, give you a life that people only dream about. Allow you to give back to your grandmother for all she has done. Give you a platform to change the world, help those in need, this is what I said I will give you, and I've so far come through, am I right?"

But now I want something. And what I want is the opportunity to make as much money as I possibly can, without any restrictions whatsoever. I pulled you in while you were not married and had no kids. In the midst of our deal, you went off and took guardianship of a child in need of help. I admired you for that, and even got you help in the form of Rosie, so that you can focus on our deal.

Mr. D, I understand everything you're telling me, and God knows, I appreciate everything you've done, but..."

"Hold up!" He interrupted, silencing me mid-sentence. "I don't want your appreciation, King. That's not what I invested in. Appreciation is nice, but not my objective. I invested in you, plain and simple! We've already capped the U.S., and until we finish the album, I can't squeeze another penny out of it.

"Now, by you not cooperating, well, I have to be honest, it's like stealing from me."

"Come on, Mr. D. stealing?"

"Yes, you're stealing an opportunity that was part of our deal. Now had your record done shit, then okay, I lose, but that's not the case here. The record's doing great, and now you're not allowing me to cash in."

Mr. D walked over to his shelf and turned around to look at me. Immediately I noticed the small glass case where he keeps the human skeleton hand, sitting right beside him, "no one's ever stolen from me and gotten away with it King, no one!"

At that moment, as if it was perfectly timed, Mr. D's phone rang and he picked it up. "D!" He said into the phone. I just stood there until he placed the phone to his chest and said to me.

"Roller Girl will get you all the details, once their ready." He placed the phone back to his ear and then turned and walked over to his window to talk.

Smiling faces popped out of their offices with a good morning. I returned the greetings, just not as enthusiastically as they were used to. It was obvious, that something was wrong.

I made it to the front lounge area where I knew I would find Sal. Sitting there like always, drinking his coffee and reading the paper.

"So how'd it go?" He asked.

"How'd what go?"

"You let him hear the song?"

"Honestly, I forgot all about it."

Sal put down his paper and watched as I plopped down onto the couch across from him.

"What do you mean you forgot?"

Roller Girl entered the room and rolled over to the couch and sat beside me.

"I'm sorry, King. I really thought you'd be excited.

"It's alright. It's not your fault."

"Fuck's going on?" Sal asked, his eyes bouncing between Roller Girl and myself.

"An overseas tour is being scheduled for this Spring!" I said sadly.

"So, what's the problem?" He asked.

"It's an Asia tour. "Roller Girl replied.

"Okay, and?"

"I can't leave them for six months!" I suddenly blurted out, and then started pacing the room.

"But King, this is great news! I mean, you know all the money you'll make?"

"I know, but it's my Grandmother, Sal. I mean, come on bro, she's fuckin' old bro, like how am I gonna just leave her?"

"All I know is you better not let her hear you say that shit." Sal said, shaking his head. "Your Grandmother's going to be fine, they both will."

"Are *you* gonna be here to make sure?" I asked, a bit sarcastically.

"You know Mr. D ain't gonna go for that."

"So then no, they won't both be fine."

"Look. I'll talk to Mr. D myself. I'll tell him to let me pick who's gonna watch out for them."

Staring at the floor, I thought long and hard, before looking back up at Sal.

"She isn't well, man." I said, my voice low and soft.

"What do you mean she isn't well?" he asked.

"I watch her, and I could see shit."

"Like what?"

"She's always forgetting shit."

"Come on, we all forget shit. That just comes with age. The great thing about it though is you now have the means to keep her comfortable. These are her golden years, King, and now she can actually enjoy them."

"What if something happened to her while I was on the

other side of the world, and I couldn't make it back...?" I couldn't even finish my sentence as I suddenly became emotional.

"Did you explain this to Mr. D?" Roller Girl asked.

"I learned something today about Mr. D that I never before realized."

"What's that?" Sal asked.

"That he really doesn't give a fuck about me."

"That's not true." Roller Girl said, shaking her head.

'He doesn't give a fuck about me, you, or you." I said, pointing at each of them.

"I'm his investment. You're hired to assist his investment, and you're hired to protect it."

I got up and started walking back toward the stairs.

"Where are you going?" Sal asked.

"Down to Rehearsal, I have to start getting ready for a tour!"

CHAPTER 5

The Long Goodbye

I stepped out of my room and into the living area where Grams, Rosie, and Porky stood waiting to say goodbye. The sadness on their faces made me want to cancel this whole trip, but I had no choice, and I wanted to get it over with. All I kept saying to myself was, the faster I get on the road, the faster I'll be back.

Porky ran to me full speed nearly knocking me over when he grabbed me. This kid was growing like a weed, and was extremely strong for his age. I kept imagining him being a man by the time I returned, even though it would only be for six months.

"I wish you didn't have to go, Rey."

"I know Pork, me too man. But it's my job. But listen, I told Mr. D, when I get back, I'm taking a break, and we're gonna go spend a couple of weeks in Disney World, wha'cha think about that?"

"All of us?" He said, gesturing to everyone in the room. I looked over at Rosie, and smiled.

"Yeah Pork, all of us!"

"Alright!" he cheered, and again grabbed me from around the waist. I don't know if I was just getting weaker, or was this kid getting stronger?

I wiggled myself out from Porky's hold and looked down at him.

"You know I'm leaving you with a huge responsibility, right?"

Porky looked up at me, and nodded. I lowered my voice a bit more, though I knew Grams and Rosie could hear.

"You're the man of the house now, and you're responsible for two very *very* special people, so you need to take care of them, protect them, you hear me?"

Porky nodded again. I then moved closer to his ear, this time so only he can hear.

"Gram's getting old, and there's gonna be a lot of things she's gonna try and do, that she actually can't. So you pay attention, okay?" Porky glanced over at Grams.

"But she doesn't *look* that old!" Obviously too loud, as Grams looked at me with this face, and Rosie turned to the wall to laugh.

"You can trust me, Rey. I'll take care of them. I promise."

I pulled Porky back into my arms and gave him a squeeze. I could feel his body sort of relax against mine. This was a child that only wanted to be loved, and he knew he had that with me. I adored this kid, as if he was my very own flesh and blood. Half of me cursed his biological parents for being such low life assholes. But my other half wanted to thank them, for allowing him to be a part of my life.

I stood up and watched as the beautiful and sexy Rosie came up to me. Man, am I going to miss her. We still pretended nothing was going on between us, but the only ones we were fooling, were ourselves. Everyone knew what was up, I think we just enjoyed the game, even though we were busted so many times. Staring at each other, smiling, and laughing for reasons only we knew.

I couldn't pass by her without touching her. Everyone caught me at least once, but Porky made a scene out of it when he yelled out, *ooh, Rey touched Rosie's butt!* He embarrassed the both of us pretty bad, but that didn't stop us, didn't even slow us down. The day Grams caught us, Rosie was doing the dishes and I reached out and touched her ass. I swore Grams was gonna smack the shit out of me, but when she didn't, that's when I realized, she knew what was up.

Rosie's room was too close to Grams, and Pork's, so in the middle of the night, she paid the visits, and we'd make passionate love. But when no one was home...We'd fuck our brains out!

We've blessed practically every inch of the house with some form of love making, starting of course with the balcony, that first night. We'd fuck in the living room, laundry room, bathrooms, kitchen, dining room, hallway. Shit, I even fucked her once in the closet when I caught her tip toeing to place something on the top shelf.

Her ass was way too fine to resist, and I knew Grams and Pork were in the living room watching a movie. I jumped in behind her and pulled down her tight jean shorts. That was the first time her and I experienced anal. Yeah yeah I know, kind of tacky, but shit... we had fun!

Sal was probably the first to know what was up, because I had to tell him when Rosie and I did it in the elevator, because we totally forgot about the camera. I gave security a thousand dollars for the tape and thought I was in the clear, until Sal paid him another visit for the copy he made. He even got my thousand dollars back.

Porky stepped back as Rosie approached. She wrapped her arms around my neck and stared me in the eyes. Hers were beginning to tear as well. She tightened her lips and swallowed the huge knot in her throat.

"You're gonna be gone for a long time."

"Yeah, I am."

"So how do we do this?" She asked, as if she was truly looking for the answer.

"We focus on the day that I come home, and we're back in this position."

I knew where Rosie was going with this. She didn't want me to promise anything, because she didn't want me to break that promise, and neither did I. My thoughts were never on women, only on the job that I had in front of me. Whatever happened in between was another story, but it was never planned. We kissed, and then she let go and went straight to her room.

Grams stepped up, and like Porky, she wrapped her arms around me and placed her head on my chest. I locked my hands around her and laid my head on hers. Everyone had my eyes flooded, but it was with Grams when my tears finally broke loose.

"You're living your dream, Mijo. That's all I ever prayed for, and my prayers have been answered. I'm good now!"

"Grams, I want you to take it real easy while I'm gone okay?"

"Oh, I'll be fine, you don't have to worry about me."

"Well that's not gonna happen, you have Rosie here to help you, let her. Also Porky's a big boy now, he can do a lot for himself, and for you, so please... "

"He's still just a baby."

"He's not a baby, he's almost bigger than you! So don't go trying to do extra stuff. If his room gets too messy, and it isn't cleaned the way you like, just leave it. I'll clean it when I get home."

"You don't need to worry about me, Reynaldo."

Grams moved in close, and tapped my lips with a kiss.

"Okay, bags are in the car, you ready?" Sal asked as he entered the apartment.

I nodded and then reached down and grabbed my duffel bag. I waved back to my family, and spotted Rosie peeking out from behind the wall, I could tell she had been crying. I looked at her, smiled, and then left.

CHAPTER 6

Six Months Away

You never truly realize just how big the world is, until you start to travel it yourself. I was pretty sad on my way to JFK, as all I could think about were those I was leaving behind. It felt wrong, maybe even selfish. After all Grams had done for me over the years, what makes me deserving of traveling the world while she stays cooped up in an apartment for half a year?

And what about Porky, after everything he's been through? His own parents, once realizing they could no longer abuse him, threw him away like a piece of trash. Thank God it was to me, and not someone who would've picked up where his parents left off. The thought alone was terrifying.

I hadn't even left New York, and was already missing Rosie. Even with her I felt a tinge of selfishness, as our relationship so far, has been about nothing but sex. No, she never complained. In fact, many times she had initiated. Could Rosie be that one that I can chill with for the rest of my life? I think so! The question is though... Does she feel the same?

Shit, in the year that she's lived with us, I don't even recall ever seeing her outside, unless it was on the balcony. And it was at that very moment I made up my mind about Rosie.

I had never been on a plane so this was all pretty exciting. It was nothing like the usual hustle and bustle that I was accustomed to from movies and television, and though I could clearly see the planes landing and taking off through the never-ending gates, the back road we followed along, was pretty dreary and desolate.

Sal slowed down as a part of the gate slid open and we pulled in. He parked beside a line of other luxury vehicles, and then we got out.

A man in a suit approached us and shook both our hands. I was too engulfed in the scene to ask any questions, and just followed when he waved us to do so.

We wound up inside the airport as the man continued escorting us to the security check point, where with a flash of his credentials he was able to bypass the long lined that zigzagged along the velvet ropes.

Once past security, we were brought through a huge double door where beside it hung a sign that clearly read, *Authorized Personnel Only.*

We found ourselves inside an airplane hanger, and in the far distance I could see a small crowd of people gathered around this cool looking private jet. It didn't take long before I realized that it was my crew, who then started to applaud as I approached. We greeted one another with hugs, kisses, and High Fives. The reunion was as if we hadn't seen each other in ages, though we spent six hours together just yesterday.

Our bags were taken and placed in the space beneath the aircraft. My crew boarded first, as the pilot and co-pilot came up and introduced themselves. Super cool guys, who really helped put me at ease for this flight.

Once on board, the Pilot welcomed us all and ran over his schedule, so that we would be familiar with the routing. When no one had any questions, he wished us an enjoyable flight, and then headed for the cockpit.

This plane was like a luxury apartment with wings, and Sal and I sat facing one another, with a small table between us.

"So I have to look at you for the next twenty-something hours?" Sal then reached down to the side of his seat and did something that allowed his chair to turn all the way around.

"Come on man, I was just playing!" I said to Sal, who replied with his middle finger.

I looked to my left, and there was Vanessa.

"Wadup Homie?" I said, reaching across the aisle until she took my hand and squeezed it.

"Sup?" she replied back.

"Excited?"

Vanessa nodded. I looked behind her, and there was Quenepa, he, on the other hand seemed a bit tensed.

"You alright, Q?" I asked, Vee followed my eyes.

"I don't know about this."

"Stop being such a pussy?" Vee mocked.

"I bet you wish I was a pussy!" He shot back.

The excited ruckus that we were creating came suddenly to a halt, the moment the plane began rolling.

The flight attendant stepped up and went over the safety procedures. To me however, none of that shit made any sense, because if this plane ever did go down, we'd be done!

None of us had ever experienced anything like this, and I could see everyone brace themselves, their heads pushed back hard against the headrest.

Sal seemed to be the only one not paying it any mind as he flipped through his newspaper, laid back and relaxed as usual.

I glanced out my window and watched as the ground swooshed by. I grabbed hold of my arm rest and pushed my head back even harder. I couldn't watch any longer, and shut tight my eyes as I felt the front of the plane begin to lift. I didn't have to look, I could feel how fast this thing was going, and what came to mind was a story I had once read where they said the two most dangerous times to fly were upon take off, and landing.

Finally, the back wheels left the ground. My heart started to slow as the plane quickly lifted into the air. My knuckles began to throb as I released the hard grip around the armrest. I turned my head to the right and looked out as the world below started to shrink, when suddenly the plane made a quick right. My heart once again sank as my window was now directly beneath me. I held on for dear life, wondering when we would finally straighten back up, as the plane did a complete U-Turn.

"What the fuck was that all about?" I said out loud. Sal shook his head, and laughed.

After completing its turn, and fighting through some severe turbulence. The plane finally chilled out, and I watched as we broke through the clouds. Everyone applauded.

"You alright man?" I asked Q, but he didn't answer. His head seemed frozen against the head rest and all that moved was his eyes.

"That sonofabitch better not throw up in here!" Vee said, her face more serious than I've seen. I shook my head and assured her that he was fine.

"Yo man, if you feel like you're 'bout to be sick, the bathroom's right there!" I said pointing right behind him, and at that very moment, vomit shot from his mouth, like a scene from the exorcist, slamming hard against the back of Vee's seat, a bit of it even getting in her hair!

CHAPTER 7

A Drive through the Jungle

Except from the extremely long flights, traveling overseas wasn't that bad. However, if you're leaving behind loved ones, it's a bit tormenting, as all I worried about was Gram's health, Porky's safety, and whether or not Rosie would be there when I got back.

For the single person, this could be the experience of a lifetime, and if you kept it clean and focused on what you were on tour to do, you can return to the states financially satisfied.

Q and I had become pretty close over the last several months, but there were some instances where I had to try and keep my distance. Unlike me, Quenepa had no one back in the states waiting for him. No girls, children, or parents. In fact, I believe that we were probably the only people on earth that cared anything about him.

Q, at times could be quite destructive to himself. The things he did I found were just plain crazy, if not plain ol' stupid. From the girls he messed with, to the weirdest people you ever saw just hanging out in his room till all hours, getting high. These were folks he didn't even know, and each one possessed their very own creepiness.

We rehearsed every morning around 6:00 am, while the tech guys would set up.

Princess always seemed more stressed than usual when he was on the road. I honestly felt like this was becoming way too much for him, either that, or he seriously just needed some dick!

Though Princess was seventy years old, he was still expected to function as he did during his prime. And I have to admit, that he did!

We'd gone through the routine so many times, that I couldn't help but zone out from time to time. I just couldn't stop thinking about Grams, Porky, and of course, Rosie. But the moment Princess would tell us to stop, I would immediately snap out of it, unable to recall anything we had just done, as if my body was on some kind of auto-pilot. But he never said anything, so as far as I was concerned, I ain't fuck up!

Vee was having a ball. I never realized how much she liked Asian girls. Every night she had a different one in her room, and unlike the girls Q was hooking up with, V's girls were all fine. The girls she brought back I would never expect to be lesbians. Shit, I wouldn't doubt it if she actually turned a few out.

I've seen Vee, in action, and I have to admit, she has some serious game, way more than I could ever dream of having. Her confidence was uncanny, considering that she didn't even have a dick. Or did she?

It seemed like no matter who she set her sights, on regardless of who they were, they would end up going back to her room. Whatever it was they did, she kept it private. Even with me, and I had a lot of respect for that.

Sal watched all of us, and knew what we were all up to, but the only one whose room he always barged into was Q's. But he had to, Q thought with the wrong head, and many times that placed him, as well as our tour in danger.

The rest of the crew was having a ball. They usually hung out together doing things like sightseeing, guided tours, exotic restaurants, and buying unusual souvenirs that they would have shipped home.

Three months had already passed, and I was counting down the days. I tried calling home as much as possible, though the time differences made it hard.

Our last stop was the Philippines. The people there were wonderful, as they were most places we went to. The only difference here was that the police officers that were assigned to protect us seemed strange. The uniforms they wore fit more like costumes, as if they didn't belong, and I wondered if they were just regular civilians hired to look over us?

Their faces looked hard, and their hands dirty and worn. Their dark eyes were sunken, and they just weren't as groomed as I was used to seeing among law enforcement. Had I been in some type of trouble, I don't know if these would be the guys I would trust to help us. There was something really off about them, and I wasn't sure if Sal had picked up on any of it.

We had three days left before heading home, and they couldn't come any faster. I was really uncomfortable, and I couldn't sleep. Something was up, and it was like I was waiting for something to go down.

I tried to explain to Sal what I was feeling, and all he said was relax, that I was just paranoid, and stressed from all the traveling.

One of the things I hated the most was how we traveled, a caravan of jeeps through the dark thick jungles of the Philippines. I had heard so many stories about entertainers being robbed, kidnapped, and even killed in places like this, that I swore we were next.

There was this one time, on our way back from one of the concerts. We were driving through the dark wet jungle when the head driver stopped. We all wondered what was up, and though he spoke no English, he did give us the universal gesture that he had to take a piss.

I looked back at the other two jeeps that had stopped behind us, each one carrying another batch from our crew. The guide disappeared into the brush, and I was becoming nervous, as he was taking a pretty long time.

I kept visualizing an army of soldiers, coming out of the bushes spraying us down with machinegun bullets.

I was becoming a panicky mess, and everyone was beginning to notice. I crouched low in my seat, positioning my back in the direction from where I thought the bullets would come, when suddenly Q stood up in the jeep behind us and started yelling in the direction of where the guide disappeared. Everyone kept trying shush him, but that was Q, and there was no telling him shit.

When there was no answer, Q did the unexpected... He went off into the bushes after him!

"Hey, get the fuck back here!" Sal yelled out, but it was too late, he was gone.

"This fucking dude!" I said to myself, though loud enough for all to hear. The set up that I had been anticipating all along was finally coming to a head, and just as others have testified in the past, yes my entire life flashed before my eyes!

We haven't been picking up any cash during the entire tour. Everything was wired back to the Funky Junky, with a small expense account that only Sal and a couple of the road managers had access to. I thought that was a great idea at first, but now I realized we had nothing to negotiate our lives with, and if we were taken out, Mr. D wouldn't just get to keep it all. He'll live to enjoy it.

Everyone suddenly started yelling for Q, the situation so intense it felt like a movie. Princess began crying hysterical, and all I could do was drop down to the floor of the jeep, and pray.

The chaos around me suddenly died down, as if something was happening. I lifted my head up just enough to look out, when suddenly the silence deadened even more. I looked back at the other two jeeps and watched as the guides lifted their machine guns, slow and steady, as if something was about to go down, we could all hear what sounded like snapping branches. I nearly passed out when the guides placed their guns against their shoulders and took aim.

I dropped back to the floor of the jeep, closed my eyes,

and covered my ears. Suddenly I felt a tap on my shoulder. It was Sal, waving me to get up, and when I did I saw Q and the Guide emerging from the bushes, the two of them laughing like old buddies. It was a strange sight!

As we drove back to the hotel, I just stared out at the passing trees. This experience was like nothing else, and I swore something was supposed to go down. I glanced over at Sal, who surprisingly was doing the same thing as me, as if he too was anticipating the same shit!

CHAPTER 8

Fucking Genius

Well, the tour was over, and finally, we were on our way home. I wasn't looking forward to another long-ass trip. But what waited for me at the other end had me in the best of moods, damn, did I miss my family! and Rosie? Man, I couldn't wait to see Rosie! In fact, I had made plans to take her out when I got home. Dinner, a movie, and then hopefully, a hotel, because this time, there'll be no keeping it quiet.

When the plane leveled off and the flight attendant announced that it was now safe to move around the cabin, I got up and reached into my overhead bin for a small gift bag. Japan was so gracious and generous that I was showered with gifts upon arrival, so many in fact that I had to ship all the big ones home ahead of time. But there was one that I was really excited to have gotten, and that was the new Sony Walkman.

One of the promoters let me listen to my song on his, and I swear it sounded as if my voice was coming from the heavens. The Walkman hadn't yet reached the U.S., and though you'd see a few people in Japan walk around with it, it was still a bit of a luxury. They even threw in a box of their most popular batteries. What good is a gift if you can't use it right away, huh?

I removed the Walkman from the box and carefully read the instructions before trying it out. After a few attempts, I realized that the radio wouldn't work from here, so I reached back into the bin and pulled out the Cuban's cassette.

I sat back down, and popped it into the player. I put on the headphones and pressed play.

My hairs stood on ends upon the opening Piano solo. The sound was even more vibrant and I could hear notes I hadn't heard before. Looking around the plane I would swear that everyone could hear what I was hearing, and a couple of times I removed the headphones just to make sure. I then stopped the tape and rewound it back to the beginning so that I could just sit back comfortably, stare out the window and enjoy the ride in all capacities.

Subconsciously, I continued searching for flaws, something, anything to convince me that he really wasn't all that. But still, I found nothing.

Everything through the Walkman sounded richer and fuller. I'm even hearing instruments that I never noticed before. Flutes and tambourines, violins and this very subtle second bassline that seemed to pop out of nowhere!

Each time the song ended, which was pretty lengthy at just over five minutes, I quickly stopped it, and rewound the tape. I had changed batteries twice already. I just couldn't stop listening to this song.

There was even a moment that my eyes began flooding, as this music was touching me in a way that I had never ever experienced. I pressed my forehead up against the window when suddenly I felt someone's hand on my shoulder. I jumped and yanked the earphones from my head... It was, Vanessa, on one knee beside my seat.

Fuck you listening to?" She asked. I stopped the tape and just shook my head. "What does that mean?"

"Nothing, just trying out this new Walkman they gave me."

"I wasn't crying." Vee tilted her head, and sucked her teeth. We stared at each other for a moment, until finally, I rewound the tape and handed her the headphones.

Once she put them on, and nodded that she was ready, I pressed play. The beautiful intro had already grabbed her, as she closed her eyes and began swaying along with it, when suddenly the hook kicked in. Vee looked up at me and opened her mouth in awe!

She turned around and sat on the floor, her back up against my chair. I could hear a bit of the music little leaking from the headphones, so I knew what part she was up to.

When the song ended, I pressed stop. Vee removed the headphones and then turned back to me.

"That's the song?" She asked, referring to the many times we talked about it. I nodded.

"But I don't get it. How? Who?" she asked, seeming very confused.

"He was the Maitre d' of the restaurant I worked at."

"Where you worked for one day?"

"More like one hour, but yeah, that's the one. You see, when I took off, I left everything in the locker. I was kind of scared to go back there, those people were too weird. Anyway, my notebook was one of the things I left behind."

"So I don't get it, the Maitre d' took your song?"

"Took it, and turned it into this." I said holding up the Walkman where the tape was still in.

He's this older gay Cuban guy, seems like he was a pretty big deal back in the day. He's got all these old black and white photos hung up all over his apartment. Instruments everywhere, including this big ass piano that I can't figure out how he got in there. I mean, he lives in a small apartment on the 6th floor.

"So how'd you find him?"

"I didn't... Q did!"

"Q?"

I nodded, then glanced back at Q who was fast asleep. I leaned in toward Vee and whispered. "He's fucking nuts, Vee."

"You ain't telling me anything I don't already know." She assured me.

"He called me one morning to meet him at this address. Sal drove me."

"You're surrounded by nuts, you know that right?" I nodded.

"So we get upstairs and Q answers the door with this

face, like a toddler who just took a shit in the toilet for the first time, and the moment I stepped into that apartment, I knew something was seriously wrong." Vanessa just looked at me, listening to the story.

"Inside was this old guy, white hair, bald spot, everything. He's tied to a chair and gagged. He was in his boxers, and a white tank top, like he was yanked from his bed. His face was fucked up, blood everywhere. His left ear, swollen, and the hair on that side matted in blood." Vanessa just stared as I continued telling her what happened, and when she saw my eyes begin to water, hers did too.

I told her the whole story, and she grabbed me and hugged me. She looked back at Q, and as usual, her face distorted.

"I don't trust him, Rey. Never did." I nodded.

"You can't say anything to anyone." I told her.

"Come on, you know me better than that." And she was right. I could trust Vee with anything, any secret, and just the same, she could trust me.

"You might want to talk to Mr. D, about getting rid of him." I nodded in agreement, and when I looked back over at Q, noticed he was now awake and staring right at us. But the plane was way too loud, and we were talking way too low for anyone to hear us. Vee followed my eyes and saw what I saw.

"So what do you think?" I asked, quickly changing the subject.

"About what?"

"About the song!"

"I love it. The guy's incredible! How come you never told me about him before?"

"Because I knew I had to tell you how I found him, and I didn't know how'd you react."

Vanessa squeezed my hand and smiled. Then turned around and headed back to her seat.

I glanced back up at Q, and he was still staring at me, his face totally expressionless. I smile, and a nodded, he did nothing.

I put back on my headphones, sat back, and rewound the tape.

CHAPTER 9

Welcome Home

"Surprise!" they all yelled as Sal and I entered the apartment. It was about 8:00 p.m. when we finally made it home, and though I was exhausted, seeing my family gave me a second wind.

It was just the family. Grams, Rosie, and Porky, who was holding a cake with one candle on it that said, Welcome Home. I looked at Sal and he smiled and patted me on the back. I greeted everyone with hugs and kisses, Sal received a similar welcome. He was going to leave, figuring this was family time, but we all insisted he stay and have dinner with us. As far as any of us knew, Sal had no family to go home to, we were pretty much it. He agreed, and stayed for dinner.

We made small talk until we were seated and ready to eat. Grams and Rosie put out the food, and then sat down with us. I noticed how Sal looked at Rosie when she did this. As far as he was concerned, she was just an employee, and this sort of behavior wasn't normal.

I watched as Rosie's eyes shifted up at Sal's then back

down to her plate. It was no secret that Rosie and I were hooking up, and I wouldn't doubt if that was the plan all along, so as to keep my ass in check when I'm not on the road. But to have her sitting here with us, and eating might've been outside of the job description.

Sal was an employee as well, but *his* position gave him a different kind of access to me and my family.

"So how was the trip home?" Grams began as she passed the bowl of arroz con gandules to Sal, whose eyebrows arched upwards, as the aroma reached his nose.

Just like he did with our coffee, Sal was now getting hooked on our food, and not just ours, he also talked about trying out different Spanish restaurants around the city. Though the funny part was when he told us which one was his favorite, it wasn't any actual restaurant, but rather a Cuchifrito joint in the Bronx.

"Long!" was my reply to Gram's question about our trip back.

"What kind of plane did you fly in, Rey?" Porky asked as enthusiastic as ever to know. I looked around at everyone, and sort of smiled, as I had no idea. But Sal came to the rescue.

"It was a Gulfstream Four." Sal jumped in, his mouth filled with food, thank God Grams didn't notice as she would certainly had said something.

"Known also as a G4, the four spelled out in Roman Numerals of course."

"So that would be an *I* and a *V!*" Porky said, showing off a bit.

"That's right." Sal confirmed proudly. I looked at Porky and smiled.

"It's a Twin Jet aircraft? Sal continued, "A derivative version of the G3. The plane's wings were actually redesigned to help reduce drag."

"Probably, so that they could fly longer without having to refuel," Porky added.

"...And to go faster!" Sal concluded.

"Where'd you learn all this?" I asked Porky.

"School," he replied.

"School? Since when do they teach about airplanes?"

"They don't exactly teach us about airplanes, but we go to the school library once in a while, and I just read all kinds of things."

"You might have a little genius on your hands, Rey." Rosie said, sipping her wine. Sal's eyes again dashed in her direction. This time it might've been because she called me Rey.

"Oh, the teachers are always telling me how smart he is." Grams bragged.

"Who, this guy?" I said, pointing across the table and laughing.

"Yeah, me!" Porky yelled back also laughing.

"What about you, Grams. How you been?" I noticed she didn't look up from her plate, as she just nodded.

"I'm fine." She said, and then took a sip of her wine. I

looked at Rosie whose face suddenly changed as she looked to her left where Grams sat.

"What's going on?" I asked. But she remained silent. Sal had just finished his meal, and wiped his mouth with his napkin and got up.

"Ladies, thank you for this incredible Welcome Home dinner."

"But you didn't have desert." Grams said. But Sal just placed his hand over his belly and shook his head.

"I will literally explode!"

"It's Flan! With coconut, the way you like!" Sal's face suddenly changed and he looked at me. I was cracking up.

"Grams would make a great drug dealer!" She waved me off, then flung her eyes toward Porky, to watch what I say. I said no more, but continued to laugh.

"Can I get it to go?" Sal asked. Grams rushed into the kitchen and came back out with an entire dish of Flan cover in aluminum foil.

"Whoa, this is a lot!" Sal said, holding the dish with both hands.

"Hey, what about us?" I protested.

"We made two of them!" Grams confirmed.

I walked Sal to the door and let him out. As he stood out in the hallway he turned and looked at me.

"If you need anything at all, you call me, okay?" I don't care what time it is." I thanked him, and reached out to shake his hand, but they were full, and so we laughed.

Rosie got up and cut a piece of Flan for her and Porky.

"Wanna go eat on the balcony?" She asked Porky, he smiled and nodded.

"You coming, Rey?" Porky asked.

"Not now, Buddy, I wanna talk to Grams for a bit."

Porky smiled, turned and headed out on the balcony with Rosie. Once they slid the door closed I turned and looked at my Grandmother who was bringing dishes into the kitchen.

"So, what's up?" I asked, helping her clean up.

"It's no big deal, Mijo, you just got home. Let's enjoy the rest of the night."

"I'm home, so believe me, I'm enjoying the night, but now I need to know what's going on?"

I watched her stop at the sink, and with both hands on its edge she looked up as if to say a quick prayer before continuing.

"I was diagnosed with the beginning stages of Alzheimer's."

I looked toward her for a long moment, neither of us saying another word.

"Isn't that when you started forgetting things?" Grams nodded, and then looked at me.

"So what, I'll forget where I put my keys every now and then." She said and then turned on the faucet.

That was about all I knew about the disease, and to be quite honest, I didn't think it was that big of a deal. Cancer was what I was always afraid of, and of course AIDS, though grams contracting that one was extremely slim.

I got up and walked over to my grandmother. She turned around and held me. I felt her tensed body suddenly relax, as we swayed slowly from side to side.

"You're the most important person in my life right." I whispered. But then I can feel her head moving on my chest.

"But I can't be." She whispered back. She pulled back, and looked up at me, "you have Victor now, and he needs you."

"He also has parents, who can at any moment..."

Grams didn't want to hear it, and quickly placed her finger over my lips.

"You don't ever allow that to happen!" She demanded.

"But..."

"No buts!" He needs you. More than he needs anyone on this earth, and believe it or not. You need him too. Remember...No buts!

I looked down at my Grandmother, who stood there, staring up at me, waiting for my response. And so I nodded.

"Victor is more related to you than anyone else in his life. Blood relatives we don't get to choose, but Victor was a choice, and he loves you. He loves you more than anyone else in this world.

"I don't know about all that." I replied.

"Oh, but I do. I see it in his eyes. He looks at you, the way you've always looked at me.

"You can't compare..." I started to say.

"Oh, but I can!" She interrupted. I'm not your mommy, but I chose to take care of you, and how do you feel about me?

"You're my world!" I replied. Grams looked at me, smiled and said.

"And you're his!

CHAPTER 10

Visits in the Night

I lay in bed, staring up at my ceiling, my mind scattered in thought. So many things, bouncing around, that I was unable to file them in any type logical order. From the tour I just came off of, to all the new business that lay ahead. Then there was the news about my Grandmother, the responsibility I now realized I had for Porky, and this incredibly selfish need I suddenly had for Rosie.

I'm back in the studio first thing tomorrow morning, this time, to begin working on an entire album, with new videos, and a major tour.

The business of music is so much easier to understand when you're actually doing it, and the science behind it all is truly remarkable.

The industry works like a machine, and every part plays a specific role important to the final outcome.

Fame and fortune of an artist is nothing more than a fabricated incentive created to keep the artists pushing with all he or she has. Had those incentives not been there, the desire to keep going would've been short lived.

True success of an artist is practically nonexistent, as success should have more to do with happiness than it does with finance! Many sacrifice that happiness early on in their careers, not realizing the importance it would play later on down the line.

The Funky Junky and Solar Records were the true partners in my deal. I was just the vehicle they used, and the moment I break down, trust me, a newer model would be rolled in to take my place.

Yeah, they were making me millions, but I was making them Billions!

I began doing the one thing many record companies feared most when it came to their artists. I began to think! I started to understand the value I held. But I also understood that that value had a clock attached, and that it was ticking, and ticking fast.

I knew that if there were any moves I wanted to make, I had to make them soon.

The game was a dangerous one, and even a hint that I would contemplate leaving could cost me in every conceivable way.

I've also been thinking a lot about Sal. I've grown to really care for this guy, but I also couldn't help but wonder whether that too was a part of the entire scheme. Our relationship had grown to where I trusted him with everything, and felt like I could tell him shit that I could never tell anyone else, except of course my idea of possibly abandoning ship.

Sal is indeed a professional, and I know that he wasn't simply assigned to watch over me. He was fuckin' planted!

I knew this. He was one of the last people I saw before bed, and one of the first I would see every single morning. Grams adored him, and Porky asked to call him Uncle Sal, and if the affection Sal returned to any of us was ever other than true... then that man deserved a fucking Oscar!

I was told that he was here to protect me, but realized early on, that the only thing truly being protected was Mr. D's investment, and if that's the case. What would happen if his investment no longer produced, or even worst... Quit?

Sal wasn't just cool, he was James Bond cool. But no matter how cool I thought he was, I also felt like something was kind of off. Sal was a crazy mother fucker, and I knew that one day, all would be revealed. And how terrifying that thought was.

We had accomplished quite a bit in just under two years, and now we were about to do it again. Tomorrow I would speak to Mr. D. Tell him I wanna write and record my own shit. I didn't see the big deal, I thought my stuff was good, and I felt as though my fans knew me, understood me, and that they will feel and understand me even more if I can give them just a little bit more of me, through *My* music!

I heard my door open and my eyes dashed to it. The moonlight illuminated my room enough that I was able to see Rosie stick her head in. I got up on my elbows and watched as she entered. She stood by the door and smiled at me. Her perfect teeth seemed to glow. Her long black hair was pulled into a tight ponytail, as she locked the door behind her and stepped to the foot of my bed in a little King T-shirt that had my picture on it.

I smiled at her. My God this girl was so beautiful that my body immediately began to react. I went to say something, but she threw her finger up to her lips, silencing me.

Her arms crossed her body as she grabbed the bottom of her T-shirts and pulled it up over her head.

Rosie then lifted the blanket and slid up under the cover. I watched as the mound of her body slowly crept upward. I could feel her hands climb my legs until her hands made their way into my waistband.

I tried to touch her, but she pushed my hand away, and so then I crossed them behind my head and closed my eyes.

In one swift motion, I disappeared down her throat. I heard a slight gag, but soon afterwards, she had it back under control. The visual alone, of her moving up and down was enough to make me wanna erupt, and she knew this.

Her timing was impeccable, and pulled out just in time. Rosie slid up my body, until her head emerged from under the covers.

"Peekaboo!" She said, and at that moment, we both lost it!

We spent some time trying to control our laughter, shushing each other which only made it worst.

Finally, we calmed down and stared deep into each other's eyes.

Rosie placed herself directly upon my shaft. I can feel her wetness, as it wrapped itself around me. She then began to slide, up and down. I couldn't tell which one of us was more wet, But together we made one hell of a ride.

Rosie pushed herself up onto her hands. I glanced down at the beauty between us, the moonlight hitting everything just right.

I watched as her upper body remained still, and her hips went into overdrive. She worked me like I have never before experienced. Her precision was incredible. As if we'd been making love for years. Her movements stroked every nerve in my body. She knew just how far up to slide, and how far down, using just her back and hips.

She applied just the right amount of pressure. Enough to make me want to explode, but not enough to actually make it happen... Yet!

She looked at me as if to say, I *run this shit,* and that she did, and God knows, I was loving every minute of it. I grabbed hold of the pillow and squeezed it tight against the sides of my head.

When I looked up, she was staring down at me, her smile bringing her sexiness to a whole other level. I bit down on my lips, trying hard to muffle my own moans. Though Rosie was enjoying every minute of it, and didn't seem to care if anyone heard us.

I couldn't believe how I was feeling, and the fact being, I still wasn't even inside her. I caught myself begging, but she had her own agenda, and was sticking to it. She had this shit down to a science and it was driving me fucking insane.

By now I knew I was being loud, but it didn't matter. I didn't give a fuck, that's how good this shit felt. Together we flowed in perfect sync. When suddenly she raised her hips and dropped herself down onto me. My dick plunged deep, and I erupted like a fucking volcano!

I held her down tight, as my never-ending spew filled her to capacity. She tightened up and together our bodies vibrated uncontrollably.

If I wasn't already madly in love with this girl … I sure as hell was now!

When our bodies finally simmered down, Rosie rolled off, and lay down beside me. The two of us, breathing heavily, stared up at the spinning fan, when suddenly I felt her hand reach over and touch mine, and so I took it, and there, the two of us stayed for the rest of the night.

CHAPTER 11

Suddenly Strange

"Come in!" Mr. D yelled out. I turned and watch Roller Girl skate backwards away from me waving goodbye.

I entered his office just as he was hanging up the phone.

"King, what's up buddy?" He said happy as hell to see me as he shook my hand guiding me the rest of the way in.

"Sit down!" He said, gesturing to the huge purple beanbag. Instead I walked over to his juice bar and sat on one of the stools, the only almost normal chair in his office beside his own.

"Can I get you something?" He asked.

"Orange Juice, please." Mr. D nodded and turned to the refrigerator and pulled out a pitcher of the freshly squeezed juice, and poured me a tall one.

"So, tell me, how'd you like Asia?"

"Besides the trip out there, it was actually pretty nice, and the people were great."

"Yes, very gracious people. I bet you came home with a

few gifts too?"

"Oh yeah, they sent me home with all kinds of shit."

"Well, I got some good news it looks like the album is heading toward platinum, and each of the four singles we picked, will be following right behind."

"Are you serious?" I asked in total shock!

"Yes, and I'll let you know as soon as it's final."

"Oh man, this is great, I said grabbing Mr. D in my arms and practically picking him off the floor. "I'm sorry" I said, embarrassed.

"It's okay." He replied, straightening himself out, "but do me a favor King, and let's not mention this to anyone until its official, okay?

"Oh wow!" I said, not sure if I could hold this in.

'It's just that I'm a bit superstitious, if you know what I mean." He told me. So I agreed with a nod, but I already knew three people who were gonna find out the moment I got home.

"Now, the real reason why I wanted to speak to you," he began, making his way over to his juice bar.

"I wanna start working on your next album," he said with a smile.

"You do?" I asked.

"Uh huh!"

"I don't get it, why so soon!"

"Well, it really isn't if you think about it. By the time we pick new songs, record them, and then create a show around it, this last album should be on its way out. Last thing we wanna do is wait for it to be completely dead before we release the next. How they say it? *Strike while the irons still hot?* So, what do you think? Mr. D asked before taking a shot of his Wheat Grass. He gestured if I wanted any, and of course I shook my head.

"So does that mean I get to write the second?" I asked, swearing that he'd be cool with it, but to my surprise...

"Write?" he sked, as if this was some a new topic we never discussed.

"Yeah, we spoke about it and you were cool."

"Well, to be honest, I don't remember, but even if I did, why would I do that?

I looked at Mr. D like he was crazy.

"Well, I figured since the first albums doing so well, why not?"

"That's not how business is done, King." He said, making himself some other supposedly healthy concoction.

"When something's working, we don't go and change it!" He said, not even looking at me.

At this point all I was hearing was some echoey voice, telling me a bunch of shit I didn't want to hear.

"If we want to repeat the success, then it's imperative that we repeat the process, which means, same artist, same producers, same marketing, and especially, the same writers!" After which he took another shot of that healthy shit.

"Man, I really thought I was gonna get a shot at writing the next album. I'm telling you Mr. D, I think I can spit out some serious shit, if you just give me a chance."

"King, I can't do it. I can't invest in speculation!

"I wasn't speculating, I was just being modest."

"I can't invest in modesty either. I need a sure thing, and the writers that worked on the last album, proved what they can do."

"But Mr. D…"

"That's it, King! End of discussion!" Mr. D took his glass around to the sink, washed and put it away.

"Now what if I don't like any of the songs?"

Mr. D stopped in his tracks and remained silent, staring at the wall in front of him. Shit became uncomfortably silent, and I watched as he turned and walked toward me. I had no idea what this mother fucker was up to, so I just braced myself.

With his face, less than a foot from mine, Mr. D placed his hand on my shoulder, and spoke in a calm yet commanding tone.

"Have I ever lead you wrong, King?" I waited a moment before answering.

"No, of course not."

"Have I done all I could for the comfort of you and your family?"

"You have, and I'm…"

Mr. D. threw up his hand and stopped me from interrupting him.

"I gave you a beautiful place to live, didn't I?" I nodded.

"All the luxury toys your heart desires? again, I nodded. Twenty-four hour security, your own body guard, a limousine, driver, private jet." Still, all I could do was nod.

"Your refrigerator, always stocked with the best of the best, shit, I even gave you a live in housekeeper that you're now fucking, and this is how you say thank you?"

That last one was embarrassing, and so bad I wanted to tell him that Rosie was more than just someone I was fucking, but that's a whole other issue.

Mr. D became louder. I've never seen him like this. I stepped back, as his words were now creating a bit of a mist between us.

He turned around and rushed to his desk and wiped everything off of it and on to the floor. It was loud and I waited for people to come rushing in to calm him down, but no one did!

By now he was yelling, turning into this person that I've never seen before.

"You ungrateful sonofabitch!" he growled, as if he was possessed by the devil himself, and picked up the oversized purple beanbag tossing it clear across the room, knocking over boxes of CDs he had stacked nicely to the side.

"Mr. D, come on man, it really ain't that big of a deal." I said, hoping to console him, but instead those words seemed to enrage him, as he rushed over and ripped from the wall his trophied Slugger, his absolute prize procession, autographed by the legendary Babe Ruth. That bat meant the world to Mr. D, proved by the many times I had to hear the same fucking story over and over of how he got it.

"Oh shit." I said to myself, as I began to back up, figuring I was his intended target, but instead he swung the bat straight through one of the many display cases he had standing around the office. I ducked as glass and wood flew everywhere, one eye on the door, waiting for someone to barge in at any moment, but no one did.

Mr. D had gone mad, as he walked around his office simply destroying shit. I waited until he turned around to try and make a run for the door, and when I finally got the chance, the mother fuckin' door was locked! I turned the knob ever way I could, pushed and pulled with all I had, until finally I started to bang on it.

I couldn't understand how no one could hear me. You couldn't fart in this place without someone hearing about it, and now you're telling me no one could hear the craziness that was coming from this office? Bullshit, something was up.

Once I realized it was no use, I stopped, but only to find Mr. D just standing there, staring dead at me.

His head low and eyes up, I swore it was Satan himself. He started toward me, his bat dragging beside him.

"Come on Mr. D, I get it man, and I'm cool with whatever you say." Still he said nothing, and stopped several feel from where I was standing by the door. Our eyes latched on to one another, and I was scared to even blink.

He then tossed me the bat, and to my surprise... I fuckin' caught it. I didn't know what to do, so I just held it in front of me by the two ends.

"Look man, I'm not trying to do this. I just wanna go. I snapped my head toward the door, as a suggestion to open it, but by this point he looked at me like he didn't even understand English.

I watched as this stupid-ass grin grew across his face, and I wanted so bad to knock his teeth out his mouth.

We stood there, just staring at each other like a couple of dicks. I had no idea what was running through this guy's head, and when he pulled that gun from his waist and pointed it directly at me, I knew I had a problem.

I stood there, like a statue, scared to even breathe. I never knew Mr. D to be violent, but then again I never really knew Mr. D. I took a breath and was about to say something when suddenly, he began shooting!

I threw the bat at him, missing him by a mile, as I jumped on the floor and covered my head with my hands, just waiting for those bullets to begin piercing my back.

All went silent, and I couldn't tell if it was because I was dead. I opened my eyes, and tried to look around without moving my body. After a few moments, I turned and looked in the direction from where Mr. D was shooting, only to find him standing over me. If he didn't kill me, I swore I would die of a heart attack.

To my relief he turned around and walked back over to his desk, placing the gun into the back of his waistband. He took his seat behind his desk, the office around him looking like a scene from a war movie.

Slowly I got back up onto my feet, watching Mr. D's every move. There was that fuckin' grin again, but this time it came with a message, and I received it loud and clear.

I heard a click, and turned to the door, thinking that someone was about to enter, but they never did. I grabbed hold of knob, and with my eyes still on Mr. D… it opened!

"Have a good day, King!" Mr. D said, grabbing the phone and dialing as if none of this shit ever happened.

I stepped out and quickly closed the door behind me. My heart was pounding a mile a minute as I rushed down the long corridor that led to the front reception area, realizing that for the first time ever, that Roller Girl was nowhere in sight.

As I passed each office along the way, I noticed that all of their doors were closed.

The Funky Junky suddenly turned into a strange place, with strange people, and as I got to the front, there was Sal, as always sitting on one of the lounges, drinking coffee and reading the News. He turned to me and smiled.

"So how'd it go?"

CHAPTER 12

Red66

It was 7:00 p.m. and we had just finished for the day. We must've gone over about a hundred songs, many of them written by some of the day's greatest songwriters, some having never even heard of Rap before they were asked to write one.

The few songs that came in from new writers were some of the better ones. They were younger of course, and actually familiar with the genre, and though me and Red liked them best, Mr. D, on the other hand said they were too black!

Red would look at me, his eyes telling me, to just leave it alone. Little did he know, after the incident in his office, I really wasn't trying to fuck with Mr. D.

We cut a hundred songs, down to around fifty before Red advised we continue in the morning, as our ears by now should be fatigued, and we don't want to overlook a hit.

Mr. D got up, and without saying a word to us, left the studio. Red and I remained quiet as we gathered our things. Red took a peek out into the hall then closed and locked it.

"Fuck's going on?" He asked.

"I don't know, he's been tripping lately."

"Who you telling? He gave me a fucked up ultimatum, produce another hit album, or else!"

"Or else what, you're fired?" I asked

"I don't know, but I'm not trying to find out."

"You're a great producer, so I have no doubt that that you'll give him another hit.

"Yeah, but look at the shit he's giving me to work with." Red plopped down onto the couch and dropped his face into his hands. "I'm fucked!"

"You're fucked?" I said, sucking my teeth. "I signed for five albums."

"Five albums?" Red asked, looking up from his hands.

I was too ashamed to nod, so I shook my head instead.

"Who does that?" He asked, and so I raised my hand.

"I was just so excited to finally get a deal, that I probably would've signed up for ten!"

"You could be stuck here for the rest of your career." Red said.

"I could be stuck here for the rest of my life!" I replied.

We stayed quiet for a minute, our minds in over-drive.

"So, what if we just buckle down and try and knock out like all five albums, say in a few months?" I suggested, but already Red was knocking down my idea by shaking his head.

"Man, how's that gonna work?" He said. "Music's no

different than fashion. The moment you create it the clock starts ticking, and before you know it, it's considered old and outdated."

"But what if we create it and just keep it in the vault until it's time to release?"

"Can't do that either. Sounds are just like material. Today's leather pants are yesterday's Polyester!

No matter what I came up with, Red had an answer for why it won't work, in other words, we were fucked... Well, at least I was!

Again we went off into deep thought, as there had to be a way out of this situation.

"What if I got a lawyer?" I suddenly blurted out. Red threw his finger up to his lips and warned me to keep it down.

"Anyone you decide to hire, is probably already on Mr. D's payroll."

"Shit! I spat, I huffed, striking the air with my fist.

"What about a buyout? What if I offered to pay him to release me from this contract?

"A buyout at this point would be according to Mr. D's speculative earnings."

"And in English?"

"The amount of money that he expects to make during the term of your deal."

"And how much you think that would be?"

"Whatever the fuck he wants it to be!"

"So basically, the only way out of this shit is if I'm dead!"

"Not even!" Red added. "He'll have you stuffed and displayed in the corner his office, until the end of the term." And at that very moment I couldn't help but think of the skeleton arm holding that piece of paper.

Red grabbed his duffel bag and slung it over his shoulder. Everyone was gone for the night, and the cleaning crew fast at work getting the Funky Junky ready for tomorrow.

"It was 10:00 p.m., and Sal wasn't expecting to pick me up until midnight, so I asked Red if he could give me a lift.

We took the elevator down to the garage, and I immediately spotted Red's car at the other end of the garage. Not because it was the only Fire Red Lamborghini down there, but because it was in fact the only *car*, as everyone else had already gone for the night.

As we got closer, the license plate came into focus and I noticed it said RED66. I thought that was so cool, as I had never seen a custom plate before.

"Yo, this shit is fresh!" I said, running my fingertips along it's sleek body.

"Lamborghini Contach LP400." Red said. I didn't know anything about cars, so he could've said this was anything, and I'd still be impressed.

"These mother fuckers aren't even out yet." Red said as we got inside.

"So, how do you have one?" I asked, confused by what he just told me.

"I produced a track for the nephew of one of the

engineers, another wanna-be rapper of course."

"Was he any good?" I asked, totally not getting the point.

"Hell, the fuck no, he sucked!" Red said, laughing hysterically. "But I got this fucking car out of the deal, so who cares?"

"So what something like this go for?"

"About three hundred thousand!" Red replied. I nearly choked on my damn tongue when he told me.

"Wait up! You got a three hundred thousand dollar car, just for producing a rap song?"

"No, I still had to pay for it I just got the opportunity to buy it before anyone else!" I looked at red like he lost his mind.

I double checked my seatbelt as we zoomed through Manhattan. I never understood people paying so much for a car, but after riding in this thing, I finally understood. Not only did I not feel a single bump, I couldn't even hear the engine, and sitting in this thing was like sitting in a spacecraft.

"King, you're a cool dude, and I trust that whatever we speak about is kept between us.

"Of course man, in fact, I feel like you're the only one I can really talk with."

"Believe me... I am!" My body jerked as Red threw the car into the next gear." I looked down at his control panel and saw the stereo. It was as impressive as the studio we worked in.

"Is that a cassette deck?" I asked him, pointing to the blue light that outlined its door.

"Yep, and right under that is the Compact Disc player."

"Compact Disc?"

"Uh huh," he nodded, and then pressed play.

I looked at Red and smiled when we both realized that the song he had inside the Compact Disc player was one of Nemesis's.

"You're kidding me right?" I asked, laughing hysterically.

"What can I say, I like the classics!" I reached down and put up the volume, and started singing along to the hook.

The sound was bright and clean, and like my walkman, seemed to be coming from the heavens. My eyes scanned the interior, as I looked around for the speakers.

"You'll never find them." Red assured me. "They're built into the interior." and again, I shook my head in total disbelief that a vehicle such as this one, actually existed.

It was pretty cool, chillin' with Red outside of the studio. He was a good guy, not to mention, extremely talented. I was fortunate to be working with him.

"Hey, do me a favor man, and make a left here?" I asked him. Red looked at me strangely, but did what I asked. I gestured him to pull over, and when the car stopped, I got out.

"What's going on?" He asked.

"I gotta talk to someone."

"Man, how long you're gonna take, 'cause I'm tired."

"Nah, you go 'head. I'll catch a cab from here." I reached back in and shook Red's hand, and then watched as he zoom off into the night.

I walked up the few steps in from of the building and pressed the button on the intercom.

"Who is it?" The crackly voice asked.

"Hey, um, what's up, this is King, you know, the one with the Yes Yes song, I wanted to know if I could talk to you for a second. I got an idea!

CHAPTER 13

Tiny Cups

I could tell he was looking at me through the peephole, but he wouldn't say anything. I just kept smiling, and waving, like a fuckin' idiot.

"What is it you want?" The Cuban finally asked through the closed door, in the accent that I had grown so familiar with, while listening to him sing my song a hundred plus times.

"Hey man, how are you? Not sure if you remember me, but..."

"...Of course I remember you. I remember all of you. Like a fuckin' nightmare. Now what do you want? I gave you your song back! I have nothing else of yours!"

"Look, I'm by myself. In fact, nobody even knows I'm here. I just wanted to speak to you, please!"

"That's exactly what your little friend said. Please, I don't want any trouble.

The door behind me cracked open, and when I turned

around, I saw a little old face peek out, then shut quickly.

I reached into my jacket and pulled out the cassette that the Cuban had given me, and held it up in front of the peephole.

"I love this!" I said, looking directly into his eye. The Cuban gave it a moment, and then replied.

"So what is it you want from me?" He asked, as if he didn't hear a thing I said.

"Look, I don't know if you have any idea who I am or not, and that doesn't really matter.

I just wanted to come by and tell you that I am so sorry about what happened." The Cuban didn't respond, so I continued.

"The guy who came here, is a friend of mine, and he was just looking out for me. I had asked him to find out who it was that was playing the song, because I couldn't figure it out, he just went a bit overboard."

I stared at the peephole and the blackness in it told me that the Cuban was still there. "I want to speak to you about the song."

"I'm listening!" The Cuban replied, still from the other side of the closed door. I looked behind me and could tell that the old lady from across the hall was now at her peephole as well. I turned back to the Cuban.

"The way you recorded my song was like nothing I could have ever imagined."

"Well, I never knew how you imagined it, so when I read the lyrics, that's what made sense to me!"

"And it was genius!" I told him. "Which is why am here."

I stood there for a moment, still holding up the tape, and smiling. But the Cuban didn't respond at all. I couldn't blame him either, Quenepa would've killed him if we had let him, and this guy had no intentions on dealing with the devil, or even the devil's friends.

After a minute of just standing there in silence, I placed the cassette on his doormat, turned and headed back for the elevator, when suddenly I heard his door unlock.

The Cuban popped his head out and looked around. He then bent over and picked up the cassette when I noticed in his left hand he held a big wooden spoon. He then looked over at me.

"Come on!"

"Go to the living room." He said, throwing his hand in its direction. "I'm sure you remember where it is"

I walked the long hallway, which sort of resembled mine and Gram's old apartment. Though the smell of fresh brewed Bustelo put me at ease, stepping back into that living room sort of fucked me up.

The Cuban invited me to sit, and so I did.

"I'll be right back." He said, before heading into the kitchen. I looked around his living room noticing even more things than before. Lots of old black and white photos hung on nearly every wall, him posing with different people, none that I recognized.

One photo however did stand out, but I couldn't see it well from where I sat, so I got up and walked over to it. It was the Cuban playing the piano in what looked like some sort of concert hall. There seemed to be hundreds of people sitting in the audience.

I realized that the photo was an actual clipping from a newspaper, and when I tried to read the caption it was in Spanish and the date said 1951.

"That was at the Grand National Theater in Havana." The Cuban said as he stepped back into the living room.

"That night I played for over fifteen hundred people. It was a dream come true."

I watched as the Cuban walked over and placed, on the table, a tray with a coffee pot, and two tiny cups.

He gestured for me to sit across from him, though I wish I hadn't, because every now and then white bathrobe would open, and I'd get flashed.

He poured coffee in each of the cups and handed me one of them. Grams use to tell me about how the Cubans drank coffee, but this was the first time I actually got to see it. This cup was no bigger than a shot glass, and I saw no sugar anywhere. It smelled wonderful, and I watched as the Cuban downed his, so I followed.

It was a little hot and though I usually like a ton sugar this already seemed kind of sweet.

I looked at the Cuban's face and saw his expression suddenly change to that of a more pleasant one than before. He smiled at me, and immediately I could feel the coffee taking effect. I'd been drinking Bustelo for as long as I could remember, and I've never experienced anything like this. My heart started to speed, and for a moment I thought, maybe he had put something in it, but he didn't. He just made it stronger than I was used to.

We stared at each other for a moment until finally he asked.

"So, what is it that you wanted to talk to me about?

CHAPTER 14

My Friends Call Me Cuba

"My name is Reynaldo Rosario, but my friends call me Rey." I said as I reached across the coffee table. The Cuban looked at my hand, and then took it in his.

"Carlos. Carlos Roberto Quiñónez. But my friends call me Cuba!" I smiled, and our hands shook. Cuba then refilled both our cups.

"I don't know if you know anything at all about me..."

"Only that you are one of the most famous rappers today. Mr. King!" He replied surprising the hell out of me.

"But how?"

"Well, your little friend sort of gave me a enough information to work with. I went to the record shop and asked a few questions, not to mention I bought this" He held up a cassette copy of I Am King. I smiled.

"So what did you think?" I asked, but he changed the subject.

"Where are you from?"

"The Bronx," I replied.

"No, I mean your nationality! Puertorriqueño?" I nodded.

"You can pass for Cubano. A white Cubano" He added. I didn't know how to respond to that so I just proceeded with why I was here.

"So the tape that you made, that music, all you?"

"Of course!" the Cuban replied *"And* the vocals!"

"And you recorded that, here?" Cuba looked at me like it was a dumb question.

"Actually, I recorded it over here!" He corrected walking over toward his piano. He grabbed a corner of the hot pink towel that covered some mysterious contraption, and unveiled it, revealing an old, yet real cool home recording set up, that consisted of a tiny mixing board, what looked like a 1950's Broadcast microphone, and Reel to Reel tape deck that was made mostly of wood. The only modern piece there was a Tascam Porta-One Mini Studio. I recognized that because I wanted one.

"You recorded all of that with this?" Cuba nodded with a smile. "But the quality... I mean, how is that even possible? The studio I work out of cost millions of dollars, and no offense, but..." I gestured back to his set up. "This equipment looks like something you got out of a Pawn Shop."

"Hmmm, a Pawn Shop, huh?" He responded a bit insulted. "I was going to say the same thing about your producer!

I looked at Cuba and laughed, accepting his subliminal smack in the face.

"This here's a four track." I said, gesturing back over to the Porta-One. "Why does it sound more like sixteen."

I don't think Cuba would make a good teacher because his patience was practically nonexistent.

"It's called bouncing." He replied within an exhale.

"Bouncing?" I asked, and it was then that I revealed the fact that I really didn't know shit. Cuba stared at me for a moment, and though it was clear that he dreaded it, he proceeded to try and explain the process.

"You see, I always begin with percussion..." He stopped mid-sentence and looked at me." You know what percussion is, right?"

"Drums?"

"Well, yes, they're percussion, but so are cymbals, tambourines, and even shakers." He added demonstrating each of the instruments he just mentioned as they were all laying around his apartment. He looked at me to see if I was following, and when he was sure I was, he continued.

"I would begin with my Conga's and lay about three minutes into track one." He said showing me with his finger, the flow of the process. Once that was laid, I would rewind the tape, set it to track two, listen to track one, and now I would record, let's say, the Shaker. On track three I would record maybe the Tambourine, and track four I'll just clap my hands. Now I get a nice blend between them until I am happy with the sound and then mix it all down to my Tape machine, erase the four track and then run the entire mix from my tape machine back down to track one. Now I have three more track to work with..."

Cuba really went out of his way to teach me the process and I couldn't help but become more and more impressed with this guy. He was so patient, and wouldn't continue until he was sure that I understood. He kept reminding me how important each step was, and continuing on without really understanding one of the steps would just be a waste of time. Not only did he teach me how things worked, he explained to me why! He said that learning the mechanics of how something works is fine, but unless we understand why it works, we would never be able to fix problems when they occurred.

I watched as he set up each instrument, and miked it just right. He'd record a few bars and then move onto the next. Each one he played himself. The Congas, Bongos, Shakers, the Cowbell, Piano, Trumpet. He pulled instruments out from everywhere. I was getting a little worried because it was late, and he was pretty loud, but he assured me that his neighbors would be fine with it.

Cuba seemed to be having a good time, as if he hadn't had company in years.

We were on our second pot of coffee, and in just the few hours that I had been there, I not only learned a lot, but also gained a whole new respect for the art of music, musicians, and for the Latin culture itself, of which I'm sorry to say, never really gave much mind.

He taught me about EQ, and other effects, and explained the concept of less is more. The shit that he produced just teaching me how it all works, sounded better than *most* shit I've heard on the radio, and practically *everything* I've ever heard coming out of the Funky Junky. There was no denying. Cuba was what you'd call, a musical genius!

Over our third pot of Bustelo, Cuba gave me a little background. Though his father was a great musician, he was known more for his guitar craftsmanship. Cuba had been his helper, for as long as he could remember, and the experience, developed in him a deep passion, not only for the guitar, but for all instruments, which by the time he was just ten years old, most of them he'd master.

His pitch perfect ear, made him the go-to kid for all instrument tunings, and had been invited several times to play for the President of Cuba.

As Cuba's father aged, his skills began to diminish, and other Craftsmen soon put him out of business. Out of desperation to provide for his family, Cuba's father got involved with the wrong people, which eventually resulted in his murder.

Cuba's mother had a nervous breakdown, and was taken away, never to be seen or heard of again. He wound up being brought to the United States by a close friend of the family who then delivered Cuba to the only relative they knew still existed, and that was his Uncle.

Tio Raul was no stranger to Cuba, as he grew up listening to all of the adventurous stories his father would tell. What Cuba never knew, was that Tio Raul was his father's twin, a surprise that nearly knocked him on his ass when he first saw him.

Life for Cuba began, once again to show hope. And though it wasn't his father, the fact that they looked identical, put Cuba in a good place, until that one night, when his uncle came home drunk…

Up until the day he died nearly six years later, Cuba was being molested by Tio Raul. His death was ruled a drug overdose, but something in the way Cuba told that story, made me think there might be more to it than that.

Life had forced Cuba to grow up quickly, and he was very smart for his age. So smart in fact, that he managed to get himself added to the lease, just before his uncle's death.

Most of the photos of Cuba with all those important looking people, though I thought were taken in Cuba, were not. It only looked that way because all of his publicity was in the Spanish papers, but they all took place here in New York City.

I was never into politics, and Cuba laughed every time he pointed to someone and asked if I knew who they were. I could only shake my head.

Cuba knew more about America than most Americans. He was proud of this country that he has been calling his own for over fifty years.

The loud buzzer interrupted our conversation.

"Who is it?" Cuba asked, with his face pressed up against the intercom.

"I'm downstairs!" Sal announced.

I got up and grabbed my things. Cuba and I chatted for a bit more as he walked me to the door. I turned around and looked at him. He had the kindest face, and I would never get over the guilt of what Q had done to him just the week before.

I extended my hand, and he accepted it with a smile.

"Thank you!" I said, and then turned and headed for the elevator.

CHAPTER 15

Warning

After my shower, and with my towel still wrapped around me, I went up to Rosie's door which was slightly opened, and peeked in.

The streetlight that bled into her room made her body glow just right, as she lie on her stomach with her face in her pillow.

She had on a little black t-shirt and a pair of red jean shorts. The back of her legs looked smooth and silky. I knew she heard me. I stepped inside and closed the door behind me. I walked to the foot of her bed and stood between her bare feet that hung a bit over the edge.

I placed my knee on the bed between her legs and then followed with the rest of my body, placing myself gently on top of her. I could feel myself wedge between her butt cheeks, hardening me even more.

I leaned around and moved her hair from her face, and noticed that she had been crying.

My urge to fuck her immediately vanished and I felt

myself begin to deflate.

"What's wrong?" I whispered. Rosie sniffed, and then wiped her eye. I lifted myself off her and onto my side.

She turned on to hers, and we faced each other. Her eyes remained on the floral design on her sheet while she traced it slowly with her finger.

She looked at me, and I could tell she was thinking of a way to tell me something, and of course I'm thinking the worst.

Half her face reflected the moonlight while the other half remained in the shadows.

As always, I couldn't help be mesmerized by her extraordinary beauty, bangs that stopped just above her thick eyebrows, her eyes and nose couldn't be any more perfect, and her lips... Damn!

"Rey," she began, her voice soft and crackly. "This job is extremely important to me, and if you haven't noticed, our cover has been blown for a while now."

"That's because I'm not trying to hide anything."

"But that wasn't the deal, Rey. We spoke an entire night about this."

She was right, and yes, I had promised. But I never expected it to be this way, for me to feel this way. I could never hide this, now. I wanted the world to know. Sal knew what was up without me saying anything, and I'd be surprised if Grams didn't figure it out by now.

"Rey, I'm gonna tell you something, and it's so important that no matter what, you don't speak about this to anyone."

This wasn't feeling right, and I dreaded what it was she was about to tell me.

"The only reason I deal with these people, is because I've been around them my entire life, and so was my mother."

"What does that have to do with us?"

Rosie became hesitant again, and looked away. There was something keeping her from telling me whatever it was she wanted to tell me. Whatever it was I wanted to know, but I didn't want to pressure her. So I just took her into my arms and held her. She relaxed into me as I laid there staring at the curtain that the cool night air was blowing into her room.

We laid there for a while, until she fell asleep. I replaced myself with her other pillow and got up and pulled her covers up over her.

I stepped over to close the window a bit when I noticed something outside, just sitting in the middle of the street. I leaned out for a better look, but I was too far up and couldn't figure it out.

I exited the elevator and started down the hall toward the door.

"Good evening Mr. King." The doorman greeted.

"What the hell's that out there?"

"It's a car. Someone came with a truck and just dropped it off there."

A crowd had already formed around the massive pile of metal that I could hardly see. I walked over for a closer look. When I got there, I swear, it looked like King Kong crushed it into a ball and just placed it in the middle of the street like some sort of art sculpture.

A gentleman stepped up beside me shaking his head as he stared at the metal clump. "They just dropped it off and left."

"Who did?"

"I don't know… a dump truck!"

As I walked around the hunk of junk, I couldn't help but wonder, how the hell did they manage to shape it into a ball? It was literally round, and compressed so tight, that I couldn't even figure out the type of car it was, or even the color. As I got to one spot, I noticed people bending down try to see something that seemed to be lodged underneath it. As I got to the spot, I did as they, and looked beneath the wreckage, when suddenly, I saw it… *RED66.*

CHAPTER 16

A Dangerous Game

Red and I had been working on the new album for nearly a year now. Neither one of us particularly happy, we made up our minds to just get it done. There was never a mention of Red's Lamborghini, and I advised him to keep it that way, and promised, that one day I will make that up to him. Besides, I'm convinced that it all happened because he was giving *me* a heads up.

The songs we were recording were getting cornier each session, and I dreaded the tour that I would soon have to embark. We had both lost so much respect for Mr. D, the genius that I once saw, was no longer there. He had changed, and I couldn't understand why.

Though my days were already filled with writing sessions, recording, and rehearsals with Princess and the crew, my evenings were even more so, as Red and I would secretly meet up at Cuba's every night after leaving the Funky Junky.

After work, Red and I would go our own ways. Sal would

drive me home, and after he left, I would call a cab and head over to Cuba's, most of the time Red was already there, geared up, and in the midst of trying out some ideas.

Everything was kept on the DL, and though it was a dangerous game, it was something we knew we had to do.

It was these sessions that I looked forward to, no matter how exhausted I might be. Weekends that I wasn't performing, I spent doing things with Rosie, Grams and Porky. Sal usually joined us.

The only other one that knew what we were up to was Rosie. I needed her to have my back in case anyone would come by or call, not to mention, I didn't want her to ever think I was messing around.

I was really digging Rosie. She was without doubt... *the* one! I felt guilty at the same time because it seemed like the only time we got to spend together was in bed. I wanted to do so much more with her, but I was on a serious mission. Rosie was a trooper though, and I was fortunate to have her in my life.

Porky had just turned twelve. His mother had passed away from cancer, and his father suddenly vanished from the face of the earth.

Porky was becoming a really big kid. At just twelve years old he was almost six feet tall and two hundred pounds. When he didn't have school I would bring him with me to The Funky Junky in the mornings and he would spend the entire day working out with Jacq.

Grams on the other hand, wasn't doing too well, and this Alzheimer's shit was really taking a toll on all of us. On some days she was her typical self, but on others, she didn't even know who the fuck I was. This was killing me more than anything, and it drove me to work harder than ever, because I needed something else to think about besides my Grandmother.

We had a couple of nurses that rotated their shifts, and that was great, but nothing put me more at ease than knowing that Rosie was there. Grams adored her, and she would always recognize her before anyone else, mainly because she's been the one spending the most time with her.

One of their favorite things to do was hang out in the living room while Grams told stories about me growing up. Some of them I don't know where she got, or who they were really about. But the ones that were true were so embarrassing.

I never understood why Rosie would want to sit around listening to these dumb ass stories about me, until one day she told me it was so she can tell them to our children... Rosie was six weeks pregnant.

We told Grams and Porky. Porky was thrilled and wanted to know if the baby would be his little brother or sister, and of course we both said yes. Grams on the other hand, didn't react as we had thought.

"Grams, what's the matter? Aren't you excited? You're gonna be a Great Grams!" I told her.

She smiled at me, and then replied.

"I'm thrilled, Mijo!" She confirmed. "But I've known this for a while now already!"

Rosie looked at me, not sure what to make of it. Grams then stepped up and kissed us both.

Quenepa was called into the studio only during his parts. He was too over the top for any of us to be around him for too long. He sensed the alienation, but I really didn't care, I had to tour with this mother fucker, and that was bad enough. This kid's issues seemed to get worst every day, and I hated having to deal with it.

Red couldn't stand dealing with him, and made sure Sal was present when it was his time to come in.

Q would always try and hang out after he laid his parts, but that shit was a no go, and he had to leave.

We still never told anyone about our night project with Cuba, something I never thought we could pull off. I knew for sure that by now, Sal would've found out, and was prepared with what I would tell him.

Vanessa had finally become Princesses' assistant, but truth of the matter was, she was really head bitch in charge! Most of the choreography we performed belonged to Vee, and we all loved it. She added a whole new twist to it all, a much cooler vibe. Her career was finally off and running, I only wished that she would find someone to share it with. Oh, don't get me wrong. Pussy wasn't a problem, Vee got plenty of it, much more than I ever did. It was that one true love she had a problem finding.

Cuba was always in great spirits. He was excited in just doing music. He never once talked about money or who gets what credit. He didn't care, he just wanted to create. Red really appreciated Cuba's talent, and was learning so much from him.

We began every writing session with a good ol' Cuban dinner that Cuba prepared for us himself. I wondered what his life was like just before we became a part of it. Besides a few of his noisy neighbors, he never had company.

For the first couple of months that we worked with him, his attire consisted of nothing more than his white bathrobe, but after the umpteenth time seeing his nuts pop out, we had to intervene, and made clothes mandatory!

Red was already an incredible musician, and with a soul that I had never before seen in a white boy. But around Cuba, he seemed like this whole other dude. He became a student to Cuba, a protégée. Whenever he did anything, he'd turn to Cuba for approval.

I personally had no interest in playing anything. Once in a while I might fuck with the Maracas a bit, but that was about the extent of my musicianship. I loved to write and Rap. That was my shit, and I wanted to focus on that and that alone.

I became cool with one of the executives over at Solar, and he sort of hinted that they'd be interested in taking over my contract. I knew they'd give me the freedom that I had been looking for, plus I'd be able to develop my label under them. And though I never once brought it up, it lingered in my mind constantly. And then one evening, as I turned to walk into Cuba's building, there sitting on the stoop, reading the paper... was Sal!

CHAPTER 17

Stoop Confessions

I stood there, frozen. Sal's, face was one of disappointment as he got up and dropped the paper on the step where he was sitting.

Wha'cha you doing here?" I asked.

He didn't say anything, but walked toward me. I backed up until I reached the wall. Sal leaned in, his face mere inches from mine.

"How long has this been going on?" He asked. I hesitated, but didn't want to wear his patience.

"Since the incident!" I replied.

"Who else knows about this?" Again, I hesitated.

"Just Rosie."

"Rosie?" I nodded.

"And she's okay with this?" Again, I nodded.

"This is really fucked up." Sal said as he turned away from me and smacked the air. "God damn it, King. You just had a fucking kid, man!"

"I know, that's part of the reason."

"Too much for you?"

I shrugged.

"And what about your grandmother, does she know?"

"Of course not, she doesn't even know who the hell *I* am anymore."

I watched as Sal paced the courtyard, running the fingers of both hands through his hair.

I was scared, I was waiting for him to turn around and blow a couple of holes into my chest. He turned and looked at me.

"and from all people?" his thumb, pointing back at the building.

"Cuba, is incredible, Sal."

"Please, I'm not trying to hear all that shit. I'm trying to figure out what the fuck to do about it."

I remained quiet and watched as Sal gave hard thought to the situation.

"Does Mr. D need to know?" I asked, Sal stopped in his tracks and turned to me.

"Of course he does, and I'm gonna tell him, because the moment he finds out. right away he's going to assume that I've known all along. Shit, he might even think I'm part of it.

"I don't know what any of this has to do with him anyway. I mean, I'm still doing what I have to do for the Funky Junky, and so is Red, but…

"Red?" Sal interrupted. I remained silent for a second,

and then continued. "Well, yeah."

"Red's a part of this too?" I nodded.

"I can't believe this shit, King. So tell me. Who's fucking who?"

"Well technically, the only one truly getting fucked is me!"

"So who's fucking you?" Sal yelled, "Mr. D!" I yelled back.

Sal flinched back and gave me a confused look.

"What did you say?"

"I said, the only one fucking me is Mr. D!"

Sal looked at me, his face distorted. He then grabbed his head with both hands and looked up into the sky, then walked over to the stoop and sat down.

"When Mr. D signed me, it was the greatest thing ever. I was on top of the world. I did what I love to do. Traveled the world, and made great friends, like you, Sal."

Sal looked up at me, and continued to listen.

"It was fun, and I appreciate everything, but I'm outgrowing this situation. I went to Mr. D and all I asked is if he would allow me to write my next album. He'd still have final approval, but damn, at least give me a shot! He wasn't cool with that, in fact, he flipped out. I had never seen him like that before and it scared the shit out of me. I didn't want to go anywhere, the Funky Junky is my home. I wanted to help take it to another level, but Mr. D just wanted to recreate the past, and I didn't want that. I'm getting older, we're all getting older. I don't want to have regrets, Sal.

"I don't understand," he said, "what does that have to do with the fagot shit?" I looked at him, trying to figure out what the hell he was talking about.

"Fagot shit?"

"Yeah," he replied. "I mean, why couldn't you just turn to drugs like most artists?"

"What are you talking about?"

"I'm talking about you, King, and all this Gay shit! Let the fans find out, and it's over!"

The girls won't want you, and the guys won't wanna be you. You'll lose everything.

"Hold up!" I said. I looked Sal directly in the eyes, and then asked, "you think I'm gay?"

"You're fucking around with Red, and the old Gay dude, what am I supposed to think? Look, I know a place where you can go and get help, they'll fix you man, and nobody ever needs to know shit!"

I couldn't help it and busted out laughing hysterically. Sal quieted down and just looked at me.

"Man, this is some serious shit, I wouldn't be laughing 'cause if Mr. D. finds out, we're both fucked!"

"You think I got something going on with the old man?" I asked, still unable to stop laughing. Sal just stared at me, with this sort of upside down look, then asked,

"You don't?"

"No man! What the fuck!"

"What about Red?" He asked.

"Damn man, if anyone I would think knows me, it'll be you. Shit, you know me better than Rosie. You know me better than grams!"

So, you're not gay?"

"No man! Damn bro!"

"What about the old dude?"

"Yeah, he's gay, but so what!"

"I don't get it though. Supposedly you leave the apartment every night."

"Who told you this?"

"Doesn't matter," Sal replied.

Look man, I wanted nothing more than to tell you, but I didn't know if you'd be able to keep it from Mr. D. and I didn't want to put you on the spot. But it was important that Mr. D didn't know about this, at least not yet."

"I don't get it, what's going on?"

"Man, Mr. D has us working on some real bullshit music. I asked if I could write this new album, and he totally rejected the idea."

"Why'd he do that?"

"Honestly man? I can't figure it out. But I'll tell you this, if we put that shit out, everything we've been busting our ass for is gonna go up in smoke."

"But I thought you guys spoke about this already?"

I just looked at Sal, as I swore he knew what went down that day at the office, but I guess he didn't."

"We've been working on all new material. The chemistry

we got going on up there is like nothing I've ever known before."

Sal gave me a strange look.

"Come on man. Serious!"

Sal takes a seat back down on the stoop, and drops his face into his hands, trying to process all that I just told him.

"I figured, we'd finish everything, and then present it to Mr. D."

"And what if he still rejects it?" Sal asked. I just looked at him, and then shrugged my shoulders.

"Why don't you come upstairs, and see what we're doing."

"I don't know if that's a good idea."

"Please man. The only thing that was missing from this whole picture was you. I hated keeping this from you. I just didn't know what else to do."

Sal stared at me, long and hard, then finally gestured for me to lead the way.

CHAPTER 18

Surprise Mother Fucker

"And you got your own key?" Sal asked while shaking his head. I just nodded. The minute we got off the elevator we could hear the music coming from the apartment. I turned to Sal as he followed me, his mind seemed to be racing, and I could only imagine what was going through it.

Using another key, we entered the apartment and made our way down the hall that led to the living room.

Red was on the piano while Cuba was on the Bongos. They didn't notice us standing there, so we just let them continue playing. I looked at Sal and he was pretty still. I myself couldn't help it, and had to bounce my body a bit.

Red and Cuba were really getting down. These two talents were incredible on their own, but together? Fucking magical!

When they finished I began to applaud, startling the two of them. Cuba smiled at us but Red, just stared.

"Surprise mother fucker!" Sal blurted out.

Red jumped up from behind the piano, knocking over the bench.

"Oh no!" He cried, as he gathered his things. "I'm sorry."

"Red! It's all good bro." I said trying to calm him down. Cuba saw how he was acting and seemed also to panic. He backed up into the corner and just stood there, watching.

"I didn't mean anything. We're just messing around a bit."

"Red! Chill out man!" I said, as I went up and placed my hands on his shoulders. At this point he was literally crying, his body shaking. I looked back at Sal as he walked over to the couch and plopped down in it. He crossed his legs and extended his arms along the back of the couch, as if he was being entertained.

"This isn't good, King." He cried out to me.

"Red, I spoke to him already. I told him what we were doing."

"Oh no, King!" He cried even harder. "Why'd you had to go and do that?"

I glanced back again at Sal. He seemed to be enjoying every minute of this.

"This isn't gonna end good, King." Red whispered to me. He was starting to get to me. I suddenly began to worry as well, but held it in.

"Come on man, you're just buggin"

"Buggin'? You saw my car man! That wasn't just my warning... That shit was dropped off in front of your building!"

"What is he talking about?" Cuba asked from his corner.

"Man, can you help me out here?" I asked Sal, who then got up and walked over to us. I could feel Red's body, shivering to a whole other level.

I lifted the bench and guided Red down onto it, because he honestly felt as if he was about to pass out.

"Can you tell him something?" I asked Sal, who then placed his hand on Red's shoulder and said.

"You need to calm the fuck down! You're acting like a little faggot!" He then turned to Cuba. "No offense!" "I just shook my head, Sal shrugged his shoulders. "Look, I'm not gonna do nothing."

"You say that now," Red cried out like a straight up baby, "and then when we least expect it, Pow!" He yelled out, making Cuba gasp.

"Look asshole," Sal continued, if I wanted to take you out, it would've been done already. Sal then pulled out his gun and placed it against Red's head.

"Boom!" He said. Cuba screamed like a little girl. Sal then placed the gun against my head. I closed my eyes, and then heard him make the same sound again.

"Boom!"

And again Cube screamed.

Sal then turned and looked at Cuba who was now hiding behind the drapes.

"You would've gotten a heart attack by now!" He said, waving him off. "So you see. If I wanted to take any of you out, it would've been done already. Now cut the shit, Red!"

Sal then returned the gun under his arm and looked at us. I didn't like feeling Sal's gun against my head, but I believe it was necessary. Sal knew the deal now, and Red had to accept that, so that we can move forward.

I walked over to Cuba and helped him out from behind the drapes when suddenly there was a knock on the door. I figured it was another one of Cuba's nosy neighbors, so I sent him to open the door.

"Yeah, we got a call saying there were screams coming from this apartment, said Office Jimmy, his sarcastic smirk letting us know, just how common these types of calls were.

I watched as Officer Jimmy and Sal's eyes met across the room. It was obvious that they knew each other, but of what capacity? Then they nodded.

"Hey!" My man, King!" called out Officer Lopez as he stepped out from behind his partner.

"Officer Lopez. How are you?" I replied as we shook hands.

"As good as it gets bro!" He then turned to his partner he ask, "member him now?" Officer Jimmy looked at me, and shook his head.

"Nah! You mother fuckers all look alike to me!" He replied. It was strange though, because as much as I stood out, he couldn't remember me... But he remembered Sal.

I laughed, and Officer Lopez waved him off.

"So I've been checking you out, you're fucking blowing up!" He said giving me five. I smiled and nodded.

"Yeah, sort of."

"Shit, everywhere I turn I see your ass. Even my daughter has your poster up on her wall. I told her I knew you, but of course, she doesn't believe me. Ten years old, you know, what do you expect?" I laughed.

"So, anyway… who's killing who?"

We all got silent, our eyes bouncing off of one another. And then suddenly, Lopez began laughing. "I'm fucking with you guys!" He said.

"Okay folks, we're outta here. Enjoy your night, and try and keep it down will you." Cuba and I nodded. Sal stood there, still and quiet. Red remained on the bench. But before I was able to close the door, Lopez turned and held the door from closing.

"Hey man. You think it's possible that I get your autograph. You know, for my little girl?"

"Um, sure," I looked around for something to autograph, when I spotted a magazine that had me on the cover. "You mind?" I asked Cuba. He shook his head. I grabbed a marker from on top of the piano. "What's her name?"

"Rosie… With an I-E"

I looked at him, and smiled, "beautiful name!"

"She'll be eleven in December." He replied as he whipped out his wallet and showed me her picture.

"She's a cutie." I told him.

"Thanks. That's my little angel," He replied.

I wrote something really nice for Rosie. Lopez read it and then gave me a huge smile. As he shook my hand, he leaned in toward me and whispered.

"If you ever need anything, anything at all!" I nodded, and thanked him.

CHAPTER 19

So Long, Grams

It was a little after six when I got home from the Funky Junky. As usual I would hang out for about an hour with the family, eat dinner, catch up on everything, and then head back to Cuba's. It was a little less stressful now that Sal knew about it, and most of the time he would even drive me. He loved Cuba's coffee, probably safe to say, he was addicted.

As soon as I got home, Pork was there. He didn't look too good. Like he was crying, and immediately I thought the worst.

"Where's Grams? " I asked him.

"They took her to the hospital, Rey. Rosie went with her. I wanted to go, but Rosie told me to wait for you.

At just fourteen years old, Porky was, six one, two hundred and ten pounds, with most of his baby fat having already converted to muscle.

"Is Sal with you?" He asked.

"No, he left. He was going to pick me up at eight, Imma

call a cab."

On our way to the hospital, Porky explained to me what's been going on. Apparently, Gram's Alzheimer's had gotten so bad that she's starting to forget how to swallow, and keeps choking on her own saliva.

I couldn't believe what I was hearing, and was upset that I haven't been around her much.

"Rosie said that there was absolutely nothing you could do but sit around and stare at her. Besides, we knew this day was coming."

I threw my face into my hands and began to cry. I felt Pork's huge hand touch the back of my neck, and then he pulled me into his enormous arms, and there we both sobbed until the cab pulled up to the hospital.

We rushed inside, and after bullshitting with the rude receptionist, we made our way up to her floor and into her room. Rosie was sitting on a chair beside Grams who was hooked up to machines that seemed to be doing the breathing for her.

Rosie jumped up and ran into my arms. Grams had been like a mother to her these past few years, and they spent so much time together.

"Where's Dora?" I asked.

Sal took her to McDonald's. They wouldn't let her up." "He's here?"

"Yeah, I had beeped him. He said he had just dropped you off at the house, but when I called the house, no one answered so I figured you left already."

Rosie started to cry into my arms. Pork plopped down in the seat where Rosie was sitting and took Gram's hand into his, he looked so big next to her, she became that mother he never had, I never seen him look so sad as he sat there stroking the top of her hand. I didn't know what was hurting me more.

Rosie and I went over to Pork who was now crying into her hand. We placed our hands on his shoulders.

"What can we do Rey? What can we do to make her better?" Pork cried out.

"All we can do now is try and keep her comfortable," said the doctor as he entered the room. We all turned to him, but Porky got up, rushed over to him, and by the front of his lab coat picked him up and held him pressed against the wall.

"Pork!" I yelled out as Rosie and I rushed over and tried to pull back his arm, but to no avail. Pork felt like an iron bull.

"If you don't put me down I will have you removed from this hospital never to be allowed back in!"

"Victor, please, put him down." Rosie said. Grams was the only other one who called him by his real name, and I think that did something, because then he lowered the doctor to the floor and then dashed out the room.

"I'm really sorry about that." I told the doctor.

"Well if he creates any problems I *will* have him arrested."

"He's only fourteen years old."

"Fourteen?"

We both nodded.

"That isn't normal, you should have him checked out!"

"Listen Doctor, I need to know what's happening with my grandmother?"

"Well, it's the Alzheimer's, Mr. Rosario, it's progressed as expected. Your grandmother has lost her ability to do almost anything on her own, and now it's affecting her breathing." I turned and looked at Grams, the pump beside her, inflating and deflating with that awful sound that would haunt me for years to come.

"Look, whatever it is that needs to be done, let's do it. If it's about the money, I have plenty, and if I run out, I can get more. I just want her to get better, Doc.

The Doctor looked at me with a sorry face, and then at Rosie.

"I'm going to leave you two alone, you have some decisions to make." The doctor turned and exited the room.

I collapsed on the chair, opposite from where Porky was sitting, and dropped my face into my hands. Rosie stepped up beside me and rubbed my back.

"This isn't fair." I cried. "She sacrificed her entire life for me, and now that she needs help, I can't do shit."

"It wasn't a sacrifice, Rey. It was her pleasure. You gave her so much to live for, and all she ever wanted was for you to be happy, and you gave her that. If she had the choice, she would do it all over again... She told me this."

Those words put a smile on my face, as I turned and looked again at my Grandmother.

"After this next tour I wanted to buy a house somewhere

on Long Island. They have the ones with the extra house attached to it. You know the ones I'm talking about?" Rosie nodded.

"I wanted us all to go to Disney next summer, do a little traveling. I mean, I had so many plans for us." Every time I thought about it, I cried even harder. It was like my life suddenly stopped, and now I have to make a left.

"She doesn't want your plans to stop, Rey. She wants you to live your life to the fullest, that's her confirmation that she did a great job!"

"She did, Rosie. She really did." I grabbed my girl from around her waist and pulled her close, my crying eyes pressed up against her stomach.

"We have to do something, Rey." Rosie said, trying to mask her cracking voice. I didn't say anything. I just listened.

"She told me, and I know she told you, that if ever she was in this position, she wanted you to let her go."

"No!" I cried out. My face pressed harder against Rosie. She squatted down and took me into her arms.

"I know, baby, I know."

"I just needed her a little longer." Suddenly, I lost control, jumped up and rushed over to my grandmother.

"Rey, stop it!" Rosie yelled as I tried to wake her up. Rosie tried to pull me off, but I just pushed her away.

"Rey, stop it!" She yelled again, and then ran to the door and called for help.

Security came in, but by then I had already lost it. Four guards and they couldn't handle me. I was becoming extremely violent, pushing anyone who came next to me. The table and chairs fell over. I grabbed my Grandmother and nearly pulled her off the bed, when another guard ran into the room, this one with a night stick. I watched as he lifted it high over his head about to bring it down hard on my head. Rosie was watching and screamed just as it began to make its way, when suddenly Porky's huge hand caught it mid-air!

He snatched it from the guard without any effort, and then pushed him out the way. The guard tumbled over the others, and Porky grabbed hold of me.

"I'm here Rey." He said. His voice, as soft and gentle as always, just the way it was when I first met him. "Let her go, Rey." It took me a second, until finally, I did. Porky turned to the small crowd of hospital staff that formed inside the room, and assured them that everything was under control. Rosie helped direct everyone out as Sal and Dora made their way in.

Rosie closed the door and then we all gathered tightly around Grams looking at each other.

I picked up my three year old and held her so that she could have a better look at her Great Grandmother. I then looked back and saw Sal standing by the door, his head lowered and I watched as a teardrop crashed to the floor. He loved my Grandmother, and she loved him.

"Hey man!" I called to him. Sal looked up and wiped his eye. I gestured for him to come join us, and he did, and together, and in our own special way, we said goodbye to a woman who played an intricate role in helping us to be, the people we were today.

"So long Grams!

CHAPTER 20

She's Still Here

I always thought my Grandmother was immortal. She was too strong to die. But today, I got a taste of reality, and that reality is life. Those final hours with her were torture. Had it not been for my daughter, I could've easily seen myself joining Grams on her new journey. I was useless. Like a helpless baby. Once she was disconnected from life support, I climbed up onto her bed and cuddled with her, and cried. There was a point where I could've sworn that I had felt her stroke my head. But that was impossible, right? I mean, she was dead!

The funeral was about as nice as any funeral could possibly be, and the people who came to show their respects were much more than what I had expected. Those from the old neighborhood knew her best, as many came up to me, to not just give their condolences, but to also tell me just how Grams had affected their lives. It was a complete surprise to know how many she helped out in some form or another.

One young woman told me about the day she was

grocery shopping and didn't realize that her purse had been lifted from the cart when she wasn't looking. She was a single mother of two, and had just cashed her check. When Grams realized what had happened, she offered to pay the bill. The woman asked if she would just cover the milk and eggs, but Grams insisted on covering it all, and she did. The woman had never forgotten that.

In the old neighborhood, Grams was always helping the neighbors who didn't speak English. She would make phone calls and write letters to the landlord for them when they had unattended issues with their apartments. There were so many that came up to me, and their testimonies usually ended with something to the effect that, *for her, Heaven will definitely roll out the red carpet!*

Her room was flooded with flowers sent from all over the world. We tried our best to keep it all private, but the press was somehow able to keep fans abreast. Everyone from The Funky Junky showed up, including Mr. D. He seemed like his old self again. He had even asked if he could say a few words at her funeral.

But the one that got me good was Porky. He hadn't said a word in days, and at the funeral he walked around like a lost little boy. I had never seen him like that before and it was a bit scary. Rosie noticed too, and sat down with him in private. She had managed to convince him to say a few words, that he would feel better. But it wasn't until she mentioned how Grams would've really liked that, that he looked up and agreed to speak.

To see a kid as big as he was, breakdown as he spoke

about his beloved grandmother, was a ride I just wasn't ready for, and neither were the hundreds of people in attendance, as not an eye would remain dry.

He talked about the things she use to tell him when he was little, how she use to sneak in his room as night to read him bedtime stories after I had already sent him to bed. Oh, and she always brought a few snacks for them to eat together.

He said that, while some kids would be sad about their parents not wanting them, Porky was grateful, and thankful to them, for if it wasn't for their un-parenting ways, Grams would've never been a part of his life.

I loved my Grandmother to death. She was my flesh and blood, and God knows I was hurting bad.

But I have to be honest. I don't think I took it as hard as Pork did. He seriously looked lost.

After the burial, we all went back to the apartment. The placed seemed so strange without her, and reeked of everything Grams. From her style of decoration, to the smell of her perfume, that lingered for months. Rosie said it was her way of letting us know that she's still here.

Every day we would find something that reminded us of Grams, a note reminding her to do something that she never got to do, a half done crossword puzzle, her favorite cup. It just wouldn't end, making it almost impossible to heal.

We decided to start looking for a house. We chose Queens, because Long Island would be too far for me to commute consistently into the City, so we settled in Forest Hills. Great neighborhood, great community!

We ended up putting Dora into a private school. Pork wanted to stay in public as he was already in High School. Still the sweetest kid you would ever want to know, but also the scariest!

Sal continued to drive me everywhere. It was like his entire life revolved around mine. The good thing was, I didn't mind, and neither did he. In fact, I don't think these orders were coming from Mr. D anymore, Sal became family. Sometimes in a day he would take Porky and Dora to school, drop Rosie off at the market, bring me to the city, pick Rosie up and take her home and then meet me at Cuba's that evening, and seemed to enjoy every moment of it.

Sal was still as sharp as ever, and just as fit, but let's face it, he was getting up there in age, and though he would never admit it, we figured Sal to be around 70, or very close to it, and just in case, Rosie and I both finally got our drivers licenses.

CHAPTER 21

No Tambourines

Cuba and Red applauded as I removed the headphones. Cuba sat on the piano bench and Red behind the tiny outdated mixing board that Cuba kept on the small aluminum TV table.

I plopped down on the couch, as it had taken me twelve takes to finally get it right, and these were just reference demos that we were recoding until my contract was up with The Funky Junky which was in less than a week. We didn't want to record at any of the major studios because Mr. D would have surely found out, and that could've cost us some legal issues to say the least.

Thank God for Sal, for he could've turned us in at any time, but he didn't. He eventually figured out what we were up to, and clearly understood, saying that as long as I continued playing by the rules, and doing everything that I was supposed to for Mr. D. which meant, five albums, tour support for each one, and that our evening hook ups weren't interfering with my obligations to the Funky Junky, that all should be fine.

Sal even hooked me up with one of his old lawyer friends that would help me to transition when the time came. I couldn't go to anyone else, because everyone knew Mr. D, and I couldn't risk a leak.

My sales were still pretty good, but the excitement from the fans was nothing like it used to be. Old King here had to make some changes, because this story would soon be over.

"So we have eighteen songs ready to go, King." Red said as he took his seat across from me. Cuba sat on the couch beside me and grabbed a handful of chips that he had laid out.

"So how many songs are we going to use?" Cuba asked Red. "I say ten songs plus a remix of Yes Yes Y'all." Red replied. "That's a good idea." I added.

"Well we have eighteen songs, how do we choose?" Cuba asked.

"I say we record them all and see which ten we like best." Red pointed at me and nodded.

"Yes, that's how we have to do it."

"I already know which ten I like best." Cuba said.

"So do I," Red replied.

"Me too!" I followed, and we all started laughing.

"So what do we do with the remaining eight songs?" I asked.

"Well, we'll go back to the studio and redo them for the next album." Red replied.

"That's dumb." Cuba added, before shoving more chips into his fat face.

"Why's that dumb?" I asked.

"We're gonna have a superior product, let's just record what's needed and move on."

"This ain't Latin music." I jumped in. "Won't these sounds outdate quick."

"Nobody's heard these sounds before." Cuba replied.

"Yeah, these won't start dating until they're released." Red added.

There was a knock on the door, and Cuba looked its way, as the only company he ever gets is us, and we're here already.

"That's Sal!" I said as I got up and headed toward the door. "He said he was picking me up early."

"That's cool, I got some shit to do too." Red said as he too got up and started gathering his things.

"Wadup, King?" Quenepa said as he stood in the doorway. We never let Q into anything we were doing, mainly because we had no intentions of keeping him around.

Red and Cuba stopped in their tracks and looked our way. Q had on a black hoodie with his hands tucked away in the big front pocket. I stepped back as he stepped into the apartment. His eyes scanned the room, the instruments, and snacks on the coffee table. He looked at Cuba with the most disgusted look ever. I've been around Cuba long enough to see how nervous he was. The only experience he ever had with Q, was one of terror.

"What's going on here? He asked with a sort of sinister smile. I watched as his eyes bounced to and from each of us. Cuba looked at Red, and Red at me.

"Just jamming," I replied.

"Jammin?" Q asked. "Does Mr. D know about this?" Again we all looked at each other. "Hmm, I didn't think so!" Q, laughed as he picked up a chip and popped it in his mouth.

"We were working on a few ideas, in hopes of presenting them to Mr. D for the next album." I explained.

"Oh, okay cool. So, how are my parts coming out?" he asked, his smile large and sarcastic. We all remained silent.

"Hmm okay, I get it." He said, nodding his head.

"Come on man, it's not like."

"Oh it's not? So what is it like?"

"Listen, Q..." and at that very moment, he pulls out a gun and points it directly at me.

"You think I'm stupid?"

"Come on, Q." Red says. Q then turns the gun on him.

"You mother fucker's are working me out of the picture."

"Nobody's working you out of nothing..."

"Bullshit!" He yelled, his eyes looking red and watery.

"Q, man, come on bro. You know I don't get down like that."

"But you do, King! You do get down like that, and now, so do these mother fuckers." He said, waving the gun back and forth between Red and Cuba, both of them looking scared as shit.

"I put you on to this fagot," he said gesturing at Cuba. "Got you your stolen shit back, as well as the mother fucker who stole it, and this is how you do me?"

I was really nervous now, as Q kept waving the gun between us. I swore that at any second it would go off, the question was… who would it hit?"

Q stepped up close to me, his gun now pressed against the side of my head. He was yelling and crying, as if he knew that once he did this, that it was over for him, but I could tell, he didn't care.

All suddenly all went quiet, and everything that moved, did so in slow motion. The sound of the hammer being cocked back on the pistol was loud and echoing. My eyes shifted over to where Red and Cuba were standing. Though I couldn't hear him, I saw his mouth say No, and watched as Cuba dropped down behind the couch.

I thought I could move out of the way, but I couldn't. My legs felt like they were stuck in cement, so instead, I shut my eyes, and raised my shoulders waiting to feel the impact of hot lead piercing my skull. Till finally, there it was. So loud in fact, that my ears began ringing. I couldn't figure out whether I was dead or alive.

I heard a thump, and felt something fall to my feet, I looked down, swearing I was having an out of body experience, when I realized that the body that lay at my sneakers wasn't my own, but rather Q's.

Sal, stood there, his gun still held out in front of him, a stream of smoke ascending from its barrel. I turned and saw

Red, then spotted Cuba, rising from behind the couch. I took a step back from Q's now lifeless body, and watched as it collapsed the rest of its way to the floor. Still, all I could hear was a constant ringing. I watched Red as he rushed over to Cuba and helped him up.

I looked at Sal, my head shaking from side to side as I tried to speak but couldn't. Sal pretty much knew what I was gonna say,

"It was either you or him," he said, when suddenly, another figure appeared in the doorway behind Sal, and when he noticed my eyes glance over his shoulder, he spun around, gun still drawn.

"No!" I yelled, my voice feeling as if it had just broke through a brick wall. It was Porky!

"What's going on?" Porky asked as Sal put away his gun and I closed the door.

"Is that Q?" Porky asked, inspecting the lifeless body. "Oh no, what happened?" he asked.

"Nothing you need to know right now." I replied. Porky didn't like the answer and looked at Sal.

You can't keep him in the dark about this," Sal said to me.

I started to pace the room, in disbelief that any of this was happening, when I noticed flashing lights outside. I rushed to the window and sure enough, it was a cop car double parked outside the building.

"Fuckin' cops!" I said, frustrated.

"Calm the down," Sal said. "we need to get this mother fucker out of here, like right now!"

"Fuck we supposed to do? Flush it down the toilet?" "No, but put him in the tub until the cops clear out."

I was hesitant to even touch him, but Porky wasn't, and scooped him up like a rag doll, carrying him into the bathroom. A huge stain of blood was left on the wood floor, so Sal grabbed the small mat in front of the door and placed it on top of the blood, and then placed the Conga's on top. He lowered the lights to try and hide any blood that might've splattered, and then waved Red over, and told him to start playing.

Cuba was still a wreck and shaking. Sal guided him over to the piano and told him to start playing.

"What should I play?" He cried out.

"Whatever calms you the fuck down!"

Cuba looked over at Red who was whacking a mellow beat, and followed along. Even in this unnerving situation, those two created pure magic.

"Now you!" Sal said, pointing at me. "Get behind that microphone, and start doing what you do. Suddenly there was a knock on the door, and everyone stopped! But Sal rolled his hands in the air gesturing to them to keep playing.

"Oh no, you guys again?" Officer Lopez asked as he and his partner stepped into the apartment, their eyes scoping out the place while he spoke.

"Hey, how's it going?"

"As good as it's going to get in the hood! Now tell me, who shot who?"

We all were thrown off from that question as we looked

around at each other.

"What do you mean?" I asked.

"Well, someone called and said that they heard a gunshot, supposedly from this apartment." Officer Lopez explained, laughing as he was sure there was a good explanation.

"Hey, you guys shoot anyone?" Sal joked. We all looked at each other and shook our heads.

"Sorry Officer, nobody shot anyone tonight. But I promise, the minute somebody does..." And suddenly, we heard what did sound like a gunshot. We all jumped and both officers reached for their guns.

"Oh, I'm sorry!" Cuba said. I was trying out different sounds using this." He held up his tambourine and then smacked the aluminum radiator cover.

While everyone was agreeing how much it sounded like a gunshot, my thoughts were on how perfect of an ear this guy had to be able to emulate it on the spot.

Everyone nodded, as did the officers.

"If you don't mind," Lopez began. "Just for tonight, please... No tambourines!" Cuba, smiled, and nodded.

"You guys have a good night okay, and if you can keep it down, at least for tonight, I'd really appreciate it.

As Sal was about to close the door, a loud noise came from the bathroom.

"What was that?" Officer Jimmy asked. We all put that dumb face on, as if we didn't hear a thing. "It sounded like it came from the bathroom." Jimmy and Lopez took out their guns and made their way toward the bathroom. My heart began to pound and Cuba fund his spot back behind the couch. I noticed Sal remove his gun from under his arm, and hold it low to his side as he headed in their direction. I stepped in front of him, and shook my head. But he ignored me.

The two officers then pushed open the door, as Sal made his way directly behind them, only to find Porky, sitting on the toilet.

Both officers grabbed their faces as the stench that came from the three hundred plus kid, hit them like a bag of bricks. They placed their guns back into their holsters, as did Sal.

Porky sat there, acting innocent and embarrassed.

"Can you tell someone to get me some toilet paper?" He asked the officers.

"Sorry kid." Lopez said as he and Jimmy backed away. I grabbed a roll of paper and brought it over to Porky, who then thanked me and closed the door.

Waving his hand in front of him, Cuba made a distorted Face.

"There's spray behind the toilet!" he yelled out.

The Officers left and Sal quickly locked the door behind them."

"That shit was close." Red said, but Sal stopped him, by placing his finger up to his mouth. We kept quiet, watching Sal as he peeked out the window, and waited for the officers to get in their car and drive off. Once he was sure, he turned and looked at us.

"He's still alive!" Pork yelled as he rushed out of the bathroom." Sal shushed him, and then went to see for himself. I followed behind.

"Yo, it fucking stinks in here!" Quenepa cried out.

"Oh my God, he *is* still alive!" I cheered, as I thanked God.

"Q, don't worry bro, you're gonna be okay." I said peeking into the tub where he laid, his eyes trying to focus. We gotta call an ambulance?" I said to Sal.

"No no, just get me a wet towel," he commanded. Cuba overheard him and met me in the kitchen. I rushed back to the bathroom and handed Sal the towel just as he was exiting the bathroom, and while with it he wiped his hands, he calmly told me,

"he didn't make it!"

CHAPTER 22

Today Never Happened

I sat in the back seat as we drove through the city back to my house. I stared out the window, watching the buildings swoosh by. Sal was driving of course, and Porky sat across from me. He was talking, but I couldn't focus on anything except the image of Q. It was all so clear. Each detail, from the blood oozing from his head, to the way his clothes bunched up under him. And though it might not have been by my hands, I would forever be tortured.

I know, had I included him in our plans, none of this would've happened. But there was no place for him. I didn't need a Court Jester. Actually, I didn't want one. I wanted to be solo, totally solo. His small size made him nothing more than a sort of novelty add-on, a freak show side kick. I wanted to break away from that shit. I hated it since day one, and now I was literally tired of it. It was corny when we first started, even more so, all these years later.

"Rey!" yelled Porky. I turned to him. "Were you listening to me?" He asked. I shook my head.

"King, listen closely." Sal said from the driver's seat. I glanced his way, our eyes meeting through the mirror.

"Today never happened, you hear me?" I just looked at him, speechless. "Erase it!" He added. But seriously, how could I? Q had his ways, was a pain in the ass, and sometimes even dangerous. But I gotta be honest, he became a friend.

My eyes became flooded so I rubbed my face and opened the window for some fresh air. I took a few deep breaths, inhaling the coolness from outside, and then turned to Porky. I couldn't believe he was now a part of all this. I felt fucking horrible, and then busted out crying,

"from all nights, why tonight?" I asked referring to him showing up. "I'm supposed to protect you from shit like this!" I cried hysterically.

"It's okay Rey," Pork replied, in his typical gentle giant voice.

"You don't know anything, Pork! You hear me?" Porky nodded. "You weren't here. In fact, I don't ever want you to go over there again. You've never been there, okay?" Porky just kept nodding, saying, Okay Rey.

I turned to Sal. "He can't get in trouble for this, man, I'll take the rap, just please, don't even mention him, ever!!"

Pork slid over to my side and grabbed me into his huge arms.

"Grams made me promise to always take care of you, and look what happened. No sooner that she's gone, and I fuck up!"

"But you didn't, Rey. You weren't doing anything but

your music, and Sal was hired to protect you, and that's what he did. Imagine if he wasn't there."

I thought about what Pork was telling me, in disbelief that this sixteen year old giant could be so smart, and compassionate.

"But what if they come around asking questions?"

"Just take what you guys did yesterday and apply it today, this way you are all on the same page." Sal said.

"What did you do yesterday, Rey?" Porky asked. I thought about it, trying to work my memory around the horrific image that refused to vacate my thoughts.

"Well, we completed the last song, and then started listening back, taking notes."

"Did you guys eat anything?" Sal asked.

"Yeah, Cuba made black beans, white rice, tostones' and palomilla. Oh, and he also made a flan."

"Mmm" Porky said as he licked his lips.

"Well, now erase everything that went down today, and replace it with whatever you did yesterday."

"But what about Red, and Cuba?"

"I told them the same thing." Sal replied.

"And what about Q, I mean, what's gonna happen with him?"

"The Cleaning Crew's on their way there now."

"Cleaning crew? What cleaning crew?" I asked.

"The one's from the office." Sal replied.

Every day it seemed I would learn something new about

the Funky Junky and everyone that worked there. This company was much more than just a record company. In fact, I started to wonder whether its main purpose had anything at all to do with music.

"We supposed to go on tour next week. What happens then?

"He's just gonna be a no show, it's not like that's never happened." Sal replied.

"Maybe a show or two, but not the whole damn tour!"

"Let Mr. D figure that one out."

"What do you mean, let Mr. D figure that one out? Like, what are we supposed to say? He's gonna eventually figure this whole shit out."

"He doesn't have to figure shit out… he already knows!"

"What?"

Who do you think is sending over the Cleaning Crew?"

I sat back and looked out my window. We had gotten onto the highway and would be home real soon.

"Rey," Pork said in a low voice. I turned and looked at him. "Can I go on tour with you?" He whispered.

"Not this one Pork, *especially* not this one.

"But you say that every time."

"It's because the road is no place for you, man. It's all bullshit, trust me!

"Then why do you keep doing it?"

"To pay bills, that's it!"

"Rey, you have enough money to pay your bills for the

rest of your life."

"Besides, you still have to go to school."

"I'm ahead… I can afford to miss…"

"I said no!" I yelled at him. "This might look all cool and shit, but the truth is, it's all bullshit! It's a dark and nasty life, full of yes people and ass kissers. You can't even tell the difference between your friends, and your enemies."

I didn't mean it to happen, but my eyes shifted over to Sal's review mirror through which I noticed him looking.

Pork slid back over to the other side and rested his forehead against the window looking out.

"Pork, look at me, man?" Porky, with his head still against the window turned and looked.

"Look at this fucking hair," My voice, now much calmer. "I've been wearing this shit for over five years. It used to be a bright gold, like a crown. The shits white now! I told Mr. D, and he said, leave it, and just say it's platinum!

I'm sick of this shit, man? I have no real life. Everything I do is according to contract. I can't just take off when I want, or even sleep late because my contract obligates me to be in the studio every day. I could barely breathe, Pork."

Look at you. I missed you growing up, and now Dora? She doesn't even know who the fuck I am."

"Yes she does, Rey. She talks about you all the time. You're her hero."

"Porky, please, focus on school. Go to college. The world is all yours man, don't throw it away on some bullshit job like this. There's so much more the world can offer you. Go and get it!"

Porky didn't respond, he just sat back, and so did I. I glanced to the front and saw Sal's eyes look away. I don't know if anything I said sunk in, I really hope it did. I love this kid, like if he was my own flesh and blood. It would kill me if anything were to happen to him. It also scared me that he was so big. He looked like a man, and anyone could easily mistake him as one.

Sal pulled up into my driveway. It was 2:00 am and I could see the light in my bedroom was still on, which meant Rosie was waiting up.

"Good night, Sal." Porky said as he continued toward the house.

"I'll be right in." I said as I stood with Sal waiting for Porky to go inside.

"Don't say anything to Rosie." He immediately told me. "I know how you hate keeping secrets from her, but there are just some things she really shouldn't know." I looked at him, and exhaled. Sal placed his hand on my shoulder and gave it a bit of a squeeze.

"Every thing's gonna be okay. I promise."

I gave him a subtle nod, before turning, and walking to the house.

CHAPTER 23

Leap of Faith

It had been over a week since Quenepa was killed. What Sal had done to the body I don't know and I didn't ask. Every once in a while his name would come up during rehearsal, but no one ever made a big deal because he basically did the same shit for every show.

Sal pulled into the garage of the Funky Junky and parked beside Red's new ride. I'd never seen anything like it before, but I'll guarantee one thing, it was expensive. We got into the elevator and went up. As usual Roller Girl was standing at the door when it opened.

"Good morning gentlemen." She greeted. Sal nodded, and headed straight for the coffee, and I continued down the hall toward the stairs.

"Reds in the studio?" I asked.

"Uh huh." She replied with a nod and a cute smile.

The office was already in full swing, everyone greeting me as I passed by.

"So, how you been?" Roller Girl asked as I pulled her along.

"Good. What about you?"

"Same ol', my days never change much. How's Rosie doing?"

"She's good."

"And Miss little cutie?"

"Cuter than ever!" I glanced at Roller Girl and though she was smiling and nodding, I could tell that something was bothering her. We stopped at the stairs, and before I went down I asked her.

"Is everything, okay?"

Roller girl looked at me, and took a second. I knew now that something was on her mind.

"What did I do wrong?" She suddenly blurted out, her eyes sad and concerned.

"What do you mean?" I asked, not sure what she was talking about.

"When you first came here, you and I spent quite a bit of time together."

"We did." I agreed, nodding while trying to figure her out.

"What is it, Mary?" I asked as I tapped her chin with my finger making her look up. Her eyes were flooded.

"I really thought we had something." She cried.

"Oh, Mary! Come here." I took her into my arms and held her. A couple of the people popped their heads out of their office and saw us standing there holding each other.

"We're friends, Mary. I mean, I don't think I could've done any of this without you."

"We made love!" She said, a bit louder than I had wished. More heads popped out of their offices. I took her by the hand to bring her to a more private spot, but she just pulled away.

"Mary, that was a long time ago, and it wasn't supposed to happen, you know that.

"What do you mean it wasn't supposed to happen?"

"I was drunk. Shit, I don't even remember what we did!"

"Is that what you told Rosie?"

"Mary, you need to chill out!"

"You told her that you were drunk? That you don't remember anything?"

"What is it that you want?"

"I want her to know. In fact, I want everyone to know.

"Why now? Where is this coming from? I'm married. I have a daughter. We bought a house, and have a life together. Why now, Mary? Why are you telling me all this now?"

"Because I know I can't hold it inside any longer. Why should you live your life in happiness when I'm miserable?"

"I can't believe this is happening."

"It's bullshit, King! You deceived me, played me!"

"Yo, I can't with you right now, and you need to keep your voice down."

"Fuck that!" She suddenly yelled out."

I tried to walk away, but she rolled beside me, yelling at the top of her lungs. Her voice now, echoing throughout the floor.

"Maybe instead of being Mr. D's assistant I should've just been a fucking maid, because obviously that's what you're into!"

"I can't talk to you right now." Again she rolled ahead and blocked me.

"Maybe if I wore a maid's uniform you would've taken me serious, huh? Or maybe if I was Puerto Rican!" "Are you on something?" I asked, as this was not like her at all.

"Oh wait, she's not Puerto Rican, she's Cuban isn't she? Which is it, King, Cuban or Puerto Rican?"

I just looked at her and turned around and headed back toward the lobby. Roller Girl skated ahead of me and then turned and skated backwards in front of me. The office doors began to close as we made our way through the hall.

"That has to be it, King. You want to keep that pure Latin blood in the family. I know your grandmother was really pro Latino." I stopped in my tracks and pointed my finger at her.

"You keep my Grandmother out your mouth!" I sternly warned.

"Oh really, and what? what are you going to do, King, huh? Kill me? I know all of your secrets you sonofabitch."

And at that moment, I totally lost it, and was about to slap the shit out of her when Sal appeared and stopped me.

"What the fuck's going on?" He asked looking back and forth at the two of us. I shrugged my shoulders, and shook my head, noticing all the heads peeking out from the offices.

"Man, I gotta get out of here." I told Sal.

"But Red's waiting for you."

"I can't do this right now. Sal looked at me and shook his head, then placed his hand on my shoulder and together we left. I followed Sal in silence as we made our way down to the garage.

"She talked a whole lot of shit." Sal said as we drove out of the garage.

"Man, I don't know what happened. It's like I don't even know her."

"I'm just surprised it didn't happen sooner."

"What do you mean?" I asked.

"Well, you did sort of lead her on."

"When? How?"

"You were fucking her."

"One time, man!"

"Get the fuck outta here!"

"I'm serious… It was one time, man. In fact, I was so drunk that I don't remember any of it, not even sure if it ever happened!"

"You never talked to her about anything, right?" Sal asked.

"Of course not." I looked over at Sal, his eyes locked on the road.

"Let's go back!" I told Sal, snapping him out of his thoughts.

"Back? You're almost home!"

"Man, I gotta talk to her."

"Maybe you should just wait till tomorrow?"

"Nah, I'll be a mess, and I rather try and diffuse this shit before it gets back to Rosie."

"Does she know anything about you two?"

"No, and now I'm regretting it. It's just that I knew I had to work there and work late and I didn't want Rosie to be worrying about anything. Let's go back, please!"

Sal made a U-Turn back to the Funky Junky, and I remained quite the whole way there, going over in my head what I wanted to tell her.

As we approached the Funky Junky we noticed a couple of Police cars and an ambulance stopped in the middle of the street, their lights bouncing off the buildings around them.

"What the fuck's going on?" I said, as I rolled down my window for a better look. Sal pulled up close to the yellow tape when a Police Officer put out his hand to stop.

"What's going on?" Sal asked as his window went down. When the officer realized who it was, he smiled.

"Oh, hey Sal. Yeah, looks like some chick might've taken a leap of faith!" He so coldly stated.

"What?" Sal asked. I immediately got out of the car, and stared across the street.

My mouth dropped as I started toward the building.

"Excuse me sir!" The Officer shouted. "You can't go in there." But I didn't listen. My eyes started to tear, and I could hear Sal tell the officer to let me go. I picked up speed, as more officers tried to stop me.

"No!" I cried out as I could see her body covered with a white sheet, I knew it was her because one leg was uncovered, and it wore a skate. I ran faster toward her. Two Officers grabbed me and held me back. One of them standing over the body turned and spotted me. It was Officer Lopez.

"Let him go!" He ordered, and they did. I rushed over to the body and he uncovered her face... I flinched, as it was practically unrecognizable. I stared down at her lifeless body, and knew that from this day on I would forever be haunted by our last conversation... Our first argument!

Mr. D appeared out of nowhere and stepped up to the body. I looked up at him, crying hysterically. Mr. D. however showed absolutely no emotion. All he could see was her skate. He looked down at it, then shook his head and walked back into the building.

The authorities couldn't find anyone related to Roller Girl. The application she filled out for Mr. D several years back was full of false information. Nothing matched. Her name, old addresses, previous employers, schools, social security numbers, nothing!

I found out that since no one would claim her body, the state would handle everything. I spoke to Mr. D about giving her a decent funeral and burial but all he said was he didn't want to get involved. I was pissed, but at the same time too torn to even deal with him. I spoke to Rosie and told her that I would like to take care of all her arrangements, and she was okay with it, however the look she gave me sort of hinted that she knew more than I thought.

Porky and Sal helped a lot. I couldn't have done it without them. Between the arrangements, police interviews, rehearsal for the up-coming tour and our continued late night meetings over at Cuba's, I was exhausted.

The day of the funeral, my family and I got there early. Roller Girl was laid out in a beautiful dress that Rosie and Dora had picked out. Her casket was white and just in case she didn't get too many flowers I had gone ahead and pretty much filled the room with my own.

It was a Saturday, and we had already been there for about five hours and to my surprise, not one person from The Funky Junky came by to show their respects. Everyone at the office knew about it and I gave everyone cards with the address and times of service. I even took out an ad with her picture in the paper in hopes that somebody might recognize her. But still, besides Red and Sal, no one else came... Not even Mr. D!

The priest showed up and asked if we should proceed with the service. I nodded.

We all took a few moments and said a little something about Roller Girl. Rosie had only met her a few times, and so they had no relationship, but she still made an effort and got up and said some really nice things. I loved her even more for doing that.

Sal and Red knew her the longest, and had some funny stories to tell, especially the ones about when she didn't know how to skate well.

Speaking of which, I had her skates bronzed. I knew they

did it to baby shoes so I took a chance and asked, and though it wasn't cheap, I did it anyway. I knew Rosie wouldn't have been too comfortable with them displayed in our home so I just kept them in a box stored in the attic.

Porky however surprised me. He had so much to say about Roller Girl, as he probably spent the most time with her. That was her little buddy whenever he came to the office. She even bought him his own skates, so that he can skate with her in the rink, though he enjoyed skating around the office better.

Porky took it pretty bad. First it was Grams, now Roller Girl. He was acting especially nice to me, so I would imagine, thoughts of losing me had been entering his mind.

After we left the cemetery we all went over to the restaurant for an early dinner. I kept catching Rosie staring at me, and whenever I turned her way, she'd look away.

It was an enjoyable dinner, as we continued reminiscing about this very special girl. But no matter how much we talked about her and laughed, I still couldn't understand what made her snap the way she did, and I felt horrible for not thinking there might be something wrong.

But there was also one bigger question that lingered, and it seemed nobody wanted to address. But I couldn't take it any longer and had to ask…

"Why didn't anyone show up?"

CHAPTER 24

Rich Kid

I stood outside Mr. D's office, hesitant to even knock. The last time I stepped foot in there, I thought I was gonna die.

"Come in!" Mr. D yelled out from inside his office. Damn, was I thinking too loud? I opened the door and as usual, he was on the phone. He gestured for me to come in and sit down on his huge purple bean bag. By now I hated the sight of that fucking thing, and fantasized of knifing that shit into shreds.

Instead I went over to my regular spot at the juice bar and waited for Mr. D to finish his call.

I was a little thrown off by his mood. His assistant had just committed suicide and he's laughing and joking like nothing ever happened, and then I thought why would it matter? He didn't even come to her funeral.

He got off the phone and looked at me with a smile, giving my shoulder, what I once considered a friendly squeeze, but nowadays I wasn't so sure. I figured he wanted to talk about what happened to Roller Girl, but instead, he wanted to talk about the tour.

It was a regular U.S. tour, and since Mr. D generated most of his money here in the U.S. He liked these best. He started talking about how the sales were already going and he expected this to be the most successful tour yet. I listened to him ramble on about all the politics going on within Solar Records, and how his deal with them was nearly up. He was setting the Funky Junky up to begin handling its own distribution as well as the distribution of other labels. This was indeed a big deal, I knew that for sure, but there was just too much shit happening for me to seem excited.

I wanted so bad to just stop him from yapping and asking him straight out why he didn't attend Roller Girl's funeral, let alone contribute in its expenses. I didn't know anything about her relationship with the Funky Junky. What was her true position, how did they pay her or did they pay her at all? We never really spoke about *her*, it was usually about *me*, and now I'm regretting it.

Mr. D kept cracking these little corny jokes every now and then, trying to feel me out. But I made it obvious. I wasn't feeling him or his jokes. I just wanted to get to the point, and then get the fuck outta there.

Mr. D was no longer the person I thought he was. In fact, I found him to be quite horrible, and I couldn't wait till I was free of him and his bullshit company.

Finally he became quiet, and his face expressionless. I figured finally he would bring up Roller Girl, and I was hoping for clarity, but to my surprise, that's not what he asked. Instead he asked...

"Where the fuck's Quenepa?" That question threw me for a complete loop, because as far as I knew, Mr. D knew all about it, and was even the one who ordered the cleanup.

I didn't know what to say. Was this a trap? Was he trying to see if I would say anything to anyone? Sal told me he knew all about it, but as far as Mr. D was concerned, he didn't know shit!

Q, was never asked about... ever! He never made it to rehearsals, which was fine because all of his choreography was improvised. Not even his no-shows mattered anymore, as Jini became his understudy, and did an even better job.

At that very moment, there was a knock on the door.

"Come in!" Mr. D yelled out, and in stepped Sal.

"Come on in and close the door." Sal did as he was told, walked over and stood beside me.

Mr. D's eye's bounced from Sal to me, and then back.

"So nobody seems knows where Quenepa is, any idea?" Subtly, I glanced at Sal, using my peripheral vision, wondering what he was going to say.

"No, it's been a minute. I did see him on the street about a week ago on my way to pick up King from his house. He didn't see me, so I didn't say anything."

Mr. D stared at us. Studying our faces for what I would think were clues. Clues of whether or not we were lying. I held my end up pretty well considering I was scared to death. Sal was beyond convincing. His poker face was that of a master player.

"Well, we have a bit of a problem, fellas."

Sal and I remained silent and listened. He walked up to Sal and stood mere inches from his face. It was the first time I'd ever seen even a hint that Sal might've been scared of anything, let alone any*body!*"

"Besides you, is there anyone else in this world that I trust more?" Mr. D asked in a low, yet piercing tone.

"No one," Sal replied with a slight shake of his head.

"Speak up!" Mr. D suddenly yelled out. I jumped, and watched as spit flew from Mr. D's mouth onto Sal's face, but he acted like nothing, and just stood there.

"No!" Sal yelled back, and though this time it was louder, I still maintained composure. I wish I knew the truth behind their relationship, because it never made much sense to me.

Sal sometimes seemed like a servant to Mr. D. He would do absolutely anything Mr. D asked, even if that meant kill someone... Shit, even if it meant, kill me!

Mr. D continued pacing in front of us. He seemed deep in his thoughts, and I wondered, what he would say next. He stopped again, his back to us, and then did a military type of about face, once again meeting up with Sal's eyes.

"There isn't even a definition, of the level of trust that I have for you."

"I know that sir, and I feel the same way." Sal replied.

"At the same time, there isn't a word that exist, that would describe the level of devastation I would feel, had you ever betray me."

Sal sounded as cool and calm as ever, his intense military training certainly paying off. Half of me wanted Mr. D to get to the point, so that I could get the fuck out of here, while the other half was terrified to find out where that point might lead.

"Now, I've seen you and King become mighty close over the years, sort of like, family! Am I right?

"You are."

"Yet, you stated many times that I was your only family, am I right again?"

"Yes!"

"The question now, is which family are you most tied to, Sal, mine or his?"

"Well, I feel like we're all one big family."

"That's not the answer I'm looking for." Mr. D. continued. "There are two families, but only one you can choose... Which will it be?"

"Well of course yours!" Sal finally stated. Though it hurt a bit, I'm sure glad that was his answer.

Mr. D nodded his head, and smiled. He seemed satisfied, and right now, that's all that mattered.

Then, out of nowhere, Mr. D says to Sal.

"If Quenepa doesn't show up between now and the day the tour departs, you're not going on the tour. I'm going to want you to stay behind and find him. Dead, alive, in pieces, I don't give a fuck!"

I felt there was much more to this whole ordeal, as I was Mr. D's prized possession, and to not have his top soldier on the road to watch over me, seemed real sketchy.

Sal nodded, but I could tell, he didn't like the idea one bit. He didn't say anything though, and I'm glad.

There was no way they would ever find Q, and now my concern was, who would come with me? The road was a crazy place, and besides Sal, I didn't know anyone else I could trust.

"Don't let me down." Mr. D said to Sal before dismissing him. He gestured for me to stay, and waited until Sal was gone. Once the door closed he gave it another minute and then looked at me.

"I have a feeling that Sal has something to do with Quenepa's disappearance."

"What makes you think that? Wasn't he the one to put him on?"

"Not at all, I've known Q, since he was a kid. His parents are very important people, and they asked that I look out for him.

"He lives in a rat infested basement."

"Because he wants to! everyone thinks he's this fuckin' gangsta from the ghetto… when all he really is, is some spoiled-ass rich kid from Long Island!"

"I thought that was just a silly rumor?"

"Not at all, and the reason I put him down with the project, was so I could keep an eye on him."

"Why didn't you tell me anything?"

"I wanted to. But once you two started hanging out, I was worried about you saying something."

This situation was getting more and more intense. My mind could barely process what the hell I was hearing, let alone how to fix it.

"Does Sal know about this?"

"Yep! Sal knows everything. That's the purpose behind me having people that I trust. Once I trust you, I'm an open book. And now, I need you to know, because we have to find him. This is some serious shit, King, and if there was any foul play... We're done. All of us, and our families!"

Mr. D gave me enough reason to tell him what happened. But there really was no telling whether it was all just a set up, a set up to see if I would snitch. I was in a fucked up place, and God knows, I wanted out.

Mr. D sat behind his desk and started flipping through his papers. It was his way of saying, this meeting's over. I turned and headed toward the door, but before exiting I turned and asked him one last question.

"So, if Sal doesn't make the tour... Who are you sending?"

I stood there, awaiting his answer, and without looking up from what he was doing, he simply said... "Porky!"

CHAPTER 25

My Stories

I took off the rest of the week and decided to just hang out with my family until it was time to hit the road again. It was bittersweet as not working was a bit tortuous for me. Every once in a while Rosie would catch me pick up a notebook and start writing, she'd take it from me and hide it. Sometimes Dora would come and sit on my lap to read to me, but my mind would wonder. I hated when that happened, I felt like a bad father. But I would try my hardest to pay attention to her, and try and strike up a conversation with her which held my attention much more.

Sal was picking Pork up every day and bringing him to the Funky Junky to use the gym, and train him on the working of a road manager. They would get back every night around 8:00 pm, and Sal would stay for dinner, and then leave.

Pork was getting huge, this kid wasn't even seventeen yet, and he was a beast. He took really good care of himself though, worked out every day, ran, ate right, he got on all of us about taking care of ourselves, but the only one who listened was Dora. She always knew that Pork wasn't her real brother, but that didn't matter, she adored him, and he felt the same.

We had a great family, one to be proud of. The only one missing of course was Grams. Dora never got to know her, though she spoke about her like she did. We even told her that she was named after her which made her feel like Gram's closet relative.

We kept a beautiful portrait of Grams in the family room over the fireplace. It was the photo we took at the Ziegfeld during my video release party. She was so happy there. Probably the happiest I've ever seen her, and I was so fortunate to have caught it on film.

When I had gone overseas I had this artist create a painted portrait of the photo and had it sent to Grams as a birthday gift, since I wasn't there. She loved it, but never wanted to take it out of the box in fear of it being ruined. I use to laugh because I knew it was because she didn't like how she looked. I thought she looked absolutely beautiful and I knew one day, when I owned a fireplace, her portrait would be hung above it.

Our last dinner together was special. Sal was invited to stay, but he felt best that we be left alone. He would be back to pick us up in the morning to take us to the Funky Junky to board the bus.

Porky was so excited even though I still had mixed feelings about it. Dora was still too young to understand why I had to go on the road, and Rosie? Well, she would always be sad when I had to leave. We had our arguments about it in the past, but she knew I was signed to a deal that obligated me to go on the road to sell records. Rosie also wasn't happy about Porky going on the road either. I never had any serious altercations on the road, and the fact that Pork was so damn big, I felt he was intimidating enough to keep it that way.

After hanging out a bit with the family, I knew we had to be up early so I advised Pork to get some rest, but I could see it in his face, he was way too excited and would probably break night. That was okay though, he could sleep on the bus. We would be on the road for thirty days, and by the time the tour was over, Pork would know for sure whether or not this was for him.

I carried Dora to her room to tuck her into bed. She was seven years old and my whole life revolved around her. After tucking her in, she asked me to lay with her, and so I did. She held me in her arms like if I was the child and her, the adult. She would stroke my hair just like Grams use to do.

She would always ask me to tell her stories at night. She never liked the regulars like Little Red Riding Hood, or the Three Bears. She liked *my* stories, the ones I made off the top of my head, those are the ones that made her laugh and ask a million questions. Stories like The Magic Bird, who would carry Little Dora off to different lands and adventures. The Flying Girl, and The Mermaid. All of which she was the main character.

The funniest though was when she would ask me to read one of her favorite *My Stories* again, and though I did my best to remember as much of it as I could, I would always leave shit out, or say something different, and she'd catch it each time and correct me.

These were very special times and it seemed like they were flying. I straightened out the dozen stuffed animals she had propped around her pillow. The big ones over her head, they kept guard, and the smaller ones were placed under the covers where they'd be safe and warm. I gave Dora a kiss and told her I loved her. The hardest thing about being on the road was leaving her, it tore me apart and the moment I left her room, I would already be anxious to get back. I know that seems a bit ungrateful, seeing that I was living a life many could only dream, but if I didn't feel that way, then I probably wouldn't be human, or at the very least... a dad!

Rosie was still cleaning up when I left Dora's room so I went into mine and placed the last few items into my bag. I undressed and got into my shower. I'm usually a cold water type of guy, but tonight I needed a serious unwind, so a hot shower it was.

I heard the door to my shower open, and when I turned around, there stood my beautiful wife. My eyes dripped down her perfectly naked body. I reached out and took her hand, guiding her into the shower. We'd been together now for several years, and still, she excited me more than ever.

We stared into each other's eyes, both flooding with tears. I wrapped my arms around her, and she placed her head against my chest, and there we stayed... saying nothing!

CHAPTER 26

Sad Goodbyes

Pork got out of Sal's car super excited. Many times he was there to help us load the buses, then stand on the curb with others to wave us off. But this time, he was coming with us, and I don't remember ever seeing him this excited.

Everyone at the Funky Junky knew and loved Porky. Shit, they practically watched him grow up. As big as he was, he was always kind and courteous to everyone. From Mr. D, to the guy who patrols the garage. To him, everyone was the same. He was a gentleman, and very charming. All he had to do was walk through a door, and he would immediately attract people.

He was the type to walk around a room and greet everyone. He would always stop and talk to them, ask them about their families, and seem to always remember something special that they might have in common.

Before taking off, Porky popped in on the other buses to say hi. Everyone was as excited as he was to have him along.

"Hey Porky baby!" the girls would call out to him and

wave. Many would go out of their way to go give him a hug and kiss, and he loved every minute of it.

Ben, one of the drivers that hauled our costumes, props and special equipment also had the responsibility of loading the truck on his own. He had been doing it for years, but now that he was getting up there in age it wasn't quite that easy anymore.

Pork saw him struggling with a few things and right away went to his rescue. He suggested Ben start up the engine, and Pork in no time loaded the truck. You could see in Ben's eyes just how much he appreciated it, and when he reached out to shake Pork's hand in gratitude, Pork hugged him instead. In fact, Pork hugged everyone, even strangers. I told him many times that he had to stop doing that. I remember Grams getting on me when he was little. She told me that if he wants to hug people, let him!

"Pork, come on man, we're out!" I yelled out. Porky came jumping out of the Dancer's bus.

You could see the entire bus lift once he was off. He rushed over and up in our bus all out of breath.

"Chill man, you're too excited."

"I Know. I can't help it!"

"You ready for this?" Sal asked Porky, who nodded like an 8 year old getting candy. "You're on the job now, kid. Remember everything we spoke about."

"I will Sal. I got this!"

"I have no doubt in my mind." Porky grabbed Sal and hugged him like a bear. I laughed when I saw Sal's feet leave the floor.

"That's enough!" Sal said, in a sort of suffocating voice.

Porky let him go, and then headed to his seat.

"Man Sal, I really wish you were coming." I said as I reached out and took his hand.

"I know, King, me too. But you'll be okay. If you need anything, I don't care what it is you get in touch with me right away, you hear?" I nodded. "And I know Porky's there to take care of *you*, but…"

"…I know." I interrupted. "I got him, he'll be fine!" We smiled and he patted me on the shoulder.

"Well what do we have here, sad goodbyes?" Mr. D asked, as he stepped up to the door of the bus, his face reeking of sarcasm.

"I'm just not use to being on the road without him." I said. Mr. D just nodded, his eyes bouncing between Sal and I, as if he was suspecting something.

"Well." Mr. D began. "Our friend Quenepa never showed up, huh?' All I could do was shake my head. Sal remained still and silent.

"This is really strange, don't you think?" again, his eyes bouncing between us. "So this is what's going to happen, you're going to go out there and put on an incredible concert. In the meantime, Sal is going to turn over every stone in New York City until he finds Quenepa. If for any reason, he doesn't turn up by the time you get back, you're going to find that the Funky Junky has made some serious changes." I looked at Sal, and remained expressionless.

"Now, if any of you, at any time, suddenly remembers what might've happened to him, I will expect you to contact me immediately, am I clear?"

"Loud and clear," I replied, and Sal nodded.

"Enjoy your tour!" Said Mr. D before turning around and heading back into the building.

"Fuck we gonna do?" I asked.

"He's going to do everything he can to break us. Make us confess, and even turn on each other. Whatever you do, King, don't fall for any of his tricks. He will tell you that I said something and turn us against one another just to get the truth."

"But he knows something's up." I said.

"Doesn't matter, he won't do anything on assumptions. He'd want to know for a fact, which to him that means a confession. If that happens, King, trust me when I tell you. We're done!"

"What about Cuba and Red? I mean if Mr. D approached them, they might crack."

"I had a long talk with the two of them. I told them, since they didn't see anything, they don't know anything. I told them to work around that entire day. That day never happened. Talk about the day before, the day after, but not that day."

"I don't know, Sal. Something isn't sitting right with me. Something's up. I could feel it!"

"I know." Sal agreed. "I feel it too. Just remember, if anything seems out of order while you're on the road, straighten it out." At that moment, Sal handed me a gun. "Keep this shit with you at all times."

"Fuck man. What am I supposed to do with this?"

"It's the same one that I have, so you know how to use it."

Sal had taken me out to the piers one night and let me shoot a few off a few clips. I had never even touched a gun before that, and wondered why he was so adamant about me learning. Now I know!

"In the overhead bin above your seat there's a small box way in the back. It has two more clips and a box of shells. Try and keep this on you at all times. And if ever you get stopped, and they find it on you, get in touch with me first!"

"You're getting me real nervous, Sal."

"You should be. Mr. D can be a real fucked up human being."

Our driver got up on the bus, excusing himself as he cut through us and got into his seat.

"Hey Rey, we're ready?" Pork yelled out from his seat. I shook Sal's hand again, and watched as he turned and got off.

I walked to my seat and watched as he just stood at the curb waiting for us to leave. The outside of the windows were pretty dark, so I knew he couldn't see me. But waved anyway, wondering if this would be the last time I ever saw him.

As we drove past the Funky Junky I also noticed, out on the balcony, the same one from which Roller Girl had fallen, there stood Mr. D. I wasn't sure how long he had been standing there, or whether or not he saw Sal pass me the gun.

I turned around and watched as Porky, went around trying out the different seats, flushing the toilet, and looking in closets. It was things like that, that reminded me of his age. Finally he came over and sat in the seat across from me. I looked at him, his smile as exaggerated as ever. I smiled back, though the feeling I had in my stomach, was quite up-setting. I would've loved to have been able to enjoy our first trip together, but I was seriously having trouble getting it together.

"Ready?" The driver asked, and before I could say anything, Porky beat me to it.

"Ready!!!!"

CHAPTER 27

Fighting For Towels

This tour wasn't showing the success it had in the past. I guess ol' King wasn't doing it for them anymore. Most of the people who attended were die-hard King fans, but there were no sign of new fans. I know Mr. D was getting the feedback, and was probably not happy. My value was fading, which I'm sure would make any decision Mr. D might wanna make towards me that much easier.

On an up note, I was enjoying this trip now that Pork was down, and I was impressed by the way he handled his job. It was like he went from a little kid, to a grown man in the time it took us to get to our first stop.

The fact that everyone liked him made it even more enjoyable. He helped everyone while always keeping one eye on me. He was great, and I prayed that we got through this tour without any altercations.

As soon as we would arrive at a city, he would go into our room, shower, change and have the driver bring him to the venue. He walked around like a show horse, happy and proud. He introduced himself to everyone. The security guards, ushers, sound and lighting people, as well as all of the opening acts and their people. I've noticed this quality of his since he was a kid. I don't even think I've ever seen him get mad, sad, yeah on occasions, but never mad.

During sound check he would stand on the side watching us in awe. As many times as he's seen us rehearse, watching us now on stage, and not just on a video brought a whole new experience. Pork wasn't obligated to do anything but hang out with me. Though technically, he was there to watch over me, it still seemed I was watching over him! Yeah, he brought it up to me a few times, but I didn't care. He would always be my little man, and I would always be protective of him no matter what the situation. No matter how old he got, or even how big, I'd always jump in front of his bullet first.

Pork could never just sit around. Especially if he knew someone could use some help. He gave himself more work that he ever needed, from helping the roadies with the equipment, and merchandise. To even helping some of the dancers with their outfits. That was his favorite!

Jini played the Court Jester, even better than Q did. She was small like him, the heavy makeup never revealed who he was anyway. She was great, and took the role serious. She even learned to walk like him, which bugged me out every time I saw her in costume.

Q's original vocals were still on the track, so all Jini had to do was lip-sync, which she did perfectly. Oh, and don't forget, she's also a dancer, and actually choreographed her own routine, something Q would've never been able to do.

Jini was smart, and totally hijacked that character. I watched her every move.

Pork and I shared hotel rooms in every city. Though I was use to my privacy on the road, I wouldn't feel safe with him being by himself, besides, he loved staying with me, I don't think he would've wanted his own room.

Every night we called Rosie and Dora. I would speak to them both, and then hand the phone over to Pork. He and Dora had a great relationship, and she could never wait to talk to him and tell him about her day's adventures.

Every other night, when Porky was hanging out with the dancers, I would call Sal, just to get some feedback as to what was happening at the Funky Junky. He kept assuring me that the waters were calm, but to me, it sounded more like shit was about to go down.

He was ordered to find Q, no matter! And though I never asked him what he did with the body, the fact that he never even considered delivering it, made me wonder what the fuck he did with it.

I suggested to Sal about me confronting Mr. D myself, and explaining what exactly happened that night. But he just laughed at my silly suggestion, and then changed the subject.

This was a bad situation, and I saw no way out. We were half way through the tour, and the fact that it wasn't doing as good as it used to, simply told me, that I would have no leverage.

Promoters didn't seem as friendly to me as they once were. Me and my crew use to be treated like royalty. Nowadays, we're fighting for towels.

Pork didn't know what it was like just a few years back, so to him, everything was perfect. I never made a big deal about it, because I wanted him to enjoy the experience. But the end was becoming clear.

On the one hand, I was feeling a bit of failure, as the fans that once pumped my music from their cars were now hiding the fact that they even knew who I was. While on the other hand, a new opportunity was on the horizon. The opportunity to change, and do shit the way I always wanted to do it. The only challenge … Will I live long enough to see it?

CHAPTER 28

Shadows

It was Sunday, around 1:00 am when we finally got home. Dora tried her best to wait up, but couldn't. Rosie however did. She also put up a few Welcome Home decorations, and made us a great dinner.

I was exhausted. Porky though, was still wired from the trip. He had a great time, and I was so happy that everything went smooth.

At past concerts, there was always something crazy that went down, but this time, shit was real peaceful. The only thing that I could come up with that made it that way was the fact that, like me, my audience was getting older.

Porky spoke a lot about the next tour. But the way things were going, and the situation happening around the disappearance of Q, I wasn't so sure there would be another tour.

We hung out in the kitchen area, eating and talking about the tour. I remember when I could talk for hours after I'd come home, excited about the whole experience. But these days, my replies seem to be subjected to nothing more than,

"Same ol' same ol'!"

Porky on the other hand was full of stories. Great ones too, Shit, I couldn't even tell if he was telling the truth or not, but either way, he made it seem like we had the greatest job in the world.

He spoke about people he met on the tour, as if they were now his new best friends.

People who I had forgotten even worked for us, like the Roadies, the sound men, lighting people, stage hands, bus drivers, and so many of my fans who had somehow become his. I swear, it was like he had his very own cult following.

After his long winded adventure stories, Porky finally decided to call it a night. He kissed Rosie goodnight and then came up and hugged me.

"I had the greatest time of my life, Rey. Thank you."

He held me a bit longer then pulled back, and looked down into my eyes and smiled.

"Me too, Pork,"

We stayed quiet and watched as he walked to his room. I looked at my wife, and she had on the biggest smile. I gestured to her to come to me, and watched as this incredibly beautiful woman approached me.

I took her into my arms, and she held me. We stayed that way for a moment, swaying gently from side to side, until finally, we kissed, I pulled back a bit and looked at her, both our eyes began to flood. We had such an incredible connection, and I could tell she loved me as much as I loved her.

I got up, and by the hand, I lead her to our bedroom. Standing at the foot of our bed, we kissed again, until she pulled back and began unbuttoning my shirt. She opened it and kissed my chest, working her way back up to my lips. I took her tee shirt from the bottom and slowly lifted it over her head. She wasn't wearing a bra, and the firm and perkiness of her still youthful breast, would have you in disbelief that she ever had a child.

Slowly, my thumbs made small gentle circles over both her nipples, and when they hardened, my tongue took over, working my way back up to her lips.

I pulled my wife into my arms. Subtly, she slid her chest across mine as her hands began unbuckling my pants. She placed her thumbs into my waistband, and in one smooth motion, pulled my pants down until her face was mere inches from my dick.

She looked up at me, her big beautiful eyes telling me that she had been anticipating this for as long as I'd been gone.

She gave it a peck, and then smiled as she watched it rise, satisfied that I wanted her just as bad. Again she kissed it, but this time, slow and gentle... My juices, now on their mark.

It was then that I closed my eyes, and felt her totally devour me. My head snapped back uncontrollably as she took me deeper than she's ever taken me before.

In no time I was at the edge, ready to erupt, but that wasn't what I wanted, and neither did she! We stopped, and Rosie stood up and pushed me back on to the bed. She removed my shoes and socks, and then pulled my pants all the way off. I worked my way backwards, up to the pillow as I watched her drop her cut jeans and little black tank top. She then climbed up on the bed, and toward me, she crawled.

Tonight was not the night for foreplay. It was straight to business! I laid back, trying my best to keep my eyes from rolling back into my head, as my wife took total control. It was like an out of body experience that I wasn't even a part of.

I turned my head to the side and noticed our shadows on the wall. They too were making love, but what I found strange was that, they weren't your typical dark shadows... These were in color, and seemed to be a few steps ahead of us. In fact, they seemed to have a life of their own!

We lay there, looking into each other's eyes, our fingers stroking each other's face. So connected we were, that it was scary. I leaned forward and kissed her, then pulled back and waited ... And there it was her beautiful smile!

"I missed you so much." She said. "Rey, you've given me, everything I could ever dream of. A beautiful home, a family, I mean everything!

"Except?" I asked, knowing there was a *"but"* in there somewhere. She gave it a moment before answering, and finally...

"Except *you!"*

Yeah, I saw that coming, and I felt the same way. I smiled at her and nodded, letting her know that I understood.

"So, before the tour, I started thinking about making some changes. I didn't want to tell you anything until I was clear as to what I wanted, and how I would go about doing it.

"Changes?" she asked, propping herself up onto her elbow.

"Yeah, I'm gonna have a talk with Mr. D, you see my contract is almost over, and I wanna do my own thing, and if I could convince him to let me out early, I'll continue to support his entire catalog, however I could."

"That's one hell of a commitment, don't you think? I mean, what if you just let the term run out?"

"This is the record business, Rosie. It's never that easy. Look, it's not like he's gonna put me back on tour. He took a hit on this one. However, cause of the way the contract is structured, yeah, he can hold on to me until all the debt is paid back."

Rosie exhaled, she understood what I was up against, and that I had to make the right decision.

"You think he'll go for it?"

"I don't see why not. The tour's over, all he has now are records that need to sell, and I'll do whatever I can to help him with that."

"How do you do that without touring?"

"Radio, TV, magazine interviews. Whatever needs to be done to move product. I don't wanna screw the guy. I mean really, I made a lot of money from him."

"And that's just a tiny percentage of the money he made from you!" She replied, and damn, she was right!

"By the way, have you heard from Sal?"

"He checked in with us, for like the first week, then that was it. I figured he had some time off, so I didn't want to bother him. You met the new guy right?"

"Yeah, downstairs, cool guy."

"Definitely not a Sal, but he does his job."

I sat up and turned on the lamp over my nightstand.

"What are you doing?" Rosie asked as I picked up the phone and pressed the speed dial button to Sal's number. It went straight to an automated voice mailbox. I got up and put on my boxers.

"Something's not right." I said before going back to the phone, and dialing another number.

"Who you calling now?" Rosie asked.

"Red!" I said into the phone.

"Who the fuck is this?" said the sleepy and irritate voice on the other end.

"It's me, man!"

"King? What's up bro, you home?" Red asked.

"Yeah, yo what's up with Sal?"

"Oh man." Red began, and I wasn't feeling the tone. "Mr. D is tripping bro."

"Fuck you talking about?"

"Man, he said he's making some changes. He told Sal to take a vacation until he figures out what he wants to do."

"Did he find out about, Q?"

"Hell yeah, we knew he would! But Sal didn't snitch on any of us. As far as Mr. D knows, Q was tripping on some shit and ran up on Sal."

"Did he go for that?"

"All I know is that Sal's still alive."

"You spoke to him?"

"Yesterday, he's staying in some crusty ass motel in Miami."

"What about you?" I asked.

I haven't been back to the Funky Junky since you left either. Mr. D said he's making changes and that he was gonna fill us all in when you got back.

"And Cuba?' I asked.

"He's good, we've been hooking up almost every night, working on shit. Wait till you hear it."

"Okay cool. I ain't mean to wake you, I just couldn't sleep.

"It's all good, King, good hearing from you bro."

"Good hearing from you too, I'll see you tomorrow!"

I hung up the phone, and then looked at Rosie.

"Everything okay?" she asked. It took me a moment to answer, and finally I said…

"I don't think so!"

CHAPTER 29

Hey Stranger

Growing up in the city, cars were never a big thing to me. Neither were houses for that matter. In fact, I use to always say, I'll *always* ride public transportation, and I will *always* live in an apartment. Funny how things change once you have a family... *and* a little money.

I had purchased a convertible IROC Z because it seemed to be the cool car around where I lived, but except for short rides to the beach and other local events, I never really drove anywhere. I went from being your typical New York City strap hanger, to being chauffeured anywhere I wanted to go, so yeah I was a bit spoiled.

I had purchased Rosie one of those Chrysler minivans because she liked to run her own errands, and most of the time she had both Dora and Porky. It was the perfect vehicle for her, though I myself wouldn't have been caught dead in it.

I got behind the wheel of my IROC and pushed back the roof, as it was already a beautiful day. You would think that my concern would be my hair, but I've been wearing this Do for so long, that the hair spray had become a permanent part of my DNA.

I pulled out before the door to my garage had fully opened, and tried to remember which way it was to the Highway. After a few wrong turns I finally found it, and though traffic was pretty slow, it was at least moving.

A car in the lane beside me rolled up playing *I am King.* I glanced their way and smiled, and for the first time, it dawned on me, my audience has aged, and so have I.

Aside from performing it every now and then, it's been a while since I last saw a car driving around bumping it. I remember when nearly every car on the road had one of my songs blaring from its system. I looked straight ahead and started to reminisce about my life and all I had done in such a short period of time.

I thought about Grams and the lies I use to tell her when she thought I was out looking for a job. How she would save up money to give me for the train. I'm so glad I came clean to her before she passed, 'cause had that secret remained, it would've haunted me for the rest of my life.

I thought about Junior, the poor kid who was killed by that truck. However, I do believe that it would've been just a matter of time before something would've killed him anyway. He was too young, and his neighborhood was too hard. But then I thought about Porky. Had that not have happened to Junior, and then we wouldn't have Porky. I justified it all as Junior's sacrifice for the wellbeing of his young buddy.

Crazy Quenepa, I get sick every time I think about him, and every night while on tour, I speak to his soul. I pleaded for forgiveness, knowing that I'll one day reach my own grave, and never would I ever hear him say he accepts my apology. His name always brought to mind the image of him, lying in that tub, dead. His neck twisted all weird and shit. I tried to imagine him at other times, at rehearsals, during shows, sitting around smoking weed. Didn't matter what he was doing, his image always appeared to me... But with a twisted neck!

The honk of a car horn snapped me out of my daydream, and when I looked to my right, the two girls driving in the convertible beside me screamed out.

"I told you it was him!" The blonde who was driving told her redheaded friend. I waved, and they screamed again. I was flattered and embarrassed at the same time.

"Check this out!" The blonde yelled out before reaching forward to turn up the volume on her stereo, from which blared my song. I smiled and nodded. She yelled out something but the music was too loud and I couldn't hear her. She reached forward and yelled out again. "Can we get your autograph?" this time signing the air with her imaginary pen. I looked around and realized that we were doing about 20 miles an hour and in the middle lanes.

"I'm sorry, I can't get off, I'm in a rush." I watched the blonde say something to the redhead and then she reached into the glove compartment and searched around until she came out with a pen and cassette cover of my album. She held it up for me to see, but all I could do was smile and shrug my shoulders. The redhead climbed into the backseat. I couldn't figure out what they were doing until the crazy blonde began to move in closer toward me.

"Yo, what are you doing?" I yelled at the driver, trying to watch them *and* stay in my lane. She paid me no mine as the redhead instructed her to move in a little closer. My car didn't have a scratch on it. In fact it still looked showroom new. Hers on the other hand looked like it took first place at the Demolition Derby.

I looked straight ahead and tried to keep my car as steady as possible because these dumb bitches were about to cause an accident. In total disbelief, I watched as the redhead climbed out the back seat of their car, and into the back of mine.

"Fuck you doing?" I asked.

"I'll probably never have this opportunity again." She laughed, making her way into the seat beside me. Cars behind us began honking at their stupidity, so the blonde threw up her middle finger.

"That shit was crazy.' I told her as she straightened herself in the seat. I glanced her way and realized, this girl was fucking fine!

"I'm sorry, it was either this, or we were just going to follow you to wherever you were going."

"You could've killed yourself." I told her.

"That's okay, it's worth it. I looked at her and believed her. She held out the pen and the cassette insert. "Please?" She said, her cute smile would've never let me say no.

She could tell I wasn't that comfortable driving, as I never really drove anywhere, especially to the city. She threw me off when she grabbed the wheel.

"I got it." She said, then handed me the pen and insert.

"Can you write it out to Lisa and Peggy. I'm Lisa by the way."

"You don't want me to write two separate ones?"

"No, we'll frame it and hang it in our apartment."

"You two related?" I asked.

"I guess you can say that." She replied nonchalant. I looked her way and smiled and then continued writing, my eyes bouncing from the envelope to the road and back. I handed it back to her and she read it out loud.

"To my crazy friends Lisa and Peggy, please drive safe! Love King." Lisa smiled at me and then leaned forward and gave me a kiss.

She waved for her friend to pull closer.

"Hey listen, why don't I just pull off at the next exit, I don't want you getting hurt?"

"Don't worry." She replied, and then stood on my seat. Shaking my head, I held tight to the wheel, keeping the car as steady as I possibly could.

Cars behind us again began honking their horns, but I couldn't tell whether it was *for* the stunt, or against it. Lisa then jumped from my car to the back seat of hers. I did notice however, that beneath her tiny jean mini skirt, she wore no underwear. I nearly rammed into the car in front of me. Lisa turned around and from the backseat and waved goodbye to me, as Peggy smiled before taking off like a race car, zig zagging between lanes until they were out of sight.

A ride that Sal usually did in less than an hour, took me nearly two. But I made it, and pulled into the garage of the Funky Junky, right alongside Red's brand new Ferrari. Red was always ahead of the game when it came to cars, I personally found them to be dumb investments, the payments on some of his cars was about as much as a mortgage would be. But Red, also owned an incredible loft in one of the ritzy parts of Brooklyn, where he was born and raised. But he had no wife, no kids. His life was his music, and his love for fast toys.

On my way up the elevator I started to think about Roller Girl, and kept wishing that she would be there to answer the door, but I knew that wasn't going to happen. I got to my floor and walked up to the door and rang the bell. As usual, I could hear music playing on the other side.

I listened as the door unlocked, and when it opened I nearly fell over when I saw who was standing there. "Hey stranger!" said Charlotte, as she stood there... On roller skates!

CHAPTER 30

Till Death Do Us Part

Charlotte rolls backwards in front of me as I step into the Funky Junky and close the door behind me. I hadn't seen Charlotte in years, I use to think about her all the time, probably up until I got with Rosie, and even then she popped up every once in a while.

Charlotte still looked fine as fuck. In fact, she looked better than she did back in the day.

"What are you doing here?" I asked, unable to pull my eyes away for even a second.

"We haven't seen each other in years, and *that's* how you greet me?" It took a moment for me to catch on, and so I hugged her.

"I'm sorry, it's just that..."

"You're surprised to see me here?"

"I mean, yeah, if that's how you wanna put it." We stopped in the center of the lounge area, and continued talking.

"To be honest, I didn't even think you were going to remember who I was." Charlotte said.

"Come on, are you kidding me? Do you know how hard I tried to get in touch with you?"

"No I don't." She replied, not really believing me.

"Real hard!" I told her. Charlotte laughed. I was too shocked to put on any other expression beside the one currently on my face.

"Are you still at the Library?"

"Oh no, I left that job around the last time I saw you. I got tired of the old bitch."

"Yeah, she was something." My eyes couldn't escape the grasp of Charlotte's beauty. I thought about this girl so many times, rehearsed what I wanted to tell her, and now all went blank.

"Why didn't you ever tell me that you were into music?"

"I really didn't have much happening."

"Well, had I known I would've introduced you to my brother."

"Your brother?"

"Yeah, Nemesis! I'm sure you know who he is?"

I stared at her, not sure if I was hearing her right.

"You're kidding me right?"

"Kidding you?"

"Nemesis? The rapper? That's your brother?" Charlotte nodded, and finally I was able to take my eyes off her. I covered my mouth with my hand and laughed into it.

"What's so funny?" She asked, bending slightly to look up into my eyes.

"Nemesis?" I asked again. Charlotte's smile vanished and she looked at me, and nodded.

"Yes… what's up?" she asked. I looked at her and simply said,

"Your brother has been a thorn in my ass since day one." I said, laughing hysterically

"What do you mean?" My brother's the biggest rapper in the world?"

"*Was* the biggest rapper in the world," I corrected, playfully sarcastic.

"He was when we were talking," she clarified, and then placed her hands on her hips and tilted her head.

I stood there in silence, trying to make sense of what she just told me, as it was the craziest thing I ever heard.

"So what are you doing here?" I finally asked, trying to change the subject.

"I'm Mr. D's new assistant." I looked to the floor, as Roller Girl suddenly came to mine. "I heard what happened with the last girl. Heard you two were close, I'm sorry."

"We were friends… That's it!"

Charlotte just nodded, but that friend shit didn't cut it.

"So what's up with the skates?"

"Cool huh?" Charlotte said doing a cool spin. I heard that's how the last girl moved around, and I love to skate.

"I could tell."

"Mr. D in his office?" I asked.

"Yeah, and he said as soon as you get here to go see him."

As I started down the hall, Charlotte grabbed hold of my arm and rolled beside me, exactly how Roller Girl use to. It kind of fucked me up, but I didn't say anything. Charlotte looked up at me, and smiled. I felt her squeeze my arm, as if she was happy to see me, and to be honest, I was kind of happy to see her too.

We stopped in front of Mr. D's office.

"I use to think about you all the time." I blurted out of nowhere, and then dropped my head. "I'm sorry."

"It's okay," she replied, then added, I didn't think you were feeling me at all."

"What made you think that?"

"Well, the time you stood me up somehow comes to mind."

"But…"

"Yeah I'm just messing with you, I know about the accident, I read the story, and how you raised the other kid."

"I hated going inside the library, I thought I was gonna make you lose your job, so I would either get there early and try and catch you before you went in, or in the afternoon, trying to catch you leaving. But the planets never lined up for me."

"Probably because the planets were over by the back entrance." She laughed.

"Back entrance?"

"Yeah, I never went through the front, and my brother usually dropped me off and picked me up."

"I can't believe this," I said.

"But look," she continued as she began skating away, backwards. "You're married, you have a beautiful wife, family, career. I mean, shit really worked out for you." I watched as Charlotte rolled backwards down the corridor, something Roller Girl would've never been able to do. "It's so good to see you … King!"

I smiled, and then noticed what she was wearing, a black Layla Storm tee-shirt and white tight basketball shorts, with the black stripe running down the sides, and when she spun around and skated off, my jaw nearly hit the ground when I saw her ass. I always knew Charlotte was fine, but damn!

"Come in!" Mr. D suddenly called out, knocking me the fuck out of a trance I should have never been in.

I opened the door and stepped inside. Immediately I knew something was up because I usually received an extra friendly greeting as well as an invite to sit in his overstuffed purple beanbag. But instead, Mr. D just sat there, behind his desk, writing.

He didn't even look up at me. No hello. No nothing! So I made the first move.

"How's it going Mr. D?" I said to him as I walked up and stood in front of his desk. Still he said nothing. No acknowledgment whatsoever. He just kept writing, so I just stood there, and waited.

Rudely he took longer than he should've, but then closed

his notebook and placed his pen down on top of it. He sat back in his chair, his fingers interlaced just over his stomach, he looked at me.

"Numbers are horrible!" He said in a calm yet stern tone.

"Well, I wouldn't say *horrible!*"

"Of course you wouldn't. That's why I'm the one who handles the business!" Mr. D stood up and then leaned forward with his palms on the desk. He looked me deeper in the eyes and repeated himself.

"The numbers are fucking horrible!" I didn't want to get into it with him, so I just kept quiet and let him talk.

"Ticket sales are down, record sales are down, merch sales are down, however the cost of having you remain on board has gone up. In other words, we have a problem, Rey!"

And at that moment, I knew we did, because he has never, in all these years called me Rey!

"Well, if it means anything, my contract's practically up." I told him, trying my best to hide the joy. Mr. D looked at me, and just stared until I was forced to look away.

"Oh, so you think that's the answer?" He asked, and that moment I knew, this wasn't gonna go right.

"Well, not the answer, but you just mentioned that it costing you to keep me on."

First off, let's get this straight. *I* have the option to extend your contract, till death do us part... If that's what I want."

"But what's the point in that?" I asked.

"The point is to ruin your fuckin' life, like you're ruining mine."

"What are you talking about, ruining your life? I made you a lot of money!"

"On the contrary, asshole, I made *you* a lot of money. I was already rich!"

"But for the last five years we've been selling out everything!"

"What, you think I just put a record out and suddenly everybody's saying, hey lets go get that new King record? Fuck no! It cost me a lot of money to make that happen. In fact, your ass is still in the red, and without any records and concerts, how the fuck do you plan on paying me back?"

"Once I'm off, you can continue to sell your inventory till it's gone. I'm sure eventually, you'll get all that money back."

"Eventually? Now since when did I become an eventually type of guy? When I signed you, did I say you'll eventually be a star? Fuck no! I made you a star immediately, and now you want me to eventually get my money?"

"I didn't mean it like that, sorry, but now what?" I asked.

"I don't know yet." Mr. D replied. "But I'll tell you this Rey, once I turn you off, that's it! You're done! You've become a novelty act, and I'm not in that business. Your audience isn't even buying records anymore, and they sure as hell aren't going to your concerts.

"But I've been telling you for a while now, let's change it up, new look, new music..."

"...If I'm going for a new look and new music, then I want a new fucking artist. That's like Putting on a new suit with some old ass shoes, it doesn't work, Rey.

Mr. D sat back down behind his desk and started writing stuff again in his pad. His way of saying, I'm dismissed.

CHAPTER 31

Signature Sounds

I opened the door to the studio, and there was Red, alone, sitting at the board. He had a little keyboard next to him and was playing cord variations and writing them down. He sensed someone had entered and turned and smiled the moment he saw me.

"King!" he said as he got up and made his way over. I stepped in and allowed the door to close behind me. We shook hands, with a slight embrace.

"So glad you're back." He said. I nodded and walked over to where he was working.

"Wha'cha working on?" I asked, as I peeked at his notebook.

"He wants us to do another album." Red said, his eyes dropping to the floor. "Sorry man." I dropped the pad back down onto the board and walked over to the couch and plopped down in it.

"Yeah, I know, I just spoke to him." Red put his one finger up as a gesture not to say anymore.

He then went to the cassette deck on the rack and pressed play. He adjusted the music loud enough to mask our conversation, and then rolled his chair directly in front of me.

"Why the fuck is he doing this?" He asked.

"I don't know, but this type of move could be disastrous for all of us." I replied.

"I heard sales are below fifty percent."

"Yeah, and so is everything else." I confirmed. "This fucking tour was an embarrassment. I'm surprised they even paid us."

"They paid you because no one wants to fuck with Mr. D. But I bet they'll never book you again!" I agreed.

We both sat there, thinking and shaking our heads.

"Man, if he would only let us do this shit our way," I said.

"I don't know, man." Red said, his head discouragingly shaking.

"Though I was just trying to stay positive, Red was being real.

"What's up with Cuba?"

"We hooked up a couple of times when you left, but, it just wasn't the same. I told him let's just wait till you got back."

"Man, I was really looking forward to hearing some new shit."

"We pulled together a couple of joints, but the vibe just wasn't there."

As I sat back, thinking, I caught myself tuning into the

music Red had playing in the background.

"You like that?" He asked.

"Love it!"

"Yeah, I've been wanting to bring it over to Cuba and let him spice it up a bit."

"Is this for a song, or a Rap?"

"I don't know, I was kind of feeling what we were doing before you left for the tour." Red answered. I stared into space, my head bopping, until finally, this melody came to me, so I started humming it. Red looked at me with this huge smile.

"Welcome back mother fucker!" Red said, as we smacked each other five.

"That's some Cuba shit right there." I said. Red agreed and laughed.

"Throw down some lyrics." Red suggested. I looked up into the air, trying to come up with something. I started with the chorus, and the word love just kept popping up. I said it. In different ways; *Love me. I Love you. We have love, give me your love, what is love.*

What the fuck. You ain't got anything else besides love?" Red asked. I thought about it, but no, nothing else fit. The melody had this sort of romantic feel to it.

Red got behind his keyboard, and with one of the "Love" hooks I came up with, he started to play. His keys inspired me, and my words inspired him, and in no time, we had written a new song, and in my opinion, it was the best song we've written yet.

We continued jamming for the next couple of hours, trying to catch up to where we had left off.

As always, we were having a blast and coming up with some really great stuff. Cuba wasn't there, but we kept imagining what he would do with certain pieces.

Red kept trying out different sounds, shit we would've never considered using before. Cuba was old school, and pretty much stuck with signature sounds. He called it style, and believed that if you changed your style you'd risk losing fans. But we were already losing fans, so basically, we had nothing to lose.

Yeah, shit was sounding a bit crazy, but it was also different, and at this point we felt different was our only hope. We were having a great time, and incredibly creative, but this wasn't King shit, and Mr. D would never agree to it, and suddenly, we both stopped, as if we had both just received the memo. We looked at one another.

"We gotta figure something out," Red whispered.

"I know," I replied as I got up and straightened myself out.

"We're just wasting our time, King."

"Wasting our lives," I corrected.

CHAPTER 32

Above The Mirror

I peeked into the rehearsal studio expecting to see the whole team, but all I saw was Princess, sitting in a chair at the front of the room instructing Vanessa with some moves.

I stepped inside and they both turned to me.

"Hey Rey!" Vanessa called out with her typical big smile of mostly gums. I couldn't help but smile back as I made my way toward them.

"Didn't expect to see you back here so soon, Princess said.

"You know I can't go that long without seeing your pretty face." I made him smile and pulled up a chair and sat on it backwards. "What are you guys doing?"

"Trying out some new stuff," Vanessa replied.

"New stuff?" I asked Princess, and he pointed to Vanessa. "Your stuff?" she nodded excitedly.

"I was just showing Princess a couple of things I came up with, wanted to get his opinion on it."

"Wow, that's great. Can I see?" I asked. Vanessa looked at

Princess, who then stepped back and he gave her the floor. She smiled, and then got into position. Vee was no doubt the most graceful dancer I had ever experienced, and even though there was no music playing, when she moved, you swore there was. There was this perfection about her that made everything she did look easy, but then when *you* tried it, you found it nearly impossible.

I glanced at Princess. The expression on his face was that of pride, as he knew just how much he contributed to her success. He caught me staring, and though he didn't smile, his eyes said it all.

As soon as she was done, I jumped up from my seat and applauded her with everything I had. Vee started laughing, waving me off.

"I always said it!!! You're a bad bitch!"

Vee walked over and sat on the floor in front of us, her arms wrapped around her legs.

"So what's up? I mean, are we using this for anything?" I asked Princess. He looked at me, then Vanessa. We could tell he had something on his mind, so we gave him a second.

"So listen, now that I have the two of you here," The tone in his voice suddenly wiping out both of our smiles.

"What is it?" Vee asked as she moved closer placing her hand on his knee.

"You guys know, I've been doing this a very long time, especially you Vanessa." She nodded, her eyes glued on to his. "I'll be seventy-seven in just a couple of days."

"I know… and?"

"And I think it's time I hang up my pointes."

"What are you talking about?" Vee said, as she got up, loud and annoyed. "You told me you'd never quit! That you'll be doing this till your last day!" and at that very moment she got quiet and we both looked at him.

Princess looked at us, his head slightly tilted, his eyes, telling it all.

Vee couldn't speak. She couldn't ask him what was wrong. She just stood there, her head shaking in denial.

"It's cancer!" He finally said. Vee rushed over to him and wrapped her arms around him and cried hysterically.

"When did you find out?" She asked.

"I've been on treatment for a few months now. I didn't want to say anything while we were on the tour."

Vanessa laid her head on his lap and continued crying. I walked over and squatted behind her, and held her. I looked up at Princess.

"Is there anything I can do?" I asked. Princess looked at me, and simply said,

"Take care of her!" I gave it a moment, and then nodded.

"Now listen, you two." He began. Vee wiped her eyes with her towel and we both looked up at him. "You two are so young, so talented, and with an incredible life ahead of you." His eyes then focused on me. "What you possess is beyond talent" He said. "It's this very special energy that you give off when you're around, pure and honest. Recognizing, and developing it will be the key to all success beyond any of this," his hand crossing the air in front of him.

"And you my love," he said as he raised Vanessa's chin until they were looking each other in the eyes. "That gift, that magnificent gift that God has blessed you with, it makes people so happy. It inspires them… It inspires me! Don't ever stop, ever!"

"Now I need the two of you to promise me something, and if you do, I'm going to hold you to it, both of you." Vanessa and I looked at each other, and then back at Princess.

"I want you two to promise me, that you both will remain friends for as long as you live."

"Of course, we will." I interrupted, until he put his hand up and stopped me.

"I know you two better than you think. You both have a deep love and admiration for the other. I saw this in no one else but you two. You will both have hardships, and heartbreaks. Depression will pay you continued visits, and the devil? Well, just remember… He ain't your friend!"

I looked at Princess, and could read between the lines. He wasn't too worried about me. I had a pretty good support system at home. He was worried about Vanessa. I remember hearing him once tell me, *"She's an incredible dancer, because that's all she has!"*

I found out later that on many occasions, Princess would hop the subway at 2:00 am to get over to Vanessa's apartment, because her depression would get so bad that it scared him. He would stay with her until he was sure she was okay. There were times when he knew, had he not gone over, she would have definitely hurt herself.

I had stopped over at the hospital one evening to see

Princess and bring him a container of his favorite soup from the Chinese spot next to The Funky Junky. It was the only thing he still enjoyed eating. We talked for a while until he asked me to get something from his bag. It was an envelope, and being that I was the only other one beside Vanessa that he trusted, he asked if I would give it to her... after he passes.

Princess wasn't worried about his condition as much as he was worried about *hers*.

When he knew he would be going into the hospital, he asked Vee if she would look after a few of his most precious belongings. From jewelry that had been handed down to him, to art that he collected throughout his travels. Vanessa agreed, unaware that she was being set up to become the heir of these very things, and the night after his funeral, I did as I had promised, and when Vanessa and I were alone, I handed her the envelope.

In it was the deed to his luxurious Manhattan apartment, which had been fully paid off for several years now. His life insurance policy claimed Vanessa as his sole beneficiary, and a bank account under her name to which he transferred *all* of his money. But the thing that seemed to move her most was a letter that he had written to her. She never offered me to read it, so I never asked, but whatever it said, made her collapse in tears.

I wanted Vee to come stay with me and the family for few days because I didn't feel that she should be left alone, but she refused. I called up Rosie and she too agreed that I should stay the night.

Vanessa and I stayed up pretty late talking. I learned a lot about Princess. He had no living relatives, and according to her the only people he considered family were those that worked at The Funky Junky, which included not just the executives, administrators, and of course his dancers. But also the Janitors, the Mailman, Jacq, and even the ladies that worked in the cafeteria, which explained why so many attended his funeral.

The only person that wasn't there, and another reason to despise him even more, was Mr. D. Vanessa on the other hand was glad he wasn't there because she always felt he was full of shit, and having him there she felt, would've been disrespectful to Princess.

Princess was indeed an odd bird, and he lived a very unique life. And though he was gay as fuck, no one had ever actually seen him with anyone. Not even Vee.

He will truly be missed, but he passed his torch over to who *he* felt, would be the best person to carry on his legacy, and that of course was Vanessa.

By the morning, I was convinced that Vee would be okay, and the following Monday she was back at the studio standing in front of the class. One of the paintings that Princess had given her was a portrait of himself that he had made during a trip to Paris. That painting now hangs above the mirror, facing the class.

CHAPTER 33

Focus

"What's up, Kid?" I said to Porky as I stuck my head into the gym at the Funky Junky. Pork was the only one there, in front of a mirror doing squats. He didn't say anything as he was completely focused on his lifting. I walked up and looked at him through the mirror. I counted four plates on each side at forty-five pounds each and did the math in my head. This kid wasn't even old enough to get into the clubs, yet I don't think there's a bouncer big enough to ever stop him.

After his final rep, Porky placed the weights back onto the rack and grabbed his towel. "Hey Rey!" he said with his typical boyish smile and a wave. It was at that moment that I realized, just how focused he could be.

"I think it's time we stop calling you Porky." I suggested as I followed him to one of the benches where his water bottle sat on the floor beside it.

"I would never change my name." Porky replied as he guzzled down the cool liquid. "Junior gave me that name." He replied before sitting on the bench and grabbing the two dumbbells at his feet.

"That was a long time ago. I'm sure he would've been the first to tell you to change it, especially now." I said gesturing to his monstrous self. I read the numbers carved into each of the dumbbells. This kid was curling a hundred pounds on each arm as if it was just a warm up.

"Well, until Junior tells me so himself, I will always be Porky". He said as he pumped each arm with perfection. "In fact, I was thinking about changing it legally!"

"What?" I suddenly blurted out, after which Porky start laughing.

"I'm just kidding, Rey."

I stood there, shaking my head at his cruel joke, while watching his veins pop out of his arms with each curl.

"So when you gonna start working out with me?" He asked.

"Man, I'd just be in your way."

"You could never be in my way, Rey!" I looked my young buddy in the eyes and knew he meant what he said. "Come on Rey, give it a try." Porky got up and I sat in his place. He took a knee in front of me and adjusted my legs in the correct position.

"Keep your back straight, Rey." He said. I then reached down to grab the weights, and he started to laugh.

"What?" I asked.

"Those are a hundred pounders. Rosie would kill me!" He and I laughed some more as he got up and brought over two ten pounders.

"Come on man, those are girly weights." I told him, but he didn't listen. He tossed the two hundred pounders to the side like a pair of dirty socks, and placed the two ten pounders in my hands. "I've eaten sandwiches heavier than this!" I said.

"I could tell." Porky laughed back positioning my body as if I was one of his old action figures. "Lifting light weight helps you focus on your form, and once you have it, then you can increase the weight." I started doing curls real fast and clumsily, when Porky stopped me, and laughed. "You see, that's what I'm talking about."

"What?"

"Rey, you know Johnston right?"

"The new guy?"

"Yeah, he came in here to work out and I saw him doing it wrong so I offered to help. Well he got mad, said that he's been lifting weights since before I was born."

"Some people are gonna be like that Pork, you can't save the world, man."

"Yeah, I know. But he actually hurt himself that day trying to show off, and has now been in the hospital for about three weeks."

"Oh damn. What happened?"

"He tore his Rotator Cuff."

"What's that?" I asked, Porky explained, walking me over to a life size photo of the human anatomy that hung on the wall. I was in awe of this kid, the way he described the injury was clear as day, and at that point I was totally convinced...

he knew his shit!

"Damn, that sucks!" Was about all I could say. "What sucks is the fact that I watched it happen."

"Didn't matter, he wasn't going to listen to you anyway."

"But you'll listen to me, right Rey?" Pork asked looking really concerned.

"I'll always listen to you Pork." I assured him, and watched as that huge smile appeared on his face. "You got a good heart kid don't ever change it, for nobody."

"I won't, Rey… Now focus!!!"

CHAPTER 34

Acid

"Hey!" Cuba yelled out when he opened the door and saw Porky and I standing there. He immediately grabbed and hugged me, patting Porky on the arm so that he didn't feel left out. We stepped inside, Cuba holding tight to my arm.

"How's it going, man?" I asked.

"When you left, everything just stopped!" I glanced over at Porky and he seemed a bit uncomfortable. The last time he was here was when we had the incident with Q.

"You okay?" I whispered to him, and he nodded.

"Come and sit down." Cuba said, gesturing Porky and I over to the couch. Porky took a seat, his eyes scanning his surroundings.

"Red should be here any minute," said Cuba. "Can I get you something, cafe?"

"No man, I'm good, maybe later."

"Porky?" Cuba asked, Porky just shook his head.

"You sure you're alright?" I asked him again. "We don't

have to be here," and again he shook his head, but this time spoke.

"I'm okay, Rey."

Maybe he's hungry?" Cuba asked, always willing to whip up a meal for anyone hungry.

"No, no thank you, Cuba. I'm good." Pork finally said.

Porky reached toward the coffee table and grabbed a magazine.

"So how was the tour?" Cuba asked, as he sat next to me with this huge smile.

"Oh man, it just wasn't the same." I replied.

"What do you mean?"

"People are tied of this King shit. I can't pull them in."

"What does Mr. Boss think about that?"

"It's hard to tell what he thinks." Cuba and I sort of stared into space shaking our heads.

"Hey, I heard about Princess, so sorry."

"Yeah, thank you, so sad."

"You know, Princess use to work for Mr. D's father back in the day. They were behind a lot of really famous people. He watched Mr. D grow up, and when his father passed, and Mr. D took over, he kept Princess on board. I thought they were close, but Vanessa told me that he only kept him on as a promise to his father. Apparently they hated each other."

"The things you find out once people are gone." Cuba said, and I nodded in agreement. "So who's taking over?"

"Vanessa!"

"Yay!" Cuba cheered, clapping his hands and bouncing in his seat. "So there you go, Some good news!"

"I guess." I replied, sort of bursting the bubble." It's just, we're trying to get the fuck out, and I feel like I'll be leaving her behind."

"And Sal?" Cuba asked. I glanced over at Porky and watched as his eyes stopped moving, as he had tuned in.

"Well, supposedly, Mr. D sent him on a little vacation until they figure all this shit out.

"Vacation?"

"Yeah, Miami."

"Wow." Cuba said, sort of strange.

"Why'd you say it like that?"

"Not for nothing, I use to live there."

"You did? How come you never mentioned it?"

"Wasn't the best time of my life," I could tell Cuba didn't want to go into it, so I left it alone.

We all remained quiet for a minute, until Cuba asked.

"You think Mr. D knows?" I looked at Cuba, and Porky looked at me.

"I think so!" Porky's eyes dropped back into the magazine, but he was listening.

Cuba's eyes dropped to the floor.

He knew what an asshole Quenepa was, and probably expected this to happen one day."

"Not only that. Sal's job was to protect you, and Quenepa was about to hurt you." Cuba said.

"I know, I know. But I think Sal might've taken it too far.

We all jumped when we heard the buzzer.

"Coño! I hate that stupid thing," he yelled as he got up and headed for the intercom.

"Who is it?"

"The Red one!" replied the crackly voice on the other end. Cuba, excited, buzzed him in as we all sat quiet waiting for him to walk through the door.

We all greeted him with small talk about the weather, and ghetto he had to drive through to get here.

Cuba was excited that we were all together, and kept offering us food and drink. Before he knew us, Cuba was dealing with personal issues that made living alone very difficult. In time, he learned to adapt, and kept himself busy by creating music.

When we came into the picture, he was the happiest he'd been in many years, then to have us all leave again, internally, Cuba was an unstable mess.

Red and I sat and spoke about what was happening, and what was not. Cuba came out of the kitchen with a tray carrying his signature Bustelo Cafe and Spanish crackers with margarine. For Porky, he made a scrambled egg sandwich on Cuban bread as he knew for Porky, coffee and crackers just wouldn't do it.

We were back, and having a great time, the coffee fueling us just as it always had.

Tonight was just a warm up. A welcome back jam to get us back on track. We started going through each of the songs we had been working on, just to refamiliarize with what we had done so far.

The time off really did us justice, because with each track we threw up, tons of new ideas for each became crystal clear.

The way we worked together was perfect. We all had our specific jobs, and trusted one another's thoughts and opinions. It was like God himself picked this team.

Red was great with arrangements and melodies. Growing up he was exposed to such an array of music, as his parents were both classically trained in a variety of instruments when they were kids. In their teens they both turned hardcore Stoners, in fact they met at Woodstock, and conceived Red in a puddle of mud.

Red's real name was Syd, which I always assumed was short for Sidney. Come to find out it was actually spelled C.I.D... and was short for Acid! The shit they were on when they fucked to have him.

I've never in my life met an actual genius, especially a musical one. But as I got to know Cuba, and watched him in action, I knew then that I was in the presence of just that!

His ancestors originated in Africa, but somehow ended up in Cuba. He only had a handful of old family photos, but the diversity of his heritage was clear.

His mother was white as snow, ghostly if you ask me, and though the old black and white photos only showed lightness to her eyes, Cuba remembers them as being as blue as the sky.

The lens through which the only photo of his father was taken, surely came from a racist camera, as his exaggerated eyes and white smile, dominated the rest of what seemed like a malfunction of the ink cartridge. And though he knew nothing about their story, I would've at least loved to know, how the hell these two ever even got together?

I could see the resemblance of both parents in Cuba's unique features. The elongated European nose and huge lips were enough to throw anyone off his trail.

The only in depth information that Cuba had of his parents was that they were both practicing Santeria's, obvious by the white clothes they wore in the photos. And though Cuba didn't dedicate his life to it, there were many things about him that showed his association. Like when he got dressed, something he didn't normally do at home, as he loved hanging out in his pajamas and robe. But when he did... yep, it was all in white, and aside for the altar that covered the top of his dresser, and a few tiny saints scattered around his apartment, Cuba was just as abnormal as the rest of us!

No question about it, I was without doubt, the absolute least talented of the crew. Yeah, I could write, but so could Red and Cuba. And Rapping? Well, I wouldn't put that past them either.

I was not irreplaceable, but they liked me, and though my celebrity might in fact be on the brink, as of now I was still relevant enough to see our plans through to fruition.

"So what now King?" Red asked.

"We wait!"

"Wait?"

"Uh huh, see whether he wants to keep me, or…"

"…Kill you?" Porky looked at him.

CHAPTER 35

Lights Out

A few days had passed by and all was as usual. I spent my mornings at rehearsals, and my afternoons in the studio. I had requested through Charlotte a meeting with Mr. D on several occasions, and each time she came back saying he was unavailable. It seemed he was doing everything possible to avoid me. I couldn't even tell when he was in his office because he had a private elevator that took him to the other floors as well as the garage where he had his own closed off parking spot and exit.

I was in the gym working out with Porky when the phone that hung on the wall rang. Porky picked it up and after listening for a moment, said okay and hung up.

"What's up?" I asked.

"That was Charlotte," he replied. "She said that Mr. D wanted to see the two of us."

"Now?"

"He's in his office." Porky replied with a nod. "What do

you think he wants, Rey?"

"Well, I've been trying to meet with him for a while now. Maybe he found some time."

It was a quiet walk through the hall. All the office doors were wide open, but they were empty and the lights were off. Everyone was gone for the night, and strangely... so was Charlotte!

We walked the long Corridor to Mr. D's office and stood just outside. I placed my ear to the door to see if I could hear anything. I couldn't. Porky gestured for me to knock, but he could tell, I was nervous!

"Come in!" Mr. D suddenly called out. Porky's eyes opened wide, as I hadn't even knocked on the door yet.

We stepped in to find Mr. D painting his office. Everything was covered with drop cloths and Red was sitting on one of the three stools set in the center of the office.

Mr. D still hadn't turned around. He just kept rolling the paint on his wall, a deep dark red, almost blood-like. I looked at Red as to say what's going on? But he just shrugged his shoulders.

"Gentlemen, excuse the mess, I've been putting off this paint job way too long. Take a seat, please, can I get you anything?"

"No thanks, we're good." I said as Porky and I walked over to the stools and sat down. I looked at Red, and gestured as to what's going on?" He shook his head, and then looked away. "You wanted to see us about something?" I asked, but Mr. D didn't answer. He just kept painting. You would think, as much money as this guy has, why the fuck would he be painting himself?

"Because, it helps me think," Mr. D suddenly blurted out from across the room.

"Excuse me?" I asked. Mr. D took a moment, and then finally turned around. He had on one of those white painter suits, but what was even stranger, was the fact that he had not a drop of paint on it.

"You were wondering why I'm doing my own painting.

I gasped!

He placed the pole and roller down into the pan and took his usual place in front of his desk. It too covered in a white drop cloth.

"I've been a bit occupied lately, and if you look around, you'll understand why. I've been doing a *lot* of thinking."

My eyes scanned over his entire office, and saw how much he had already done. His work was as meticulous as I have ever seen, and the red, white and grey that he chose, were used in ways that I would never have thought. His attention to detail was like that of an artist, and the fact that he didn't even use tape to mask his edges, reminded me of his unusual focus.

"I pride myself with the many great decisions I've made over the years." Mr. D began. "Two of those great decisions are right here in this office." Red and I looked at each other. "Because of these, and many others, I've learned to trust my decisions. Never second guess them, and ultimately, put behind them absolutely everything they might need to flourish.

So many people, not just in the music business, but business in general, cut corners. They expect the ultimate result, without the ultimate effort, and when things don't work out for them, they blame everyone but themselves."

Red and Pork seemed a bit lost; I on the other hand was used to his parables, and understood everything Mr. D was saying. However, I wasn't yet sure why he was telling it to us.

"All due respect Mr. D," I finally said. "Where are you going with this?" Mr. D looked at me with an irritated face. He always loved speaking in riddles, but today, I just wasn't in the mood. I had shit to tell him, and now that I was here, I wanted to get to it.

Mr. D stood up from the edge of his desk and started pacing in front of it. Staring at the flooring while scratching his head, made it obvious, he was in deep thought, and about to tell us some shit we probably didn't want to hear.

Suddenly, I heard the ring of some sort of bell, and when I looked, Mr. D's private elevator door opened and out stepped Sal.

"Sal!" I yelled out about to rush over to him, but he held out his hand and stopped me, his eyes focused on his steps as he made his way over to where we were sitting. I looked at Red, then at Porky, as I had no idea what the hell was going on.

I noticed Porky's eyes drop down to Sal's hand, and when I followed, I noticed he was holding his gun down tight against his thigh.

I heard a whimper, and quickly turned to Red, he was losing it. I shook my head, trying my best to calm him down.

Porky on the other hand, was calm, too calm in fact. I tried to get his attention, as I didn't want him doing anything stupid. But his eyes were locked hard on Sal, as well as his every move.

Mr. D just stood there. His arms crossed, and a smirk I would've loved to smack the fuck off his face. It was at that moment that I suddenly realized what was happening.

The drop cloths, the white suit, red paint, and the fact that Sal has been checked into a motel in Florida for nearly a month told me that this was all a set up for the perfect murder. A triple one at that!

"Porky had nothing to do with anything." I pleaded.

"Well, he does now!" Mr. D replied. I looked at Sal, but he refused to look back.

"Sal, this is crazy man, I know you're not gonna do this."

"When you start paying him the way I do, maybe then he'll listen to you." Mr. D said. I looked over at Porky and he was still staring at Sal, like if he was sizing him up. I was terrified, 'cause though Porky was strong and could probably take him. Sal was a pro!

"Please Mr. D." Red cried out. "Don't kill me. I've always been loyal to you. I'll tell you everything, I swear." I looked at Red, disappointed that he would sell us out like that. Even Sal looked his way. It was then when I notice Porky tense up. Like he was about to plunge, but I patted his leg, and when he turned to me, I just shook my head.

"I pretty much have all the information that I need, Red. But I do appreciate the offer, and your willingness to snitch on your friends." Red dropped his head.

I then watched as Mr. D gave Sal a slight nod. Sal then raised his gun, and pointed it directly at Red's head. Red busted out crying. He closed his eyes as tight as he could, and clenched his fist. He sat to my right, and so I leaned toward Porky, hoping to avoid any flying fragments. I placed my hands over my ears and also closed my eyes.

"Wait!" Mr. D called out. Sal, with the gun still pointed at Red turned and looked at Mr. D.

"You know what? Let's not do him now. I might still need him." Sal dropped his hand back down as Red exhaled, thanking both Sal and Mr. D for sparing his life.

"Do the kid first!" He then said.

"Wait! Hold up!" I shouted.

Red leaned forward and looked at Porky.

"I'm sorry, bro." he told him. Porky sucked his teeth and waved him off.

Porky stood up, and stared directly at Sal.

"Sal, don't do this, man. Think of Grams. She treated you like family man. We all did!"

"Porky stepped forward, and Sal quickly raised his gun directly at Pork's forehead. I jumped up and forced myself between them, but Porky was too tall, so I couldn't block.

Instead I pushed Sal back, but he didn't budge much. I kept jumping up between him and Porky.

"Don't do this shit, Sal!" I yelled hysterically. I grabbed Sal's arm and placed the barrel of his gun to my head.

"Sit the fuck down!" Mr. D yelled out.

"It's okay Rey!" Porky said.

"Fuck no!" I cried out. You might as well blast right through me." I ordered.

"Move, King!" Sal commanded.

"I'm not moving. If this is what you're gonna do, then do it. But I'm going first!"

"Rey, stop it!" Porky said as he stood up and moved me out the way.

"Do it now!" Mr. D yelled out. Sal looked at him, not sure what to do as Porky and I pushed each other back and forth. Sal's gun went from my head to Porky's and back. Mr. D ran up beside Sal, and directly into his ear, he yelled.

"Shoot that mother fucker right now!" Red passed out, and fell off the stool. Mr. D rushed back to his desk and yanked the drop cloth off so he can get to a draw that had in it his own .38 revolver. He made sure it was loaded and then cocked it. Mr. D then charged forward with his gun aimed directly at the back of Porky's head. I yelled out.

"No!" And with everything I had, I was able to push Porky out the way just as Mr. D's gun went off. I immediately felt a stinging in my left shoulder, and I knew I was hit. I caught my balance and turned back toward Mr. D. The entire moment moved in slow motion, and I watched as Mr. D turned his gun back on me. I could actually see the hollow-head inside his barrel. I tried to move out the way, but my legs felt as though they were trapped in cement. I knew at any moment it will be lights out, and so I stood my ground and shut my eyes tight.

Bang! I suddenly heard, waiting for that final impact… But it never arrived.

I heard a loud thump, and when I looked, there lay Mr. D on his face, his arm still extended, his gun still in his hand. I was lost, no idea of what had happened, until I turned, and there stood Sal, his smoking gun pointed still in the direction of Mr. D's lifeless body.

My ears were still ringing after the shot was fired. Aside from that, all else was silent, and still. I looked down at the body, the bloody stain on the drop cloth widening around his head. I looked at Porky who just stood there, also staring down at Mr. D. God I wish he didn't have to see that. Red was getting up from the floor, he too had his eyes locked on Mr. D.

Sal stood there, still in position. You could tell there were a million things running through his mind. I knew this wasn't his first murder, but I could tell, this one was special!

Slowly, Sal's hand lowered to his side.

"I need you guys to get out of here." Sal said, still not looking at any of us.

Red, jumped up and was about to run out.

"Wait!" Sal called out. "Not you!" Red looked at him, even more terrified than he had earlier.

"Man, I wasn't really gonna say anything, I was…"

"Shut the fuck up!" Sal demanded, and immediately Red went silent.

"No!" I told him. "We're not going anywhere, we're doing this together. You too Red, and I swear to God, you ever pull some shit like that again, Imma kill you myself!"

"You two finish up the painting, and then clean up. How's your shoulder?" I pulled up my sleeve only to reveal a graze.

Okay good, give me a hand." Sal commanded then slid his gun back into its holster and then took Mr. D's gun from his hand, and went through his pockets to make sure there was nothing in them. He folded Mr. D's arm down to his side, and neatly, began to fold the ends of the drop cloth around him like a Pastele complete with ties made from nylon rope he found in the closet.

We loaded the body onto a mail cart and wheeled it into the elevator, and down to the garage. Placing first some plastic garbage bags to line the trunk of Mr. D's BMW, Sal and I lifted the body off the cart, and then placed it into the trunk and closed it.

I started looking around for any cameras.

"There's none on this side of the garage." Sal explained. "And as far as anyone knows, I'm still out of town, and you guys came up there to help Mr. D paint. He went home and you guys stayed to finish up."

"Let me go with you." I asked.

"No King, the less you know the better. Go upstairs, finish painting, and make sure you clean up good when you're done." I nodded, and again, Sal repeated. "Clean up good!"

I stepped back and moved the cart out the way as Sal got into Mr. D's BMW, backed up and pulled out. I watched as the automatic door opened and then closed immediately behind him.

CHAPTER 36

To The Grave

I drove up to the Funky Junky around noon and noticed a couple of squad cars parked in front along with one unmarked. I wanted to turn and go back home, but I was going to have to face the situation eventually. I drove down to the garage and parked beside Red's, the thought of them questioning him suddenly sent my heart racing. I began taking deep breaths to try and calm myself, but it wasn't helping.

I got upstairs and instead of Charlotte opening the door, it was Officer Lopez.

"There he is!" Lopez said patting me on the shoulder as I entered. The entire staff was sitting around moping.

"What's going on?" I asked.

"Seems your boss has gone missing."

"My boss?"

"Yes, Mr. Donald Duck, aka Mr. D?" Lopez added. "Missing?"

"How are you Mr. Rosario?" said the small Asian man. I just nodded. "My name is Detective Chin, and this is Detective Soto. I shook hands with him and his female partner. I noticed her wipe her hand on her pants after shaking mine.

"When was the last time you saw Mr. Duck?" Detective Soto asked.

Last night. I helped him paint his office."

"Last night?" Detective Soto asked. I nodded.

"So, tell me about that night?" Detective Chin asked.

"Well, I went by to talk to him."

"Talk to him?" Soto asked.

"Yeah, we hadn't had a chance to meet up since I'd gotten off tour."

"Is that typical?" Chin asked.

"Um, pretty much. Sometimes a couple of days would go by before I saw him."

"So, you stopped by to talk to him?" asked Soto.

"Yeah, not for anything in particular," I watched as both officers took notes. Seemed like they'd been writing every word I said.

"And then what happened?" asked Soto.

"Um, he was painting his office."

"So you left?" asked Chin.

"No, I hung out and we talked for a while.

"About?"

"About the tour,"

"What about it?" Soto continued. These were vague questions. They were precise step by step questions, so I had to make sure not to trip."

"Do I need a lawyer?" I asked. Both officers stopped writing and looked up at me.

"Do you *think* you need lawyer?" asked Chin. I gave it a moment, and then answered.

"No." I replied, and the two then looked back down at their notepads and continued.

"So how long did you stay there Mr. Rosario?" asked Soto.

"Well, Mr. D supposedly had been painting most of the day, and I guess the fumes were getting to him because he complained of a headache. I suggested that he call it quits till the next day, but he said he didn't want to come back to this mess, so, as much as I hate painting, I volunteered." The Officers looked back up at me. "There wasn't much more to do, a couple of walls, and of course the cleanup. Porky was in the gym..."

"Porky?" asked Soto.

"Victor, he's sort of my adopted son. He likes the gym here so when I have to work, I usually bring him with me, when he has no school of course. I called down there and asked him to give me a hand. He ran into Red, and they both came to help."

"Red?" Soto asked.

"Yes, that's my producer, he works out of the studio right

across from the gym." The way the Officers looked at me sort of told me that they weren't really buying my story, either that, or it was just part of their tactic.

"Do you think Red, and Porky would mind answering a few questions?" Chin asked.

"I don't see why not," I replied, so Chin handed me his card.

"Would you mind, asking the two of them to give me a call sometime tomorrow morning?"

I took the card and nodded as the two officers closed their pads and each shook my hand before heading out.

I couldn't wait to get out of there as the first thing I was going to do is meet up with both Porky and Red and give them a heads up.

We invited Red over for dinner, and of course the same role we had to play for the cops, we practiced on Rosie. I never liked keeping things from her, but this time I had to, for everyone's sake. Red always loved Rosie's cooking, and so did Sal as the two of them had been over for dinner many times. Dora came out and told us all goodnight, after which Rosie took her upstairs to tuck her in.

Porky, Red and I grabbed whatever it was we were drinking and went out to the back yard. We pulled close some chairs, and there talk about what happened, what *was* happening, as well as what *will* happen, depending on how all else goes.

I made their story as simple as I possibly could and their involvement to the absolute minimum. I laid it out in a way, that by the time they got up to the office, Mr. D was already gone. Supposedly Red had some nice clothes on, so he just touched up edges, I finished up the job, and Porky cleaned up. The drop cloths were folded neatly and placed inside the closet along with the brushes, rollers, and remaining cans of paint.

I made the story a simple one, and warned them of tricks and lies to get us to say things we aren't supposed to.

Once I was sure we were all on the same page, I held up my drink, and they theirs, and together we toasted...

"To the grave!"

CHAPTER 37

A Meeting with the Angel

Whenever a tinge of guilt would come upon me, I'd remembered Mr. D was trying to take *us* out! Sal saved our lives and probably the lives of my wife and daughter. Last thing I would ever do is flip on him.

No one had even an idea of the whereabouts of Mr. D was an extremely private dude, and until his disappearance, none of us even knew where he lived.

Business continued as usual, as everyone expected him to just one day walk through the door. We on the other hand knew better. It sort of pained me whenever I heard staff members include his name in decisions or that they would have to get his approval first. So many times I wanted to jump up on the coffee table in the reception area and yell out. *Mr. D is dead! Move on with your lives, mother fuckers!* But that sort of statement would surely put an end to mine.

I realized that Mr. D had no partners; no VPs or Presidents to take over if something were to happen to him. He was the owner, president, CEO, COO, and CFO, and though this was a great opportunity for me, there were people on the job who were going to be fucked. One of the senior administrators had a wife who was undergoing chemotherapy. Another had just gotten married and bought a house, and another had twins on the way. Ah shit and there I was, feeling guilty again.

To stop working would make us look suspicious, so it was important to continue as if Mr. D was still around. Every day, Red and I would continue working on music, while Vanessa continued working on our show. The only difference now, was the fact that we practically scrapped all that bullshit Mr. D had us on, and began finally recording our new material.

With the loss of Princess, working was the only thing that kept Vanessa going. There were at least two dozen employees at the Funky Junky, and everyone continued to come in as usual.

Charlotte was still pretty new at the job, and seemed, not only concerned about her job, but more importantly, the meeting she got to set up between Mr. D and her brother.

This was supposed to be a secret, so that I wouldn't feel like my spot was in jeopardy. Little did anyone know, I would've gladly had given it to him.

For about a month after the incident, I would enter the Funky Junky, each day surprised that its doors were still open. Until one day, Charlotte introduced me to Mr. Beckler, apparently the attorney that was handling Mr. D's estate. As it turned out, the state was about to step in and claim what they were owed, as Mr. D was in default of an arranged settlement.

In order for a person to be declared dead, proof must be given that they are not alive, and this default made that clear, as well as the many other taxes and unpaid bills.

The idea of what might've happened to Mr. D was now split between being dead, or evading taxes.

Mr. D and the Funky Junky became a regular on the News and in the papers. DEAD OR INDEBT, one of the headlines read.

That evening Rosie and I had a long talk about what was going on, and she suggested I inquire about purchasing the Funky Junky. I laughed. The sight of that place already made me sick, owning it would probably kill me. But then she explained how it really wasn't The Funky Junky, or even the people that made it unpleasant. It was Mr. D. And when I thought about it... she was right! The next day I called Mr. Beckler and he agreed to meet with me at his office.

Mr. Beckler warned me against the purchase, explaining that what they were asking exceeded its actual value. That I would be better off starting a new company from scratch, and believe me, it didn't take much to convince me.

The price they wanted for the Funky Junky and all of its possessions including studio, masters, building and so on was 2.5 million dollars, a number that was a bit out of my reach. I laughed my way out of there.

That evening I met up with Red and Cuba at Studio in the Funky Junky, as There was no more sneaking away to Cuba's apartment. When I told them about my meeting, and how much they were asking, Cuba's eyebrows nearly hit the ceiling, but Red on the other hand, didn't flinch. He began to ask me things about the deal that I hadn't even thought of asking, 'cause once I heard 2.5 million dollars, any further questions would've been just a waste of time.

"King, when they say 2.5 Million Dollars they're not expecting you to pay for it all in cash." Red told me. Since I had purchased my home in cash I didn't have the experience of dealing with the banks and getting a mortgage. Red broke it down for me, and it made so much sense. I asked him if he would come in as a partner, but he just laughed. He wasn't interested in the day to day dealings of a company such as The Funky Junky, but told me, that if I decide to buy it, that he'll introduce me to a friend of his, who is what they call, an Angel Investor, a term I had never before heard, but with the word Angel attached, it sounded like a blessing.

I gave it a couple of days, while Rosie and I gave it much thought. She was all for it, and so was Porky, and then one evening, I called Red and told him to set up a meeting with the Angel.

Though the interest seemed a little high, and the small piece of equity wasn't something I was expecting, in just a couple of days, three million dollars was wired to my account.

Apparently my celebrity status played a bit of a role, as the Angel claimed to have been a fan. For the first time in years, I felt like I was once again on top of the world, and now I was anxious to get started.

I kept the staff abreast of what I was trying to do, so that they would hang around just a bit longer. Some did, and for those I had big plans. But most of them left.

I had Rosie arrange a meeting with our now tiny staff

which also included Porky, Red, and even Cuba. We all piled up in the reception area, and with Mr. Beckler beside me for confirmation, I made the announcement that I was now the new owner of The Funky Junky!

CHAPTER 38

A Threat Come True

The transition went smoother than I had anticipated, as if there was some invisible force helping me out. Once all the assets were transferred over, and the deal closed, it seemed as if the entire investigation regarding Mr. D went away.

One of the biggest shocks was when we learned about the ties Mr. D had with the mob. Originating with his father, Mr. D maintained these associations, and kept it all very private. Over the years I've seen many strange characters come in and out of the Funky Junky, however, none of them I thought ever had that mobster thing about them, but now that I know the truth, I realize that yes, a few of them could've very well played the part.

Questions I've always had, but was scared to ask were now being answered, and the more that were answered, the more I realized just how much danger, not only was I in, but also my family.

The authorities were giving up hope, and began saying that due to his ties, the chances of his body ever being found were zero to none, and you know what they say... *No body, no crime!*

Rosie began coming to the office on the regular, and so I made her my personal assistant, because it was important that she knew absolutely everything that went on.

Rosie only use to come for parties, and on special occasions, so she didn't really know the building. But after the first week, while getting shit back in order and how we wanted it, she knew it like the back of her hand. Porky even showed her all the secret rooms and hiding places he use to play in when he was a kid. Most of them he couldn't even fit in anymore.

We had lost most of our employees, and so I figured we'd start interviewing, but Rosie, after a bit of research, realized that most of those employees should've never been hired in the first place. It turned out that though most of them were nothing more than stand-ins with no real responsibilities, they received incredibly substantial paychecks.

Going over the books, and the employee contracts of those who had quit, left us with a bunch of questions, questions that we needed clarity on, and when we tried to reach back out to those former employees, and hopefully get some answers, strangely, no one was able to be found... No one!

It was as if the people who had left never even worked here. Everything about them was phony! Names, addresses, even social security numbers were all fake.

I started to think about when I first started, how every single door would be open, and everyone made sure to show their face and greet me. I always thought they were just a bunch of hard working people who helped me get to where I was, now they seem to have been nothing more than a bunch of actors.

Not a day went by that someone didn't either call or come by to try and collect money that was supposedly owed to them. It was all illegal, but seeing the people that Mr. D was apparently involving himself with, I didn't ask any questions. Mr. D's personal debt was costing me a fortune, but I was already too deep in, so I had no choice, thank God for my angel, who helped keep me afloat.

The place needed some minor repairs, and though I didn't have a problem hiring a contractor, Porky insisted on doing the work himself. I was amazed at how much he knew and how handy he was, shit, I couldn't screw in a light bulb without reading the instructions.

Red practically made the recording studio his second home. Hold up! Correction! His first home! He would even swing by and pick up Cuba every morning and bring him in.

Cuba seemed like a whole new person. Always excited and in a good mood. His work was already incredible with just his limited home set up. But now, with access to pretty much any piece of equipment he can ever want, the shit that he and Red were spitting out was like nothing I've ever heard.

Cuba was so fascinated with the technology, that he would geek-out on a piece of equipment, and by the end of the day, would master it, having it do things you never thought was possible.

I loved popping in on Vanessa during rehearsal. Unlike

Princess, she was always glad to see me, as were her dancers. She stopped whatever they were doing and invited me in.

I haven't seen her this happy in quite a while, another reason that made everything I did, well worth it.

We were between projects, but Vee still kept a steady schedule, and took advantage of the downtime. There was no one left from the old crew. Once Princess died, everyone left. And though it did hurt Vanessa a bit, it also gave her a clean slate to work with. No old baggage or attitudes. She was the sole decision maker when it came to her dancers, and from what I could see, no one could've done any better.

I then went across the hall to check in on Porky who took charge of our Fitness Department. You heard right, Fitness. Porky's idea of course, and why not, he spent most of his time there anyway.

Jacq didn't change much over the years. Same look, same attitude, however, he was up there in age, and we were becoming concerned. Porky had been going there since he was a kid, and everything he knew about fitness, he learned from Jacq.

He started helping out a few years ago, and has since trained several people. He scheduled everyone in a way where he can work with few at a time, and on different days, trying his best to leave Jacq with nothing much to do, except maybe dust the equipment every now and then.

We placed Dora in a private school close to the office since Rosie and I spent most of our time there. Porky was Dora's designated chauffeur, upon her request of course. It worked out perfectly. On his way to the office every morning, he would drop her off at school, and then pick her up in the afternoon. Porky took the extra supply room at the back of the gym and converted it into Dora's very own room, complete with a television, radio, games, books, everything you can imagine to make her comfortable. She even had her own telephone in it so she can talk to her friends, she was twelve years old and in the 7th grade, beautiful as can be and pretty popular with the other kids.

A lot of her friends knew who I was, mostly because of their parents. Some of them had actually been fans, and didn't hesitate to let me know. Others obviously weren't, and they didn't hesitate to let me know either.

Dora use to have a hard time dealing with that. She couldn't understand how people didn't like my music, or even *me*, for that matter, and once Grams was no longer with us, she took the spot as my number one fan.

I explained to her that music was an art, and that what made it art was the fact that not everyone loved it. They weren't supposed to. We had a long deep conversation regarding the topic, and explored many examples from the various art forms, and of course… she got it!

It was at that point I believe that Dora really took to the arts, all types, from music to dance, film and fashion. Not to mention the works of Rembrandt, Picasso, Warhol and Basquiat.

I loved what she had become so far, and was excited to see where she'd go.

When Dora's friends were dropped off to either hang out or do homework, and though they themselves didn't really care who I was, their mother's did, and would go nuts when they saw me. Rosie had prepared little grab bags that she kept close by, so that I can quickly autograph and they can be on their way.

Sometimes I would go down and check up on Red and Cuba, just to find Dora sitting in the studio. I wasn't too crazy about it, because both those guys had dirty mouths, but they would promise to behave, just so she can hang out.

We kept Charlotte on, because she was really good at what she did, and though at times I still got butterflies when I saw her, I adored my wife, and therefore knew we were all good.

I mentioned to Rosie that we knew each other from the library, but that was it, I didn't see the point in making anyone uncomfortable. Besides, we never did anything, anything at all!

I use to think that having the receptionist rolling around on skates was just some weird fetish that Mr. D enjoyed, until after running this place for a while, that I realized what a fantastic idea it actually was.

The Funky Junky was huge, and there was a lot of going back and forth. If anyone had to do all that walking, I couldn't see them lasting a week. Rosie even considered getting a pair herself… But Dora put a stop to that idea real quick.

Charlotte was skating beside me, reading off some of the messages that had come in, when out of nowhere I decided to ask her about her brother. I didn't like the dude, and had made it obvious on many occasions.

It was no secret that his career had totally flat lined, as his fall from grace seemed to have caught more press than his climb. I suddenly felt fucked up, as she went silent and just looked ahead. I knew how he was doing... Damn, what did I do?

I was hoping that she would say something like *I don't want to talk about it*. But she never did. Instead, she stopped in her tracks and turned to me, then... She told me the story.

The company he was down with went under, along with everything they owed him. His wife left him for one of his bodyguards, and they ended up moving out of state. Nemesis attempted to follow, so to be near his children, until one night while he was sleeping, some guys broke into his apartment and nearly beat him to death, a threat come true!

Charlotte begged him to go and stay with her, and that together they're work on getting him at least his visitation rights.

He did small club shows from time to time, practically begging promoters to put him on. The pay was humiliating, and that was *IF* he even got paid!

With his tail between his legs, Nem finally caved, and moved in with his sister. He got a job as a bike messenger, being paid according to the amount of deliveries he made. His co-workers were cruel, his bosses even more so, as they would give him the runs that no one else wanted to do, making in his first week, a mere twenty-seven dollars.

Charlotte had come to Mr. D to try and see if he could help resuscitate his career. He told her that he'd rather hire her than him, and so she took him up on the offer. Charlotte had a lot going on for herself, and she seemed to have given it all up for her brother, but he did the same for her, and was the one paying for her college. The same college she had to drop out of, because he was no longer able to pay the bill.

Though at first, I really didn't give a fuck. I couldn't help but be moved by this story. Yeah, I thought he was a dick. But he probably thought that I was one too. Shit, we were both artists, rappers at that, going after the same fans, trying to headline the same tours. Were we ever supposed to be cool? Probably not! But I'm no longer in the position that I use to be, and neither is he. Why are we still competing? Well actually, why am I still competing?

I stood there and listened to the rest of Charlotte's sad story, and I have to admit, it hit me. It hit me hard!

I ended up telling her to bring him in, that I was sure there something we could fine for him to do here.

"You told her what?" Rosie yelled out. I gestured for her to lower her voice, as I'm sure Charlotte wasn't too far away. She hated when I did that, and would purposely get louder.

"Rey, we pay so many people for shit we don't need, that the things that we do need, we can't afford!"

"I know, Rosie, but Mr. D left a lot of people high and dry. What are we supposed to do, just throw'em away?"

"Yes! They'll be fine, most of them would've had jobs already and living happily ever after, besides, Nemesis had nothing to do with Mr. D."

"There has to be a way to put him on."

"There isn't Rey."

"So, we'll make one!"

"Make one? Do you hear what you're saying?"

"Come on Rosie, its Charlotte's brother, and she's part of the team."

"To be honest, we don't need her either!"

I didn't know what else to say. I plopped down into my seat and threw my head into my hands. I remained that way for a bit, trying to think what I was going to do.

I felt Rosie's hands on my shoulders, then she placed her head on top of mine, then wrapped her arms around my neck. We stayed that way for a moment until finally she whispered into my ear.

"You are indeed your Grandmother's child!" She said, and I knew what she meant and smiled.

"Ten dollars an hour," Rosie suddenly blurted out. I turned and looked at her.

"What?" I asked.

"Ten! That's how much we can spare, plus that's what we give his sister."

I got up and grabbed my wife and gave her the biggest hug.

"Really?" she said, "and for someone you don't even like?"

"Oh man, this is great, Rosie." I said, pacing excitedly in front of her. "I'm telling, you this is gonna be great, you watch."

"Oh I'll be watching alright, starting with what it is you're going to have him doing for that ten, and it better not be something stupid, Rey!"

"It won't, I promise."

CHAPTER 39

A Bucket of Salt

I prepped myself mentally for this meeting with Nemesis the next morning. He and I never really liked each other and now he was coming to me practically begging for a job. Oh how the tables do turn!

I couldn't help but contemplate being just a little fucked up with him, because I could imagine him walking through the door with his broke ass trying to be all hard. Little does he know, that the only job I have available at the moment, is that of another Janitor!

I had cleared out Mr. D's office and made it my own. It had all the fixings of a successful artist and businessman, and I couldn't wait to see Nemesis' face when he walked in.

I set the tone just right. In the background, playing continuously was a CD that simply said Epic Instrumentals. The lights, adjusted so that the gold and platinum plaques that decorated the wall behind me, smacked the shit out of him!

Framed Billboard listings along with magazine covers

and front page newspaper articles covered the wall to my right, while photos of me with practically every major celebrity and politician hung to the left.

I got rid of all of Mr. D's corny furnishings, including all that creepy shit that he called Art. I had the room stripped bare and then totally refinished, including a fresh paint job. The only thing I kept was that big purple bean bag which I sinisterly fluffed in front of my desk. Oh Mr. D, how now I understand!

I kept looking up at my clock, as our appointment was a 10 am sharp, and it was already three minutes to. I had hoped he'd come to his senses when he woke up this morning and be a total no- show. Boy would that make shit easy. But if he did show up even one minute late, I was just gonna send him home, and have Charlotte reschedule his appointment in about a month. Why I still hated this mother fucker? I don't even remember. All I knew was... I still do!

Thirty seconds to ten, Nemesis still wasn't here, and I was a bit relieved. I picked up the phone and called Rosie's office to joke about the situation when suddenly there was a knock on the door. I looked up at the clock, and it was ten on the dot.

"Come in!" I yelled out, just as Mr. D use to do every time I came to see *him*. Charlotte rolled in and held open the door as her brother stepped inside.

"Page me if you need anything," she said with a smile that seemed to have thanked me once again. She whispered good luck to her brother, then rolled on out, closing the door behind her.

"I'll call you back, Rosie. My 10 o'clock just arrived."

I looked across the room at Nemesis, and watched as he just stood there, his head bowed and his eyes to the floor, contrary to what I had expected. I had imagined his entrance over and over, and had rehearsed in my mind how I would've handled his arrogant ass when he arrived. But he rendered my plan useless.

"Come on in, man." I invited, a bit thrown off by his disposition. Nemesis walked forward, his head still bowed as if there wasn't even an ounce of pride left in him.

I couldn't help but stare at him, wondering if this was the same dude that practically tormented me for the first few years of my career.

"Can I get you something to drink?" I offered, my tone softening by the minute. "No thank you," He replied in voice I didn't recognize.

"Take a seat." I said, gesturing toward the big purple beanbag in front of my desk. Nemesis, thanked me, and without any hesitation was about plop down in it...

"Wait!" I called out. Nemesis looked up, not sure what was going on.

"Don't sit there, bro." I told him, kicking the Beanbag to the side and replacing it with one of the new chairs I just had delivered.

As he sat down, I could see his eyes take in quick glances of his surroundings. And though for me this should've been a glorious day, one of pride and victory. Instead, I felt shame!

I now had to search for something to say, as the rant that I had rehearsed over and over, had totally vanished from my memory. This scene was nothing like what I expected.

"So how you doing?" I began. Nemesis took a moment to answer.

"I'm good." He lied, still unable to even look at me.

"I was surprised when I found out that Charlotte was your sister. I've known her for a while now. Cool people." Nemesis just nodded. I could tell that he just wanted to hurry up and get through this tortuous meeting.

I started imagining him walking around in the Janitor's uniform I had all ready for him. Nemesis the Superstar, cleaning my toilets and emptying my ashtrays, a vision I couldn't wait to bring to life, no longer seemed as exciting as it once did. This guy had certainly been wounded, and here I was with a bucket of salt.

Nemesis sat there, like a criminal awaiting his execution. Whatever they did to this guy they did it good, as he was stripped of all dignity. Charlotte had no idea what my true intentions were, me agreeing to hire him wasn't because we were friends, but because I planned on beating him over the head with it. I wanted to humiliate him. Make him my bitch. I even thought about getting this mother fucker a pair of roller skates.

I looked at his clothes and they looked as if they had been donated to him by some old fat guy. His shoes were scuffed and the toes were bent upward. His trademark Kangol was replaced by a raggedy ass knitted hat, old and covered in lint balls, and though I never got close enough to tell, from where I stood, he looked like he stunk!

I stood there in silent, watching as this pitiful mother fucker stared at the floor. I dug deep into my memory bank, pulling up absolutely anything I could find that would remind me of how this sonofabitch and his mutant crew treated me and mine. But no matter what came up, I just couldn't help it... I felt sorry for him.

This was the part of me I didn't like, the part that came from Grams. No matter how people treated her, she always managed to find their light, and show compassion. I ain't wanna be like that. I wanted to be cold and callous to those who were cold and callous to me. I wanted to step on mother fuckers who stepped on me, kick'em to the curb and watch'em suffer... But I couldn't!

I couldn't even move myself to hiring him as the janitor. I glanced over at the uniform I had draped over the chair. The one I couldn't wait to give him.

I had that shit custom made just for him. Green work pants and a yellow shirt with my logo covering the entire back. I had it cut a size too small, with pants that dangled just above the ankle. Yeah, I was gonna make this bitch pay, one way or the other... But I couldn't do it!

Damn! What was I gonna do now? I tried to think up other positions that might be available, but they were all filled, even the ones Rosie thought shouldn't even exist.

The room was still and awkward. I didn't even know what to say. I knew about his career as a Rapper, probably better than most, as his and mine ran parallel most of the way. Do I have him fill out an application? Conduct an interview? What?

I stood up to try and loosen up a bit when I accidentally knocked over my coffee.

"Damn it!" I yelled out as I looked around for some napkins. Nemesis immediately jumped up and grabbed the roll of paper towel I had on the counter. He rushed back over to me and quickly began to clean up.

He caught the spill before it reached any of my papers, then continued down the side of my desk.

I handed him the wastepaper basket to toss the dirty towels, then stood there as he wiped up the mess that splattered around my sneakers, as well as the few drops that hit them.

"Where do you keep the bags?" He asked, and I pointed to the closet. He went over, grabbed a new bag, and relined the trashcan.

I watched as he tied up the trash, then looked at me, and simply said…

"I really need this job!"

CHAPTER 40

The Soul of King

The Funky Junky was back in full swing, but with just one artist, and that being me. We were able to acquire the entire King catalog along with the company, and did a pretty good job licensing out to film and Television. But that would never sustain us. What we needed was growth!

Every Monday morning we would all meet in the conference room. It was usually just me, Rosie, Red, Porky, and just recently we began including, Cuba. The topic at hand was new signing artists. The businessman in me knew without doubt that this was the logical thing to do, yet that arrogant artist that still lingered, felt that no artist could do a better job.

"But you're always complaining about being on the road." Rosie said.

"We could keep it local!" I suggested. "I mean, come on guys. We just recorded a whole new album."

"Without the proper promotions it's gonna flop," said Red, "and it's gonna be very public."

"We can't afford that Rey." Rosie added.

"I threw my hands over my face and rubbed hard. I could feel my wife, rubbing my back to console me. All I ever wanted to be was an artist, and now that I have the chance to do it the way I always wanted to do it… It's too late!

"You had a fantastic run." Rosie said softly as she placed her head on my shoulder.

My eyes glanced over at Red.

"They're not buying your records anymore!" He said, shaking his head. I then looked over at Porky.

"My friends don't even know who you are, Rey… I'm sorry."

I took my final glance at Cuba, prepared for another stabbing. But he did something worst. He turned away.

"King, think of it this way." Red began. "All of your resources and experiences can now be used to help someone else's career."

"Nobody helped me." I replied. "Don't you think they'd appreciate it more if they had to do for themselves?"

"That's not true!" Rosie protested. "Your grandmother helped you, you told me that yourself. Had it not been for her you would never had been able to do any of this!"

Rosie was right, and I felt horrible about my statement. I apologized to my grandmother in a quick prayer and looked back at my wife and nodded.

"Normally the bulk of an artist's career is spent making mistakes," said Red, "many of those mistakes being quite stupid. However, if you are the one to give artists an opportunity, the bulk of their careers could now be put into making hits, hits that will benefit The Funky Junky."

I looked down at my empty notepad and rubbed my forehead, it was like my brain was becoming claustrophobic, wanting to bust out of its tight quarters. I had to make a decision, one that would totally change, not only the course of my career, but also, my life!

Everyone remained quiet and just stared at me, waiting for an answer. I couldn't adjourn this meeting, this was a do or die situation and I had to make a decision. The room was absolutely still, and silent, and I swore everyone could hear my heart pounding.

I looked at my wife, who was giving me the most pitiful look, as if the plug was about to be pulled.

I asked Grams if she could somehow guide me, hoping she wasn't mad at me for the stupid comment I made a minute ago.

I suddenly began to feel an unusual amount of tension building up in the room. I was never one to sweat much, especially just sitting, and asked if there was a problem with the AC. Porky assured me that it was cool in the room when suddenly we heard a loud crash. We all jumped and looked in its direction when we noticed it was one of the many framed posters that hung on the wall. Porky rushed over and propped the busted frame against the wall, and when he realized which poster it was he looked at me. It was the poster we found in my Gram's bedroom when we cleared it out.

"That's weird. The nail's still in the wall." Porky said. Red picked up the phone and called for the Janitor, then he and

Porky sat back down..

Al eyes were back on me. I took the deepest breath I could take, and held it in. Everyone watched in silence, when finally, I exhaled! It was as if I could feel the soul of King, suddenly leave my body.

My heart was pounding and I tried desperately to catch my breath. Rosie took my hand, and squeezed it, watching me closely until I began to calm down. When I did, I looked at everyone, and with a smile asked.

"So how do we find artists?" and immediately it was like a window was opened and all pressure in the room blew out. Everyone stood and applauded, and it seemed as if at that very moment a huge weight had been lifted, and the room suddenly turned bright. Those butterflies that practically lived in my stomach back when I started, now seemed to have magically reappear, and everything finally made sense.

I noticed the door open, and in stepped Nemesis. Porky pointed toward the mess to where Nem walked and began cleaning up.

"We run ads. Like the ones you use to *answer*." Rosie suggested, to a room full of nods.

"And we can hold auditions down in the rehearsal studio. Red added."

"What about talent contest?" Porky asked, a bit hesitantly, and everyone loved the idea. Porky got excited.

"And you guys are sure about this?" I asked them all, and together they all gave me a loud YES!

We continued throwing ideas back and forth, and my

once empty notepad was now on page three. We discussed everything, like whether we wanted a male, female, trio or group. I was becoming really excited, and every idea thrown out seemed to be a great one.

I glanced over at Nemesis, who was now on his hands and knees, making sure every piece of glass was picked up, when the voices in the room suddenly became muffled and I began fantasizing about what it must feel like to be Nemesis at this very moment. Whereas Rap History was being made, and his only involvement was cleaning up a mess in the room where it took place.

I snapped out of my little trance and jumped back into the conversation, making sure I spoke loud and clear. I purposely threw out names that were once direct competitors of Nemesis, knowing damn well we would never use them. Rosie caught on to what I was doing and gave me that look, Porky however, got me good when he said those artists were, "madd old," knowing damn well, that I was older than they were.

CHAPTER 41

Upside Down

I stepped into the studio around 4:00PM. Red and Cuba were at the console, Porky and Dora sitting on the couch just watching them work.

"What's up King?" Red said. Cuba waves and I look at Porky and Dora.

"Pork, do me a favor and bring Dora upstairs, her mother's leaving in a few."

"Red was going to let me sing something, Daddy."

"We can't play now Sweetie, we have work to do," I replied. Porky got up and waved Dora to follow.

"But that's not fair!" She said.

"We did kind of promise her that we were going to record her singing something." Red responded.

"Guys, are we not busy enough?" I asked them.

"She has a nice voice, you should hear her." Cuba added.

"I've heard her. She has a beautiful voice." I replied though I hadn't never really listened to her. "Sweetie, I promise you, we'll come in, maybe on a weekend, just me and you and record something, okay?"

"You don't even know how to use any of this stuff." She replied gesturing toward the console. I looked at the guys and they looked away, I wonder where she got that from? "Besides, I wanted to record Take Me."

"Take Me?" I turned to the guys. "Are you crazy?"

"What's wrong with Take Me?" Red asked.

"That shits about Love!" I replied.

"And what's wrong with love?" Cuba asked.

"She's fucking ten years old, that's what's wrong with love!" I shouted.

"Come on man, you're buggin' out' bro." Red lashed back.

"That's my daughter. I'll bug the fuck out as much as I want. Now unless the song's about roller skating and eating Ice Cream, I don't want her involved." I looked up at Porky. "You were cool with this?"

"I didn't see anything wrong with it." He replied, shrugging his monster shoulders.

"What the fuck's wrong with you guys?" I said, looking at all of them, as if they lost their minds.

"Go 'head, bring her up!" I ordered, and watched as they left the studio "And unless I know about it, she's not to set foot in this studio again." I yelled up just before the door closed. Everyone was silent, but they stared at me.

"What?" I asked.

"Don't you think you were a little too hard on her?" Red asked.

"No I don't."

"She loves music, King." Cuba said.

"And she has a brand new stereo system in her room." I replied sarcastically. I went over to the couch and plopped down in it.

"You gotta ease off her a bit, King, She's not a baby anymore."

"Fuck you talking about, Red? of course she's still a baby!"

"She's *your* baby" Cuba jumped in, "and will be so no matter how old she is, but she isn't *a* baby!"

I sat back and placed my hand over my face and stayed that way for a long moment.

"I don't want her doing this." I said in a calm tone. Red and Cuba looked at one another.

"Why not?" asked Red.

"Because it's a mean and nasty business, that's why!"

"Is it?" Cuba asked.

"You know it is!" I said to Cuba. "You yourself told me the stories. Not to mention, I have a few of my own. And so do you Red!"

"It wasn't the business that was mean and nasty, King. It was the people that you and I had no choice but to have to deal with." Red explained. "Dora doesn't have to deal with those people."

"She's got us, King," Cuba interjected. "and we wouldn't let anyone hurt her."

I looked at the two of them. I believed that they really loved Dora, and would do anything to look out for her, but handing her over to this business would be a huge sacrifice on my part.

"Maybe I'm getting overworked for nothing." I began. "I mean, most kids go through this type of phase."

"Phase?" asked Cuba.

"Yeah, you know, they start to dream about the fame and shit, until they realize that it doesn't come easy, not to mention, you gotta have the talent."

"Well, I don't know if this is a phase she's going through." Red said. "But as far as the talent? She's got it, bro."

"She really does." Cuba confirmed with a nod. This took me for one hell of a loop because I personally had no idea, and my face proved that.

"You've never heard her sing, have you?" Cuba asked. I wanted so bad to lie, but shamefully, I didn't. Instead I just shook my head."

Red quickly picked up the studio phone and paged Porky. "What are you doing?" I asked.

"You gotta check this out." Red replied.

"Okay, maybe she sounds cute." I continued. "But we're talking real life here guys, and the last thing I want to do is let her down." The phone rang back and Red picked it up.

"Pork!" Red said into the phone, "Dora still with you? Okay cool, bring her back down? Don't worry about that. Just bring her here." Red hung up and looked back at me.

"I don't know about this shit," I said to them. "if I'm not feeling her, what then?" "I don't think that's gonna be the case." Red replied.

"Does Rosie know about this?"

"Yep!" answered Cuba.

"And what did she say?"

"She told us that you were going to react exactly the way you are reacting right now."

The door opened and in stepped Porky and Dora. Rosie followed behind them. Dora had a face on her that sort of reminded me of my Grandmother when she got angry. It was the first time I ever really noticed their resemblance.

"Come here baby." Cuba said waving her over to him. She stood beside him and gave me the look of death. Red gestured Porky and Rosie to take a seat on the couch.

"Your daddy didn't mean anything bad," Cuba began, "he just loves you so much that he wants the best for you. She looked at Cuba and her stern eyes suddenly softened. "How come you never let him hear you?" Dora shrugged. "Can we let him hear you now?

She looked at me, and exhaled. Damn, she was so pissed, she looked like a grown up, but then she nodded.

Cuba took her by the hand and led her to the booth. I turned and looked at my wife, her eyes were a bit watery. Red spun around and set up the board and tape machine. I watched through the glass as Cuba adjusted the microphone to her height and then placed the head phones snuggly on her head.

Red reached over and pressed the intercom button so that we could hear what they were saying.

"Do you need the words?" Cuba asked.

"No," She replied. "But what if he doesn't like the way I sing?" She asked. It put the biggest lump in my throat and sent Rosie weeping.

"He's going to love you!" Cuba told her as he took her by shoulders and looked her in the eyes. "But I want you to sing exactly the way you sang for us today. Don't change anything. Forget any of us are even here."

"Can I close my eyes again?"

"Absolutely," he replied, before kissing her on the forehead and exiting the booth. He smiled at us as he stepped back into the control room. "She's so cute." He said. "You sure she's yours?" He asked me, and then turned to Rosie and squinted.

Cuba's jokes lightened up the room, and though she couldn't hear us, Dora could see us all laughing and that made her smile, and more importantly, relax.

Red looked at Cuba and smiled at him, as he saw what he just did.

Cuba reached over to the intercom button and held it down.

"Okay sweetie. Are you ready?"

Dora gave a great big smile, followed by a thumbs up, my heart suddenly dropped, as this was the first time that I realized that my baby wasn't a baby anymore.

"Hit those lights." Cuba said, and so I did. The entire control room turned dark, aside from the equipment and whatever light seeped in from the booth. Rosie and Porky stood up, just as Cuba again pressed the intercom button.

"Okay Dorita… from the top sweetie!" He gestured to Red to press play, and so, the music began!

I hadn't heard the music to Take Me yet, and got goose bumps from the first bar. It was a different kind of sound, a sort of mixture between Rap and Latin, upper-mid tempo type of joint, which allowed you the option to either dance, or just chill out and listen.

I watched as Cuba raised his hand, ready to count her in, then finally, THREE… TWO… ONE! He points to her, and at that very moment… My entire world turns upside down.

CHAPTER 42

Goodnight Daddy

It was a cool evening as I sat in my backyard, watching the flames as they danced in my fire pit. The screen door opened and out stepped Rosie with two cups of coffee. She handed me one and took the seat across from me. I took a sip and then sat back and continued staring into the fire.

We both remained quiet for a moment and I can feel Rosie staring at me. I turned and looked at her and she smiled.

"You okay?" She asked. I just nodded, so she sat back and took another sip. I had so much going on in my head that what I needed most was to just be left alone so I could try and sort shit out. Rosie knew it, but hung around anyway.

Many decisions she's allowed me to handle on my own. But this wouldn't be one of them.

"She's really good, Rey." And when she said that, it was as if someone suddenly punched me in my chest. I just sat there shaking my head.

"This isn't the life I want for her." I said, still looking at the fire. "No one said it's going to be her life."

"She doesn't know what she wants."

"Maybe... But until she figures it out, I think we need to support her. "She could do so much better than this, Rosie."

"And she will. She has you... She has us!"

At that moment we both heard a sound and looked around. I glanced up at my house and saw the curtain moving in Dora's window. She must've been listening. I looked at Rosie and she gave me that look as if I better go fix this. I placed my coffee down on the table, and headed inside.

I stood in front of Dora's slightly opened door and waited a moment before sticking my head in. She hadn't quite fixed the curtain as it was still bunched to the side a bit. She played sleep, her beautiful face, glowing from the moonlight that seeped in.

I sat at the edge of her bed. She did the old make believe I'm waking up routine, and opened her eyes with a yawn,

"Hey Sweetie!"

"What's wrong, Daddy?" she asked.

"Just wanted to say goodnight," I placed my hand on her head and began to stroke gently. Dora closed her eyes. She looked so much like her mother it was scary.

"You sounded beautiful today." I told her. Her eyes opened a bit, and she smiled before closing them again. I wanted so bad to just give her a kiss goodnight and leave, but I knew this wasn't over.

"So where did you learn to sing like that?" I asked.

"Cuba." She replied.

"Cuba?"

"Uh huh, he showed me a few things."

"Like what?"

"Like how to breathe, and sing from the diagram."

"Diaphragm!" I corrected.

"Diaphragm!" She repeated with a giggle.

"So how long has he been teaching you these things?"

"Not long. I heard the song and memorized the words while they were working on it.

Cuba turned around and caught me singing along, and asked me to sing it for him. He was surprised that I knew all the words and started helping me with some of the lines."

"Helping you?"

"Yeah, a few of the lines I had a hard time singing so he showed me why, and then showed me how to fix them. He's a really good singing teacher, Daddy."

"I see that."

Dora turned around and sat up.

"I really want to sing, Daddy." She suddenly blurted out. I can see it in her eyes, she was serious. "I always wanted to tell you, but I was embarrassed."

"Why would you be embarrassed?"

"Because I never thought I was any good. I think if Cuba hadn't caught me I would still keep it a secret."

"Singing's a wonderful thing, Dora, but only when you

do it for yourself. Once it becomes a business, it sort of changes things."

"What kind of things?"

"Mostly the fun of it!"

"I don't think that would ever happen with me." She replied.

"Most people don't, until it does, and by then, it's usually too late." Dora looked at me, and I could tell she didn't understand.

"All I'm trying to say is that you have plenty of time to do this."

"But what I really want is plenty of time to enjoy it. That's why I want to start now."

Dora's face and voice were without doubt that of a child, but her mind was something else. The way she thought and the expressions she made while doing so seemed to me like she was Grams reincarnated. All I could do is look at her, either way I was fucked, so I opted to give her my blessings. She grabbed me around my neck and hugged me so tight I had to pull her arms loose because she was actually choking me.

I hadn't noticed Rosie standing in the doorway, but there she was, with the biggest smile.

I tucked her back under the covers and closed the window as it was getting pretty cool out. I kissed my daughter on the head, and before exiting I turned and gave her one last look. I smiled at all the little girl decorations, toys and posters that covered her room, knowing that not long from now, this will all change. My eyes started flooding and a huge lump got stuck in my throat. And just as I was closing her door, I heard her say,

"Goodnight Daddy!" I looked back, and smiled at my little angel, and then replied.

"Goodnight, Sweetie!"

CHAPTER 43

Frank or Frankie

I had a few meetings to attend to and would be back at the office around noon. Porky had driven Rosie in, and of course took Dora to school. It was a pretty good day, met up with some really important people who will play a huge role in the success of our company. I felt great about everything and the light at the end of the tunnel was looking really bright.

I parked my car where Mr. D used to park his, and took the private elevator up to my new office. The bell rang and the doors opened, and to my surprise, there was Rosie and Porky standing in front of my desk. The strange thing was the guy sitting behind it.

"What the hell's going on here? I asked as I stepped out of the elevator. Porky glanced to the side, and that's when I noticed the two men, one standing by the door, the other right next to the elevator, their hands in their leather jackets.

"Mr. King!" The man behind my desk said before crossing his feet up on it and latching his hands behind his head.

"Who the hell are you?" I asked, as I made my way toward him. One of the guys followed closely behind.

"He says he's your partner." Rosie blurted out.

"Partner?" I laughed. "Look man, you obviously have the wrong place, 'cause I ain't got no partners. The man laughed back.

"Obviously, you didn't get the memo... because yes you do!"

The man stood up and walked around to the front of the desk and sat, knocking over my framed family photo. I glanced over my left shoulder, as I could feel his boy practically breathing on my neck. He and his partner were focused on everything being said... as well as every move.

"Look, I have no idea who you are, I settled out with all the families that had their hands in this company so I don't know what to tell you."

"First off, asshole," the man said as he stood up and made his way toward me. "You don't tell me a fuckin' thing!" I saw Porky kind of jerk, and prayed he wouldn't do anything stupid.

"So tell me, who are you?" I asked, my eyes following as he walked to the wall to admire my collection of celebrity photos.

"You can call me Frank, or Frankie, whichever you prefer," he said, his eyes still on my wall.

"I prefer to call you neither."

Frank turned and looked at me with a serious look and

then laughed. "You're a real smart-ass, aren't you?"

"Look, you're the one coming up in here, saying you're a partner and talking in riddles. Tell me, who are you, what do you want, and what the fuck I have to do to get you out of my office, and out of my life?"

"Okay, straight to the point. I like that!" He said nodding his head and smiling at his boys.

"I have a note signed by a Mr. Donald Duck. I still can't get over that mother fuckers name." Frank said, laughing at the thought.

"Keep on!" I told him.

"So anyway, he borrowed one million dollars from me at 30% interest compounded over five years."

"But that has nothing to do with me. You need to hit up his estate."

"Listen kid, don't fuck me. This *is* his estate. It's the only thing he fucking owns."

"But he doesn't own it anymore, I do! Mr. D's dead."

"Yeah, I know. And I wonder how that happened?" Frank replied, giving me a look as if he knew what actually went down.

"So now, because he's dead, I'm supposed to just forget about my money?"

"Look, you need to get the fuck out..." I began, as I took a step toward Frank, but was quickly stopped when his boy placed his gun up against my head.

Rosie screamed and when Porky was about to step

forward as well, I grabbed him.

"Good choice!" Frank said to me as I guided Porky over to a chair to sit. I didn't answer, but watched as Frank picked up the calculator from my desk and began pushing buttons until a smile grew on his face. He looked at me.

"We could settle this right now for let's say a flat three!"

"You sonofabitch," I said, again stepping toward him, but this time he pulled out *his* gun, and aimed it straight at my face… and cocked it.

"Keep this in mind." He said, the gun still pointed at me, "If I blow your face off, your family will still have to pay off the debt."

"Please." Rosie cried out. Frank looked at her, and slowly lowered his gun. "Look, we don't have that kind of money right now."

"Rosie, don't do that!" I yelled, trying to get her to be quiet

"Shut the fuck up!" Frank yelled back, then turned back to Rosie, and nodded for her to continue. Rosie looked at me apologetically.

"We exhausted all of our funds acquiring the company, so we'd need some time." She said. Frank looked at her and licked his lips. That pissed me off even more, and made me wanna rip his tongue out his mouth.

"This is bullshit." I said into the air. Frank looked at me, and then at her.

"Twenty-four hours I expect the first payment, along with a plan of how you'll be paying off the rest." Frank looked at me. "That's because she's smart. Your dumb ass would've gotten your entire family killed."

"Fuck you!" I shouted, until his boy quieted me down by shoving the barrel of his gun harder against my temple. Frank walked pass me and toward the door, his boys with their guns still drawn walked backwards until they met up with their boss.

"Well it was great doing business with you all... I guess I'll see you guys tomorrow. Same time, same channel." He said laughing. One of his boys opened the door for them to leave when standing on the other side was Sal.

"Sal?" I said in a low yet excited voice, as Porky grew a huge smile.

Sal held his gun to Frank's forehead as he stepped into the office, Frank stepping backwards. His boys had their guns pointed directly at Sal, but he didn't look phased at all.

"I guess you never told them about me?" Sal said to a petrified Frank.

"Put'em down!" Frank yelled out, his head perfectly still. His boys didn't listen, so Sal cocked his 357 and raised his eyebrows. "Put them away, now!" Frank cried out, and finally they obeyed. When all seemed okay, Sal removed his gun from Frank's forehead.

"I thought you were dead!" Frank said.

"Surprise, mother fucker!"

"You have no business here and you know it." Sal scorned, his gun pressed against his nose.

"Man, Duck checked out without paying his bill." Frank

wined, suddenly sounding like a little bitch. His boys looked at one another in disbelief.

"But that has nothing to do with these folks."

"Heard that they were making right with everyone else, just figured we'd come get ours."

"And how much was that?" Sal asked, but Frank remained silent.

"Three million!" Rosie said.

"Three million dollars?" Sal said giving Frank a disgusted look. "This mother fucker I bet doesn't even have three hundred to his name!" again his boys looked at each other and then put their guns away.

"Come on Sal." Frank pleaded. "Just trying to get a little piece you know."

"You guys don't owe him a penny."

I exhaled, and smiled at Rosie and Porky.

"Now, you get the fuck out of here. And if I ever hear that you're fucking them. You're done!"

Frank nodded and headed for the door. One of his boys exited with him, but before the one that stayed with Sal left, he stopped him/

"That mother fucker's gonna get you and your man killed." The guy looked at the door, then back at Sal and nodded.

"Make him disappear, and then, you and your partner come by around this time tomorrow. I got some real work for you. The guy nodded a thank you and then took off.

Sal closed the door and locked it, and then turned and looked at us. The first one to rush up to him was Porky. He grabbed Sal in his arms and hugged him. Sal started to laugh.

"Goddamn, it's like hugging a bear!" Sal joked, as we all joined in on the hug.

CHAPTER 44

All Began to Spin

Come to find out that the money given out to repay Mr. D's debt was all bullshit, and the person behind it all was Mr. Beckler, yep, Mr. D's estate attorney. Having some of his thug friends pose as representatives for the different families they were able to extort quite a bit of money from me. Mr. Beckler had warned me that this might happen, and when it did, I didn't ask any questions, I just paid!

I ended up confiding in Sal about the payoffs, and when I mentioned the name of one of the guys I thought were a part of a particular family. Sal laughed and asked what made me think this, and when I told him... he flipped!

According to Sal, Mr. D owed no money to the Mob, or anyone else for that matter. Suddenly, all began to spin as I realized that I had just been robbed, not once but several times and for substantial amounts of money, most of which I borrowed from my Angel, and still had to pay it back.

Sal took me with him as we visited each of the families of which I thought we had to pay. I was in awe of the amount of love and respect they all showed Sal. This man never failed to amaze me. A lot of people got in trouble for this action, and a lot of heads rolled... Literally! I got some of the money back, which I immediately sent over to the Angel toward my huge debt, but a good portion of it would remain uncollectable.

Without saying anything to me, Sal had finally caught up to Mr. Beckler, who had gone out of town on some business. He had made a promise to Sal that the remainder that was owed, he would pay within thirty-six hours... Mr. Beckler hung himself in twenty-four!

Sal explained that the reason he went back to Miami after Mr. D's death was to protect *us* from the inevitable wrath that was sure to come.

To keep Q's father from trying to figure it out himself, and possibly hurting others in the process, Sal decided to confront the situation head on.

Quenepa's father, who everyone called Jefe, though agreed to meet with him at his mansion in Key West, also warned, that if unsatisfied with the explanation, that he would be executed on the spot.

Three of Jefe's soldiers picked up Sal from the little dingy motel he stayed at by the beach, and brought him to the mansion. It was a long, silent trip. Upon entering the grounds, Sal, again was searched thoroughly, and once cleared, was brought up to meet their boss.

The mansion was bigger than the White House and employed a staff of over two hundred. Sal knew he could be killed and no one will ever know, nor would his body ever be found. He had killed not only his son, but also, one of his greatest investments... Mr. D! Sal couldn't even tell which one hurt him more.

Jefe's office was like nothing Sal had ever seen before. Black and white Marble, smoked glass and gold set the theme. Sal was surprised when he was greeted so friendly, and when Jefe waved off his boys and left them alone, he was even more in shock, as he was sure that Jefe was aware of the fact that Sal didn't necessarily need a weapon to take him out.

Sal took the drink that he was offered, and the two men began by getting acquainted with one another. Sal followed Jefe's lead as the two spoke about various topics which included the weather, politics, sports, and of course, family. About an hour in, Jefe's entire personality switched up as he looked Sal directly in the eyes and said.

"You brought great sorrow to my family, and to my establishment."

"I understand." Sal replied. "And I am deeply sorry."

Sal knew that men with the wealth and success of Jefe, didn't make hasteful decisions, they were successful because they were smart, and extremely patient. Sal knew that if Jefe really wanted him dead, it would've already been done. The mere fact that Jefe agreed to meet with him was all Sal needed to know.

Sal knew better than to go into an explanation unless he was asked, and so the two men just stared at each other.

Sal never finished telling me what happened. But the fact that he was even still alive, told me that it all somehow worked out.

He did assure me however, that everything was taken care of, and that the Funky Junky was free to grow and prosper without any interference from anyone, and actually... That's all I wanted to know!

CHAPTER 45

Falling Down Steps

Our bank account was now financed and we were able to move forward with our plans. We began holding auditions, pulling in talent from around the Tri-state area. There was a lot of talent indeed, the only problem being, that no one really stood out.

I decided that in order for the Funky Junky to do something spectacular, we needed acts that were spectacular, and we knew that if we wanted something different, we couldn't keep looking in the same place.

Rosie thought about organizing a National talent tour, which I thought was great. The only question was who would go?

Red and Cuba were needed in the studio, and Rosie basically ran the entire operation. I myself couldn't possibly go on the road, besides it was too much like back in the day and I'm not trying to be there.

What I needed was an A&R person. Someone who knows music, and what it takes to be a great artist, and at that absolute moment, as if God had planned it way before I even thought I needed it, in walked, not just the one who qualified the most, but rather the one whom I would've considered the least... Yup, you guessed it!

Nemesis didn't even look my way when he entered, his trademarked garbage can, rolling beside him. I watched as he made his way over to the wastepaper basket, and emptied it like a pro. Our eyes finally met, and so I smiled, while Nem gave me just a nod and headed for the door.

"Hey man!" I called out just as the door was closing. Nemesis stopped and looked at me. "Can I kick it with you for a second?" I asked.

His face suddenly tensed up and I watched him choke down the large knot in his throat. I then waved him over, and gestured to take a seat. When I think about it now, I kind of feel bad, because he thought I was firing him.

He was having trouble looking at me, as I watched his eyes roam the office.

"You know, we never really got a chance to talk." I began. He looked at me, his face void of any expression whatsoever. I paused for a moment, then asked. "So what happened, bro?" His head tilted, as if he didn't understand the question.

"Your career man, what happened? I mean, you were the shit, on top of the mother fuckin' world!"

"And so were you!" He replied.

He caught me off guard with that one, but damn he was right!

"Look man." Nemesis began. "This music shit, bro. It's all

one big game. In the beginning we're not so sure how good we are, so we're careful, and treat everything like its important.

But after a while, after we make the hits, and enough people tell us how great we are. We relax. We feel like we got this, and like nobody could take it away.

We become careless, and we swear it's never gonna end… until it does!

Next thing you know, there's a new nigga in town, bright and shiny, with that new car smell. Now that's the one everybody wants to ride.

As hard as I tried to be, this dude's story just fucked me up. His downfall wasn't just a straight drop like most. His was like falling down steps, where each one hit in its own painful way. So many times I thought he was in a better position than me, I now know, that wasn't the case at all. In fact, what he didn't have, was everything I took for granted. His only support system was his sister Charlotte, and she herself had depended on him for years.

I never knew anyone who had a nervous breakdown, but if you ask me, I bet that's what happened to Nemesis. You see It's one thing to go broke and have all your possessions taken away, those things you can sometimes reclaim, but for that to happen to your pride and dignity? Well, that could sometimes be irreversible!

I'm not gonna lie. I always hated this dude. From the first time I ever laid eyes on him, I thought he was an arrogant bastard. But now that I've gotten to know him a bit more, I suddenly realized … So was I!

"But you have a huge name, why didn't you ever try capitalizing on it somehow?"

Nemesis looked at me in a way that said he wanted to tell me something, but was hesitant. I remained patient, and gave him time to decide, and then finally, he did.

"It was that crazy mother fucker that works for you." He suddenly blurted out. At first I had no idea of who he might've been talking about, as I have a bunch of people who work for me, and then out of nowhere, it hit me!

"Sal?" I asked staring deep into Nem's eyes that now seemed to resemble that of Frank's when Sal walked into the office.

"Don't worry, he won't touch you." I assured him, but Nem didn't care about that.

"I'm worried about my sister. He can do whatever the fuck he wants to do to me. I just don't want him messing with her, she ain't got nothing to do with any of this. Once Nem opened up, there was no stopping him. It was like he's had this all bottled up for so long, and now, with the opportunity to let it out. He didn't wanna leave anything behind. It seemed to have all started back when we were on tour.

Sal would break into Nemesis' room every night, for nothing more than to let him know. *I can get to you whenever I want!* Nem tried to figure out ways to better secure his room, but no matter what he did, every night, from in a chair across from where Nem was sleeping, Sal would wake him up. This went on for the entire tour, all the way up to the night that the albino disappeared.

I wondered why Nemesis' career seemed to suddenly

come to a complete stop, and now, it all made sense.

And though, getting Nemesis out of the picture, totally helped boost *my* career, I still think it was done to protect Mr. D's investment. But either way, it was definitely fucked up.

"Look, I really have to get back to work." Nemesis said as he stood up.

"Hold up a second!" I told him. He stopped and looked at me.

"I wanna make you a proposition." Nem looked at me and let out a short laugh.

"You've already given me the best proposition I've been offered in years... a job!"

"How about heading my A&R?"

"A&R?"

"Yes," I replied, "artists and repertoire."

"Oh, I know what it means and I truly appreciate the offer, but to be honest, it sort of sounds like a handout"

"Trust me, it isn't. In fact, this janitor job I gave you, well now, *that's* a hand out. Anyone can throw out trash, "A&R, however, no, not just anyone can do that, but I believe *you* can!"

"I don't get it, man. Like, why me?"

"Because then I'd have to find someone just like you."

Nem went silent and fell into deep thought. I stood there and watched as he pondered over the offer I just made him. I hadn't even spoken about numbers yet, but shit, he took a janitors job, and I'm sure he's aware that A&R pays more... A lot more!

When Nem finally came out of his trance, he looked at me, and upon his expressionless face, grew the first smile I'd ever seen since he's been here.

"When do I start?" He asked. I looked at him, my smile, even brighter than his.

"As soon as you're done emptying all the trash cans!" I replied, extending my hand toward him, in which he gladly took.

CHAPTER 46

More Dangerous Than a Gun

"You hired the Janitor? Rosie yelled at me from across the conference table as Sal paced back and forth in front of the windows.

"So who's gonna take out the trash?" Red asked, half-jokingly, sitting to my right.

"I'm sure we won't have a problem finding another Janitor." I replied.

"This isn't good." Sal said, still not looking at any of us.

"What's the big deal? It's something we needed and he's already a part of the staff."

"He's not a part of the staff." Rosie corrected.

"He is now." Red whispered to himself as he sat there doodling on his note pad. I then turned to Cuba and asked.

"What do you think?" Cuba looked at me, then at Rosie, and then at Sal who stopped and turned to him.

"I think I should stay quiet." Cuba replied.

"You see, this is the problem." Rosie began. "Nobody

wants to say what they feel. I personally feel that Nemesis should be removed from the position."

"So do I." Sal said. Rosie looked at Red awaiting his thought. He looked at me and mouthed, *"Sorry bro!"*

I threw my elbows up on the table and dropped my face into my hands.

"You guys didn't even give him a chance." I said to them. Sal turned and walked over. Placed his hand on my shoulder and looked me in the eyes.

"Some people you can't give a chance to. You took his spotlight, and now he throws out *your* garbage and empties *your* ashtrays. Do you really think this guy's gonna help you?"

"So are you going to tell him, or should I?" Rosie asked, as she stood up and gathered her things.

"So it's like that? You guys decided, and now he's out?"

"We didn't decide, Rey, we voted, and the majority is in favor of removing him from the position of A&R."

"What about Porky's vote?" I asked.

"Porky isn't here right now, and the longer you keep this guy thinking that he's A&R, the harder it's going to be to let him down." Red and Cuba also gathered their things. I stayed put, thinking about this fucked up situation I was in.

"You should also reconsider his position as the Janitor too." Sal suggested.

"What do you mean?" I asked.

"A Janitor has the keys to every room, and sometimes a

key can be more dangerous than a gun."

"This is bullshit." I spat, as everyone headed for the door, just at that moment, Porky entered.

"Hi everybody," he said with his typical jolly face. I immediately smiled, as I was so glad to see him. Everyone looked at him. "What's wrong?" He asked as he read the room.

"Porky! I said as I hugged his waist, and then ushered him in.

"It's not gonna matter, Rey." Rosie said, but I just had to hear it for myself. I explained the entire situation, cutting off anyone who tried to interrupt.

"So, the question is," I asked, "Should Nemesis remain as A&R, or return to being the Janitor?" We all stood around, each of us burning a hole into Porky. He could feel it, as the pressure was certainly on. I felt confident that Porky would vote in favor of Nem staying as A&R because Porky always proved to be a fair dude, and would never allow himself to be negatively influenced.

He asked a string of questions, and tried to make sense of everything he was being told. He assured both sides that he understood their stance, but then he had to make his decision, and just as I had expected, let alone hoped for... He voted in favor of Nem remaining as A&R.

"Yes!" I cheered in victory.

"It's still three to two Rey." Rosie said, busting my bubble of course.

"Come on guys. If anyone should be taking this personal,

it's me. I never liked dude. He made my life miserable for many years. But just like we could use a second shot at this, so can he!"

"I say yes!" Cuba suddenly called out his hand raised high."

"Yes what?" Rosie asked.

"Yes, I think he should stay on as the A&R."

"Boom! I shouted as I jumped up and did a cool spin."

"You said you didn't want to get involved." Sal said to Cuba.

"If I have to work with an artist, I need it to be the right artist, and King is right. He fits."

"Thank you!" I said, kissing Cuba on the top of his bald spot.

"Okay, so that ties us up, three-three." Sal said. And at that very moment, Red raised his hand.

"You're fucking kidding me, right?" Sal said to Red.

"Cuba made a serious point there. You guys don't have to be in the studio with these people. We can't risk bringing in someone who's only trying to hook up their sisters and uncles. We need someone who understands what's at stake here.

"Why don't we do this," Cuba suggested. "Why don't we put him on, give him some sort of time frame, and see how he does? If he doesn't work out, he has the option of going back to being a janitor, but if he does, well, we all win!"

"There you go!" I said to everyone, gesturing toward

Cuba. Rosie nodded as did, Red and Porky. Sal however wasn't happy with that either, but there was no way out at this point, so Sal just went along.

It was a productive meeting. Everyone got up and gathered their things. Rosie and I walked everyone to the door and watched as they all continued down the hall still talking about the meeting.

I closed the door and looked at my wife, then exhaled a smile.

"Look, I'm not trying to be an ass..." Rosie began, but I cut her off and kissed her.

"You were incredible." She said. My face twisted in confusion.

"What are you talking about?" I asked.

"Here's a guy that will go down in the history of Rap music as *your* arch enemy, and here you are, not only giving him *a* job, but rather. *The* Job! And when those closest to you, including your beautiful wife go up against your decision, you fight for him! Why Rey? Why would you do that? Why would anyone do that?

My eyes shot to the floor as I thought about her question. *Why? Why would I do that?* I looked back at her and just shook my head.

"I don't know." I told her, and at that moment, Rosie turned around and moved over all the papers that were on my desk.

"What the hell is this?" She asked, holding up a huge cup full of some nasty green shit inside.

"That shit ain't mine!" I laughed.

"Porky!" We both said at the same time, shaking our heads and laughing. Rosie placed the green drink over on *her* desk, then came back over mine, and pulled my pants down to my ankles. She then lifted her skirt, dropped her panties, and sat up on the edge of my desk.

She was soaking wet and so I entered her with ease. Though the moment was fast, it was super intense and no sooner that we had begun... it was over!

We looked at each other laughing, as we pulled our clothes back together.

I gathered my things to head down to the studio as Rosie got behind her to finish up some work.

"I'll be in the studio if you need me." I said as I leaned over her desk to kiss her.

As I was about to step out, Rosie called me back.

"What's up? I asked. She looked really weird, and I had no idea why, until finally she asked.

"Where the fuck is that green drink?" My eyes opened wide, and immediately I started looking around for it. I looked back at Rosie and she had her face in her hands.

"Oh my God, Oh my God, Oh my God!" Was all she could say.

"You always lock the door." I told her. But she didn't answer, but rather continued.

"Oh my God, Oh my God, Oh my God!"

At that moment, the phone rang. I looked toward Rosie to

answer, but she couldn't, so I picked up.

"Good afternoon, Funky Junky!" I greeted.

"It was me, asshole!" The voice on the other end said.

"Sal?" I asked.

"Lock the fuckin' door next time!" he said, and then hung up.

CHAPTER 47

Repairing Damages

In just a couple of months, Nemesis had proved my idea of making him A&R a brilliant one. His eye and ear for talent was beyond anything I had ever seen. He was nothing like the Nemesis that just a few months back was emptying my trash. In fact, he was nothing like the Nemesis I once toured with. It was like he took all of his experiences and created this whole new talent.

Nem seemed like a different person. He seemed taller, healthier, and for the first time ever, I even spotted a bit of handsomeness. His confidence was through the roof, and it should be, as he had brought in some of the greatest new talent I had ever seen.

The crazy thing about it was, Nem never advertised his searches.

"Any talent searching the classifieds for an opportunity is not the type of talent I'm interested in. The one's I'm interested in are the ones who haven't yet discovered their talent!

Nem didn't even search the clubs, or even hold talent contests. He took shit a step further, by simply visiting neighborhoods and just asking around. This is how he found what he was looking for, those kids that only sang in church, or who would geek out on an instrument while all the other kids were outside playing. This was the story behind most of our current developing roster.

Nem felt that he not only exhausted the five boroughs, but rather the entire tri-state area. He wanted now to expand his reach, and explore other cities around the country. The system he created to discover the caliber of talent that he had already discovered, had been proven over and over again, and he knew for sure, that by going outside of New York, that he would definitely find that one gem. That one artist that will take the Funky Junky over the top, providing the resources needed to support the rest of their repertoire.

The only problem was the budget. We just didn't have it. I fought tooth and nail to be able to just hire Nemesis. Asking now for more money would simply put me in the doghouse. He knew what I had already been through, and respected my position, but then came to me with a proposition.

Nem was so sure that he would hit the jackpot that he offered to put up twenty-five percent of his own salary to cover expenses. The deal sounded great to me though I knew it really wasn't fair to him. That was until he mentioned his one condition.

"If you hired me for this job, it means that you feel I'm qualified."

"I do." was my reply.

"Then whoever it is I find, I need your one hundred percent support!"

"Yeah of course, we'll bring'em in, and see what they…"

"…No!" Nem cut in.

"Huh?"

"No we'll bring him in, and we'll see!" He said.

"I don't get it."

"When I find that *one*… and I tell you, *that's the one!* I want everyone to give me a hundred percent.

I looked at him, a bit hesitant of the whole idea. Not because I didn't trust him, but rather that we were all so used to being a part of that entire process.

One of the first requests we granted for Nem when he came aboard as A&R, was the rigorous screening process he had in place. This system was well thought out, and ran pretty smooth.

Everything that came back to us was in its purest form. The demos were always recorded by Nem himself. Acapella's sung straight into a portable recorder. No fancy microphones or voice processing. What you heard was what you got. He would also take just one head shot photo of them with a Polaroid camera he took with him everywhere.

I once asked him why he doesn't take at least two, one head, and one full length. He told me that he didn't want us judging them by anything else but their voice.

For those artists that Nem wanted us to consider, he would actually write their short bios himself, just so we have a better feel for their character.

But now he wanted to put an end to all of that, and have us give him full rein, with one hundred percent backing. It didn't take long for me to agree, as I trusted him and his talent for talent. And though yeah, I pretty much had final say in shit, I also respected my crew, and so, I'll have to have a talk with them.

Mr. D had left a pretty big mess behind, and without old King releasing hit after hit, Solar Records watched us careful, and kept their hand steady on the eject button. The record deal we had was eventually downgraded to a production deal, and the company was no longer obligated to put out everything we gave them. From here out, if they liked what we brought them, they'll release it, but if they didn't, well then, we were fucked!

Solar had a good run with me, and so their deal was more so a handout, because they knew as well as we did, that no other company wanted to mess with us.

Nem and I would make multiple trips throughout the day to the studio where Red and Cuba worked endless hours trying to produce new music to match our new talent.

Though we were sending Solar a new record every single week, they on the other hand were accepting just one every few months. And when it got to the point where we weren't making them any money, they started invoicing us.

They billed us for everything! Mastering, pressing, shipping, advertising, you name it, they charged us for it. They didn't want to just break even. They had to make a profit, even if it was just a few bucks.

Even records that did okay, barely made us enough to

pay off the last record's debt. It seemed as if we were stuck on this continuous roller coaster and though I tried to stay positive, it was beginning weigh on me.

Every release we put out we celebrated because we were sure that this was it! But afterwards that celebration played a more important role as a write off because once again, we hit a wall.

We knew the records we had were hits, but without the proper support, it would never be realized, and they would just go to waste.

Our meetings soon became shouting matches, as everyone blamed everyone else, while the Funky Junky slowly sank to the bottom.

Many times I would stay late at the office, just walking around my empty establishment trying to figure out what went wrong. I dedicated so much time, money and energy into this place and it was betraying me.

My staff was being paid from my personal account, because the Funky Junky was practically broke, and the only one who knew this was Rosie. She was also the voice of reason and a huge supporter, but it had gotten so bad that even she was beginning to lose faith.

School was about to be out for the summer, and we had nothing to release. We lost all hope. And when I held a company meeting smack in the middle of the day, everyone knew something was up. As my staff, including Vanessa, Nemesis, Charlotte, Sal, Rosie, Red, Cuba, Porky, and others who relied on us for their livelihood piled into the conference room, I was embarrassed to even look at them. I looked at

Rosie, and she nodded, as a gesture for me to speak. I looked out at all of these people who trusted me, relied on me, and now I will have to let them down.

I took a deep breath, and then spoke. I couldn't believe what I was saying, and the more I spoke the more I solidified my failure. But instead of just letting everyone go, I gave everyone one month off with pay, writing it off as vacation. I noticed Rosie twitch when I said that, because it wasn't planned, but it was too late to turn back now. I told them to try and have something to fall back on, and if I was able to turn the company around by the time their vacation was up, then they could return to work, if not, I thanked them all for their service and dedication to the Funky Junky. I apologized for what I had to put them through. I saw tears running down everyone's face, and one by one they each came up to me, hugged me, thanked me, and then left.

This was a moving experience for me. I stayed in the conference room looking up at all the photos, plaques and newspaper articles hanging on the walls. Rosie could tell I wanted to be left alone, so she cleared out with the rest of them. I stayed in there until everyone was gone, and stood there till I was able to pull myself together.

I told Rosie to go home, and that I would meet her there later. Our offices would be closed for a whole month so I wanted to make sure everything was locked tight. Sal helped me, and then drove me home, what a sad day.

When I got home, Porky and Dora were already asleep. Rosie was on the couch reading a book.

"Hey!" She said. I looked at her and smiled as I locked the

door behind me.

"It's almost two o'clock."

"I couldn't sleep. You're hungry?" she asked, I just shook my head and plopped down beside her on the couch. I turned and looked at her.

"I'm sorry." I said, and she stared at me for a long moment.

"There's really nothing to be sorry about, you did everything you could."

"Did I?"

"I think so." She replied. I appreciated her saying that, even though I didn't really believe it myself.

"Look, I have an idea." She began. I turned and looked at my wife, her beautiful face soft and warm. I waited. "Let's take a vacation!" She blurted out with a big smile, as she turned her entire body toward me bouncing excitedly in her seat.

"Vacation?" I asked with a laugh, knowing she couldn't possibly be serious.

"Yes, a vacation. I was thinking Miami Beach. You like it there."

"Rosie, we're in the middle of a crisis here and you're talking to me about going on a vacation?"

"What does one thing have to do with another?" She asked.

"First off we practically laid off our entire company because we didn't have any more money."

"No, we didn't lay them off, we gave them the summer off with pay."

"I needed time to think, and try and figure this shit out."

"So why not figure this shit out on the beach?" I looked at her and pictured myself sitting on the beach looking out into the ocean, thinking."

"You can't organize messy file cabinets without first emptying them out." She said, suddenly making a whole lot of sense."

"It's the money, Rosie!" I said. "We don't have it." She looked at me with a serious face, and then smiled.

"Yes we do." She replied. I looked at her tilting my head like a puppy. "Wait right here." She said, then got up, and rushed upstairs, returning a moment later with her bank book. She tossed it onto my lap.

"What's this?"

"A few dollars I've been saving up in case it rained." I opened it and immediately my eyes started to water."It's not a lot, but it's enough for the four of us to get away, clear our minds and figure out what we need to do next. Besides, when was the last time we took a family vacation?"

"This is your money, I can't..." I handed the bank book back to Rosie.

"Rey, we're married... Everything we have is ours!"

"But to spend money on a vacation, I don't know Rosie."

"But I do... Start packing!"

Rosie talked me into renting a family van so that we

could drive instead of fly. At first I was against it, feeling that we would be wasting time driving, but she explained that no time together is wasted time, and once again, I couldn't agree with her more.

Porky and I took turns driving, him doing the bulk of it. We stopped a couple of times and got to Miami just as the sun was setting. We rented a house on the beach, and I could already feel this trip repairing damages.

Porky and Dora hit the swimming pool as soon as we settled in, while Rosie and I went out onto the balcony that overlooked the ocean. It was a perfect night in so many ways. The full moon cast a peaceful glow on the semi-calm ocean. Porky and Dora were enjoying themselves in the pool, as I sat cuddled on the lounge with my wife drinking wine. I could feel the pressures of the world rolling off my shoulders as we both sat quietly, staring at the waves as they stretched their way upon the sand.

"So, I was thinking…" I began, but Rosie reached up and placed her finger tips over my mouth with a calm shhh.

"Not tonight Rey, tomorrow." She suggested. I smiled, and relaxed and for the next few hours… there we stayed.

CHAPTER 48

Evolution

We chose Miami's beach over Orlando's Disney for the simple fact that all I wanted to do was chill, but no sooner than the sun came up our first morning there, that we were out and about. Porky was more excited than any of us and had planned out our entire trip.

From Aquariums to Museums, Historic sites and a slew of excursions that included snorkeling, water skiing, and a swim with the Dolphins. Every night we ate at a different restaurant and afterwards a walk on South Beach.

Rosie would look at me and could tell by the look of my eyes that I would be calculating the money we were spending, but she would just tippy toe up to me and give me a kiss on the cheek. *Have fun.* She would whisper and then give me a calming smile.

The kids were having a blast. Porky and Dora would walk ahead of us holding hands, Rosie and I walked behind them doing the same. We couldn't help but laugh at those two. Though Porky was huge next to Dora, just like her mom, she always wants to run shit. But Porky didn't mind at all. He adored her, and did whatever she wanted.

Nearly every club in the area had their promotions people on the street giving out flyers. These were usually young kids, not even old enough to get into the clubs themselves. However, they were good at what they did. It was hard to tell though whether they were hired by the clubs, or by the artists because they sold both just as well.

During the course of our walk I must've accumulated around forty or so flyers and when I looked, so had Porky and Dora. She held them out like a deck of cards, and we all laughed.

"Can we go see one these groups, Daddy?" Dora yelled back at me.

"Sorry sweetie, you're too young. They won't let you in any of those places. She pouted, and Porky laughed at her, she smacked his leg and then they both started to laugh again..

Shuffling through my stack of flyers, I was amazed at just how jumping a place Miami was. The only time I use to come out here was to do shows, and that was on a whole other vibe. I never realized it was like this.

We came upon what looked like an open club / restaurant.

"Mommy, how do you say that?" Dora asked pointing up at the huge aqua-colored neon sign.

"Agua!" Rosie said.

"It means water right?" She asked, and her mother

nodded in confirmation. Porky and Dora had stopped and we all gathered in front looking at the unusual layout.

"What happens if it rains?" Porky asked.

"Everybody gets wet I guess."

"It's all outdoor furniture." Rosie replied. "And you see that blue thing?" pointing above the stage. "that's an awning, they pull it out to cover the performers."

"Wow!" Dora said.

"That's cool." Porky followed.

"Can kids go in?" Dora asked.

"Yeah look." I said pointing at a couple of other kids sitting with their parents."

They even have a kids menu." Rosie said looking at the display menu hanging by the entrance, and they have ice cream!"

Porky and Dora both cheered. The hostess was escorting us to a table when Dora asked.

"Can we sit there?" She asked, pointing to a table right in front of the stage.

"Sweetie, I don't think anyone's performing..."

"Actually there is!" The hostess corrected. Dora and Porky looked at one another and smiled.

Rosie and I ordered ourselves a couple of Mojito's while Dora ordered a Banana Split and Porky, a Double Cheese Burger with Fries and a Vanilla Milkshake. Mind you, we had just eaten dinner at the last restaurant. But it was cool, and we were used to it, as Porky was still a growing boy, even though he was already six feet six and God knows how many pound.

The kids were enjoying the different acts that performed, and so did we for that matter. It was a breath of fresh air compared to what we had to surround ourselves with back at the Funky Junky.

Rosie and I fell into a pretty deep conversation regarding the company, even though we promised each other not to talk business.

But it was something about the vibe here that made us think, and knowing that the end of our vacation was almost here, it almost seemed necessary.

As Rosie dove deep into one of the bigger issues we were facing at the office, I couldn't help but be distracted by this unusual sound that came from the band that was currently on stage.

Though their music was similar to some of the acts we had already signed back in New York, they added to theirs, this sort of robotic sound that was made by singing with what looked like a plastic tube they held in their mouth. I loved it!

I looked around and watched everyone suddenly stand up and dance in place, Porky and Dora following along. Rosie and I looked at each other, and so as not to seem like the odd balls, we also stood and kind of bopped in place.

Their sound was so different, and as I attempted to dissect it, I discovered within it Hip Hop beats, a variety of Latin percussions, the energy of Rock, and the Soul of R&B. I never even knew anything like this existed, and when I tried to categorize it, it was impossible, as this music seemed free of any one particular style of music.

Each song that this group played sent the crowd roaring even louder than the last. I looked back and noticed that not only did a crowd form outside the gate, it continued out into the street disrupting even more, the already disrupted traffic of the South Beach strip.

It was a great night and I was glad to have been able to enjoy it with my family. As we were about to leave, Dora noticed that the group we liked were out in front of the stage signing autographs.

"Daddy, can we go and get one?" She asked. I looked at Porky and he seemed as excited as her. I nodded, and watched as the two of them hurried over to the growing crowds that surrounded them.

"Why don't you go over and say hi?" Rosie asked when she saw how I was looking at them.

"I don't feel like fucking with that crowd." I replied.

When Dora and Porky returned holding their autographed photos, my eyes immediately shot to the bottom where printed was the group's name... Evolution!

CHAPTER 49

It's Never Alright

As I walked through the entrance of the Funky Junky after such an incredible vacation with the ones I loved most, the building seemed strange as the hustle and bustle that usually went on throughout the day, was nowhere to be found.

Rosie headed straight for the office, as I headed down to the studio to see Red.

"There he is!" Red said as he stood up from behind the console. I was surprised though to see Cuba and Nemesis there as well. We spoke about my trip for a few minutes before getting back to business.

"So tell me, what are we doing?" I asked. They looked at each other, and then at me.

"Man, we lost all our talent." Nemesis suddenly blurted out, wasting no time in updating me on the bullshit that I didn't even know was going on.

"What do you mean, by lost?" I asked, my eyes jumping around to the each of them. Cuba dropped his head.

"Word got out!" Red said.

"Yo, guys, I'm not here to solve riddles, what the fuck is going on?"

"Everyone knows the Funky Junky's broke!"

"What? Where they get that from?" I said in defense. They all looked at one another.

"Look bro." Nemesis began. "This is the mother fuckin' music business, and the Funky Junky has always been in the spotlight. You think they ain't gonna find out shit."

"But we're here!" said Red, Nemesis and Cuba nodding their heads.

"Though it was kind of fucked up that you took a vacation knowing this," Nemesis said, and he was right.

I walked over to the couch and plopped myself down in it. The guys all sat back down.

"So it's true?" Red asked. At first I was hesitant, but then nodded.

"So what's the plan?" Nemesis asked. I gave it a little thought before answering.

"Well, the building's paid in full." I began. "I could probably take out a loan against it, just to cover a few salaries, at least for six months or so and see if we can possibly rebuild this thing."

"I could donate about three months or so, King." And I'm sure Charlotte would too." Nemesis said.

"You would do that?" I asked, surprised that he even offered.

"Of course, you looked out for us at a critical time, bro. It's the least we can do, really." I reached out, and shook his hand.

"You know I'm here for the long run." Red said. I looked at him, trying to suck in the tears. I reached out and shook his hand as well. We all then turned to Cuba who looked up at us and smiled.

I have no choice. I already threw away my bathrobe?" He said, making us all fall out laughing.

Suddenly, we heard a noise, and when we turned, there was Rosie, standing at the door, crying.

"What's wrong?" I asked her. But she just shook her head and smiled.

We all came together and got into a huddle, when into the studio stepped Porky.

"What's going on here?" He asked, but no one answered, instead we just pulled him in, and though he had no idea why we were hugging he still wrapped his huge arms around us all.

For the next few hours, we all sat around the studio, discussing the situation while drinking coffee. The calm music that blanketed the room set the perfect tone, as we turned over every possible stone. Rosie as always worked from her infamous Pros and Cons list. And I have to admit, for the first time ever, I didn't think it was stupid!

It helped us to realize that we were actually in a much better position than we had been. Though Nemesis had an incredible eye and ear for talent, there was still something missing, and I knew that it was just a matter of time before we figured it out.

Porky had gone up to the game room to get Dora and brought her back down to the studio. As usual she took her regular place on the floor under the light, where she was able to sit and read, probably her most favorite pastime.

She usually had no interest in anything we would be talking about, but this time I kept catching her looking our way. Tuned in to whatever it was we were saying, and the moment I'd spot her, she'd immediately turn back to her reading.

The studio became a much more energetic and creative place for these meetings, way better than our old conference room that was pretty cold and uninspiring.

We talked about the kind of artists we needed. Whether or not we should explore other genres, as Rap was all we ever knew, or even tried.

Cuba kept trying to convince us to go Latin, and though he had many great points, my inability to speak the language, kept me from even considering it.

Red loved Rap, but said he'd consider R&B giving me a bunch of examples. I loved a lot of that music, but I felt I wouldn't be able to do it justice. Let's be real, our crew didn't particularly fit the bill as to what an R&B label would look like.

Rosie was a huge Pop fan. Michael Jackson, Madonna, Prince, and so on. Those were the superstars and she didn't understand why we didn't just shoot towards that.

"Pop is short for Popular." Nem explained. Anything can go pop, it all depends on how the audience receives it.

We debated a bit on that topic, as I believed Pop was a genre in itself, even if it wasn't accepted by the masses.

It was already late, and Dora had fallen asleep on the couch. We decided to call it a night, though all agreed, it was a good day, and very productive. What I enjoyed most about this particular storm session was that we were open and honest with our opinions as well as our suggestions. Porky picked up Dora and carried her to the private elevator that led down to my section of the garage. Me and Rosie said goodnight, while Red, Cuba and Nemesis stayed to clean up.

When the elevator door opened we were all surprised to see Sal standing there. It had been some time since we last saw him.

After greeting one another, Sal asked if he could talk to me for a moment.

"Goodnight Sal." Rosie said as she headed for the car. "Why don't you come over on Friday, I'll make a nice dinner!" She said from a distance.

"I'll be there!" Sal said with a smile and a thumbs up," after making sure everyone was in the car, Sal reached behind his back, and of course I tensed up, but then he pulled out a large envelope and handed it to me.

"What's this?" I asked.

"It's for you." He said. "Well, for the company!" He corrected. I opened it and looked inside. It was full of money, all hundred dollar bills. I looked up at him.

"Three hundred thousand," he said.

"I don't understand," was all I could say.

"I want you to have it."

"What?"

"I want you to rebuild this shit. Turn it into what you envision."

"Sal man, listen."

"No, you listen. I don't need it, King. I would never be able to spend that money in my lifetime, but you, you'll be able to put it to good use, I know it."

"Sal. Please bro..." But he didn't want to hear it. He shook his head, and pressed for the elevator.

"The two assholes are still upstairs, right?"

"Yeah, I replied with a slight laugh. "Man Sal, Thank you!" was the only thing I could come up with.

Sal extended his hand, but I bypassed it and grabbed him instead. He seemed cold and stiff, as if he hadn't been hugged in years, but after a moment he seemed to relax. The bell rang and the elevator door opened.

"I'll see you Friday!" He said, and the door closed."

"What was that about?" Rosie asked as I got into the driver's seat, strapped myself in and drove up to the garage door.

As it slowly lifted I could see the heavy rain bouncing off the sidewalk. I pulled out and turned up the block to head home.

"So?" Rosie asked, still waiting for me to answer her

question, but instead, I handed her the envelope. She took it, and then waited a moment before looking inside.

"What is this?" She asked.

"Three hundred thousand," I said. Porky sat up and leaned forward to see.

"Rey, those loans are what messed us up in the..."

"...It's not loan!" I interrupted. Rosie went silent. I can feel her staring at me, the only sound we can hear are the wipers.

"He just gave you three hundred thousand dollars?

"He wants to help us get back on our feet."

"Wow." Rosie said, and without me even looking, I could tell she was crying.

"But why's he giving you all that money Rey?" Porky asked.

"He's my friend, Pork," I replied.

"Shoo, I need some new friends!" He suddenly blurted out sending us all into a loud laughter that ended up waking Dora.

"Where are we going?" Dora asked.

"Home sweetie." Rosie said looking back at her. "Go back to sleep."

I heard Dora in the back ask Porky for her book.

"What book?" He asked.

"The one I was reading!"

They both looked around the back seat, but nothing.

"We'll get it tomorrow." I told her.

"No, I need it."

"Sweetie, we already left, we'll be home soon."

"Please Daddy!" She said, as she began to cry. I looked at Rosie who just shrugged her shoulders, and so I turned around and headed back.

As we drove around the building to get to the front entrance so that Porky can run in, we spotted Sal standing outside messing with the garage door. He was drenched, as the rain had picked up even more since we left.

"What's wrong?" I yelled out over the loud rain. Sal looked back.

"I got it!" he yelled back. "Same shit happened last time it rained." Porky saw Sal struggling and got out to help.

"Shit, now he's gonna be in this car all wet." I said to Rosie. I watched as Porky patted Sal on the back and jogged up to the entrance of the building, and waited to be buzzed in.

Sal smiled at us and waved and was about to rush to his car, when a man, holding his umbrella down close to his head, walked past Sal, cutting him off.

Sal stopped in his tracks, and looked at us as if to say, what the fuck! When suddenly, the man turned around and lowered his umbrella. Immediately I saw the gun, and when he pointed it directly at Sal, I yelled out, but my window was up, and the pouring rain too loud. I couldn't hear the gun go off, but I saw the flash, and when Sal dropped to the ground, I knew he was hit.

"Stay here!" I told Rosie, and then pushed open my door

and dashed across the street, nearly getting hit by a car. Porky heard the gun shot and got to the scene before me, but the shooter had already taken off, leaving behind his umbrella, upside down in the gutter.

Lying on his stomach, I watched as the hole in the back of his head spit blood like a volcano. I looked up at Porky just standing there, unable to say or do anything, when suddenly we heard a scream. It was Charlotte standing at the door of the Funky Junky. Porky snapped out of it and ran inside to call an ambulance.

I felt Sal move a bit and tried to make him comfortable.

"Hang in there buddy, help's on the way.

Sal struggled to open his eyes.

"Relax man, you're gonna be alright."

"King," He whispered.

"I'm right here Sal." I said, moving closer to hear him.

"I've put lots of bullets in the back of people's heads. It's never alright!" He then laughed, sending a clot of blood onto my shirt.

When the Paramedics finally arrived, they moved me out the way and immediately began trying to revive him, but it was too late. In fact, I think I knew exactly the moment he died, as I could've sworn I saw his soul leave his body.

I looked across the street at Rosie and Dora in the car, their hands pressed against the window, and though I couldn't hear them, I can see, they were hysterical.

CHAPTER 50

Little Metal Rings

When Sal had disappeared for that time, it was strange, but something always told me that he'd be back. But this time I knew for sure, he wouldn't. Everything seemed strange, and quiet. Everyone seemed suspicious. I never worried about any of this in the past as Sal had it covered. We spoke about bringing someone else on board full time to protect the family, even interviewed a few, but it wasn't the same. Having a stranger on board seemed no better than having nobody on board, and in the meantime, we just had to be careful. Very careful!

Most of my work I could do from The Funky Junky, but every once in a while I had to meet up at other people's office. I sometimes drove myself, other times I took a taxi. Porky always volunteered to drive me wherever, but I always declined his offer. Porky was as special to me as Dora was, and I would lose my mind if anything would ever happened to him, especially if it had anything to do with me.

Porky lived with us for free, and was welcomed to live

with us for as long as he wanted.

I paid him a small salary to maintain the gym and help out with some of the employees who were interested in working out. He also trained at a couple of other gyms in the area, went to school in the mornings, and pretty much played bodyguard /chauffeur for Dora.

It was good that he stayed busy because losing Sal was pretty devastating to him, not to mention the fact that he actually witnessed the murder. Porky always blamed himself for not going after the guy, but I told him, the guy was armed and dangerous, and Sal would never had wanted him to put himself in that situation. Porky would nod, and say that he understood. But in no time, it'd wear off and he'd be back blaming himself.

Porky had gone to a health and fitness resort. It was a thirty day intensive workshop, somewhere upstate. Ever since I stopped touring, I was never away from him that long, and had really wished he didn't go, however, Porky was grown, and there wasn't much we could do to stop him. Besides, he was a good kid, and always made good choices, so we tried not to worry.

Until Porky got back, Rosie worked at the office only while Dora was in school. After which she would pick her up, and the two would head home.

I was never one to stay out all night Though Red, Cuba, and sometimes even Nemesis would work into the wee hours, I never did. I always got home at a reasonable time, but was usually the first one at the office every morning and found Rosie sitting on the couch, drinking tea.

"Wha'cha doing up?" I asked as I went over and gave her a kiss.

"I couldn't sleep." She replied, and immediately I knew, something was wrong.

"What is it?" I asked, and immediately, her eyes began to flood. Rosie got up and placed her cup down on the coffee table. I followed her downstairs to the basement, which Porky had converted into his very own apartment. I've never gone down there without him, so it didn't seem right.

"We shouldn't be here." I told Rosie as we both stood in the center of his living room area. My heart was starting to pound as I had no idea what was going on, but there was something Rosie wanted to show me, and I became terrified to find out what it was.

"I don't know about this, Rosie."

"This is our house, Rey." She said, throwing me a stern glance. My eyes scanned Porky's pad. It was a nice spot, and he had it decorated to his liking. He had only a few close friends, close meaning that they were welcomed to come over. Girls on the other hand were out of the question, not because of us, but because he was still very shy, and kept that part of his life very private.

He had a nice little kitchenette that I think he only used to make his protein shakes and popcorn, other than that it looked practically unused as he always ate with us upstairs.

I felt bad walking through his place, but I followed Rosie to the back where his bedroom was. She pulled a credit card out from her pocket and used it to open his bedroom door.

"What are you doing?" I asked. She didn't answer. She opened up the door and I swore I was about to see something that I didn't wanna to see.

But so far nothing, it was an ordinary bedroom, a few cool posters on the wall, sports memorabilia on the shelves, and framed photos of all of us scattered on the side wall, including one very unusual photo of him and Sal. Unusual because... Sal never took pictures. I tried to figure out where and when that photo might've been taken as I stepped in for a closer look.

The background seemed like some sort of desert, and they both wore beige camouflage uniforms. Rosie stepped up beside me.

"That was the first thing I noticed too."

"Where was this?" I asked. Rosie turned and walked over to his dresser and pulled out the top draw. I walked up beside her and looked inside, and there, lying on top of socks and underwear was a Nine Millimeter pistol.

"Did you know anything about this?" Rosie asked.

"Of course not," I replied. Rosie then turned to the bed and got down on her hands and knees, she reached under the bed and pulled out a huge black case and opened it.

"I guess you didn't know about this either?" She said as I looked down at four assault rifles packed neatly in the case. My head began to spin as I had no idea what the fuck was going on.

Rosie took me around the room and showed me more weapons that she had found. More guns, knives, brass knuckles, you name it. We found a small wooden box in the closet and when I opened it, it was filled with hundreds of these little metal rings. We couldn't figure out what they were.

"Come here Rey." Rosie said as she stood in his closet." I entered, and followed her finger as it pointed at the stack of magazines way on the top shelf, they were partially covered with a towel.

"Let's not forget, he *is* a man!" I said, suggesting that they were without doubt adult magazines. Besides, I really didn't want to touch them.

"Please, Rey." She said, and though I was totally against this, I grabbed a chair, and used it to reach the shelf. I grabbed a stack of the magazines and brought them down with me.

"I knew it!" She said.

"What do you mean, you knew it?" I asked.

"I found one in his bathroom." She relied.

"I grew up around Mercenaries! I know what they do!" Rosie suddenly blurted out.

"What are you talking about?"

"He's dangerous, Rey, and we have a little girl living here."

"Come on, you know better than I do that Porky would never put any of us in danger. Especially Dora! Besides, this is probably just another phase he's going through. Like that time he wanted to be a stuntman, and practically fucked up the whole house! "

"This is not a phase Rey. There are enough weapons in

here to arm a small army." Rosie said as she exited the closet.

"Why are you walking away?"

"Because if you can't see the danger in this, then there's nothing I can tell you, except that he has to go!"

I followed her out of the room, through Porky's place and up the stairs. Rosie waited for me at the top and started on me as soon as I made it to the top.

"He's gotta go, Rey." She said, her face mere inches from mine.

"Go where?" I asked.

"I don't know, but it can't be here." She said and continued into the living room where she picked up her cup of tea and headed to the kitchen.

"Come on, Rosie this is crazy."

"No, what's crazy is having him living here. He's not a little boy anymore, and he's definitely not doing little boy things."

She emptied out her cup in the sink, washed and put it away.

"We can't just throw him out in the street."

"Maybe you can't, but I can! I don't give a fuck how big he is, when it comes to my daughter, there is nobody too big for me!" Again she turned away and headed for our bedroom. I followed, and just as I got to the door, she went in and closed it.

"Rosie, come on, stop." I said, wiggled the knob, though it was locked. "Come on, open up."

Suddenly I heard it unlock, but she only opened it a bit and stuck her face out.

"I can't believe you're even saying this."

"Well believe it!" Rosie walked up to me, and again got in my face. "Rey, one of the things you need most when being a parent, is instinct, you know why?" I didn't dare respond, but she continued anyway, "Because if you ignore that instinct, later on it might be too late to do anything."

"Why don't we just sit down and talk to him when he comes home?"

"Because this isn't his home anymore, it's ours, mine, yours, and Dora's. We live here to be warm, dry, and safe, and I am not willing to compromise any of it."

"But it's Porky."

"You did your job. You saved him from the streets. You gave him a place to call home. Fed him, clothed him. You gave him a life he would never have had. Bravo, Rey, you should be canonized a saint, but it's over now. He's got his wings, let him fly, let him fly the fuck out of here before we regret it."

"But Rosie, hear me out…"

"I'm going to bed now, so figure out how you plan on doing this, or I will." and she closed the door.

I started to pace my living room, playing out the situation in my head of how I would ask him to leave, and no matter how I said it, I saw his face, confused, and scared. Porky might've been a grown man now, but he still had the same face he had when I met him. How could Rosie be like that with him? He loved Dora with all his heart, and this would definitely break it. In fact, it would break both their hearts. I walked over to our picture wall and began looking over all the wonderful pictures we had such great times. I never realized just how many of the photos included Porky, shit, Dora might've been my flesh and blood, but Porky would always be my first.

The pictures on the wall began back when he was still in the hospital after the truck hit him and Junior. Even bandaged up the way he was he still smiled and said hello to everyone. Here also were a couple of photos with Grams. She absolutely adored him, like if he was her very own. It was Grams who convinced me to take him in. She said he will be a special kid to me, and she was so right. So many photos of him at different points of his life, here he is as the Ring Bearer at our wedding. He was an only child then, and though we tried desperately to spoil him, we never did. This was the time when he and Rosie really bonded. After Grams had passed, it was all about those two. This is why it's so hard for me to accept what Rosie's saying. How do you love someone the way I swore she did, but then be able to just throw him away like that? I always thought love was unconditional.

The pictures that really jumped out though were those of him and Dora. From when she was born he always wanted to hold her, feed her, we even let him change her a few times. I believe those times really solidified their bond.

CHAPTER 51

Worthy of a King

I had a pretty busy day running around the city and now I was back at the office finishing up paperwork. The only one's still here besides me were Red and Cuba. Charlotte and Rosie had gone home, and Nemesis was back on the road.

I looked up when my door opened, and it was Porky. I immediately got up and gave him the biggest smile.

"Pork!" I said so happy to see him. I came out from behind my desk and we hugged. He looked good, happy as always.

"Just got back?" I asked as I watched him walk to my fridge and grab a bottle of juice.

"No, I got home around noon, took a shower, changed and then ran a few errands." I sat on the edge of my desk, my eyes following him as he plopped down into one of the chairs in front of me.

"So how was the trip?" I asked. Pork looked at me and remained quiet. It was at that moment that I realized that he knew what was up. His head dropped and he shook it.

"Porky, listen man…"

"…I'm sorry Rey." He interrupted.

"But what's going on?"

"First off, let me just clarify. The guns, they were Sal's."

I exhaled in relief. I knew there was some logical explanation.

"But what were *you* doing with them?"

"He just gave them to me. I don't know why. I asked him, but all he said was, *don't worry.*"

"You can get into a lot of trouble having those things, Porky." I said, and then he looked at me and shook his head. I didn't know what that meant, until he got up and handed me a card. It was Federal Firearms license. I looked at him, baffled as fuck.

"A long as they stayed in my designated living area, it's all perfectly legal." He said. I got up and started to pace a bit, trying to make sense out of it all. I then stopped and looked up at him.

"I use to see Sal's gun under his arm, and was just so fascinated. I thought it was so cool. One day, he had picked me up from school. He spotted someone he knew and made a stop. He got out and started to talk to them. They were there for a while, and out of nosiness, I popped open the glove compartment and saw another gun in there."

"Yeah I know. He kept them everywhere."

"Anyhow, the next day, I was in class and I saw Sal walk in and say something to the teacher. She told me to grab my things and that she'd see me tomorrow. Sal walked ahead of me and wouldn't say anything to me. I couldn't figure it out. He got into the car, I into the passenger seat, and we took off.

"Where we going?" I asked. But he didn't answer. We pulled into a small industrial area and parked. Sal turned to me and held out his hand.

"Hand it over." He suddenly said. I was about to act like I didn't know what he was talking about, but I could tell, he wasn't in the mood for games.

I reached into my book bag and pulled out the .45 I had taken from his glove compartment."

"He never told me this."

"Well, he promised he wouldn't. Anyway, he got out the car and told me to follow. I was so nervous. We went inside what looked like an abandoned factory, and I swear Rey, I thought he was going to kill me!"

"Sal would never have hurt you."

"That's what I thought, but there was something about that day."

"So keep going."

"So the building turned out to be a shooting gallery."

"For junkies?"

"No, an *actual* shooting gallery!" He corrected, his fingers shooting an imaginary gun. This was getting intense, and so I gestured him to continue.

"This gallery was different, this place let you shoot anything you can get your hands on. Anything!"

I listened to the rest of Porky's story, as Sal from that

point on began teaching him about guns. To respect them, clean them, repair them, and of course... shoot them!

"I've learned to shoot so many different weapons. I've even thrown a few hand grenades."

"Wait, so those rings..." Porky nodded.

"Okay, so a few hundred!" he added correcting his previous statement. I couldn't believe what I was hearing, and that Sal would do such a thing.

"I wanted to tell you, Rey. I swear, but Sal made me promise not to, that you would never understand.

"And he was right, because I don't."

"He felt that curiosity would eventually get me killed, so He figured, that by feeding it to me, that I'd get it out of my system."

"Fuckin' dude!" I said to myself, shaking my head."

"He meant well, Rey, he really did. It just didn't work out as he had hoped."

"And now you're hooked!" I said, a slight smile trying to sneak in. Porky nodded.

"Rey, you did an incredible job raising me, and I owe my life to you."

"No you don't..."

"...Of course I do! But no matter how much you tried to protect me, I was still exposed to the dangers that surrounded you."

"I'm sorry."

"There's nothing to be sorry about. That's just the nature

of this business." I took a deep breath and was about to tell Porky that he would have to leave, but he stopped me mid-sentence and smiled.

"I know Rey, and I understand." He said, relieving me of the pain I was about to endure.

"Maybe if you get rid…"

"…No Rey! He laughed. It's time, and I will never blame Rosie. She's just protecting Dora. She would've done the same for me if it was reversed.

"We know you would never do anything to harm her."

"Of course not,"

I couldn't believe what I was hearing. I sucked back the tears, and not because Porky was leaving, but because he understood the situation, probably better than any of us.

"Listen, there's no rush, take your time, if you need me to help you find…" "I already did." Porky blurted out.

"You already did what?"

"When Sal gave me the guns, he also gave me the title to his car, and the deed to his condo."

"He did?"

"Uh huh!"

"Shit, he never even *invited* me to his condo."

"Well, you'll finally get to see it!" Porky said with a smile.

"Oh, and about those magazines? Those were Sal's also, I love them though, you have to check out, some of those stories are crazy!"

I looked at this kid who I would forever claim as my own.

Everything that I was worried about, he made sure to explain, putting me totally at ease.

"I'm good, Rey." Porky once again assured me. And though his body has definitely changed over the years, he still carried around that innocent cherub face. I did feel better though, because it seemed as though Porky didn't ever want to leave on his own, had Rosie not given us this ultimatum, he probably would've never moved on.

I hugged my overgrown buddy, squeezing him with all I had.

"Let's go grab a bite!" Porky invited, attempting to lighten the subject a bit. "My treat!" he added.

"*Your* treat?" I asked, surprised.

"Yeah!" he replied with a huge smile. I grabbed my jacket and keys on our way to the door.

"So which Hot Dog stand you're taking me too?" I teased.

"Come on, Rey. You know there's only one place worthy of a King!" I looked at him, waiting for the punchline, and there it was.

"White Castle!"

CHAPTER 52

Lit Like Times Square

"This is fucking ridiculous!" I yelled as I got up out my seat in the control room and began to pace. Red, Cuba, and Nemesis sat there watching me.

"I mean the stuff isn't bad." Red said. "With the right marketing at least"

"If we have to rely on marketing to have a hit, then we already failed." I replied.

"But every major company relies on marketing, King."

"Oh really, every major company?" I asked, and Red nodded. "Like who?" I watched as he gave it some thought, and then blurted out.

"Coca-Cola"

"Coke already had a superior product, Red. All their marketing did was put the product in front of the masses, and that's what our problem is, we don't have a superior product."

"King, those artists are some of the best voices in the

country." Nemesis added. "Not to mention all the time we invested..." added Cuba.

"Not invested, wasted! There's a fuckin' difference, and yeah, beautiful voices. But nothing special, sorry!

"But you liked, Sarah." Nem said.

"Which was Sarah?" I asked.

"The one you said sounds like Whitney Houston."

"Oh, that's Sarah! Yeah, she was great. Sounded just like Whitney. I just wish I knew what the fuck *Sarah* sounds like!" They look at one another and then back at me.

"Guys, we don't need any Michaels, Madonna's or Whitney's. Those artists already exist. We need new shit."

The door opened, and it was Rosie. She realized we were in the middle of a serious discussion, so she stopped just inside the door and waited.

"Come midnight, *these days* are over, and *tomorrow* arrives. I don't want the shit that's happening these days. I want the shit that's happening tomorrow!"

Cuba began rocking in his chair, giving me this really obnoxious look. So obnoxious that all I wanted to do was kick him in the fucking face. I took a really deep breath to try and calm myself down, before continuing.

"Record stores sell records!" I said low yet stern. "We... need hits!" I added. I stood up straight and looked at Cuba. "Does that make sense to you?" I asked him. His eyes darted toward Red who I could see through my peripheral vision nodding, so Cuba nodded.

"King man, we're doing exactly what everyone else is

doing." Red said.

"Again, that's our problem." They all looked at one another, confused. "We're doing what everyone else is doing."

"It's called following trends." Red replied. That's what businesses do.

"Yes, businesses *follow* trends. I added. "But successful ones set'em." I leaned against the console and looked at each of them, I could tell, I had them thinking.

"People, in just this room alone, I feel we have gold, each of you, are the top in their respected field, mother fucking geniuses if you ask me." I watched as each of their egos began to resurface, including Rosie's. I had to hit them hard because they needed to hear me loud and clear, and now that they were listening. I had to get us all on the same page, with the same goal, and then we had to go do the job.

Red stood up and walked to the wall scratching his chin. His eyes glanced at the photos that decorated it, and then turned back to me and asked. "So how do we know when we're setting trends?"

"Well, that's the fun part, Red. We don't!" I replied with a smile.

"So if we don't know when we're setting trends, how would we know when they'd been set?" Nemesis asked.

"The fans will let us know." I explained.

"But the fans won't know unless we release the track, which means we have to actually create it." Cuba added. "And that's the problem."

"You're absolutely Right!" I answered.

"You're fucking us up, King!" Red responded with a weary laugh. I watched as the other two shook their heads in confusion. Rosie just stood there, against the door.

"So how will we know when we're right?" She joined in.

"You won't know when you're right." I replied, everyone looked at one another as if they were all agreeing, that I was nuts. I gave them all a moment, until I was certain that my last statement had sunk in, and then I added. You'll only know when you're wrong!"

I saw each of their blank and confused looks snap back to life. Their crinkled foreheads began to throb as if the blood that stood still within suddenly broke free.

I remained quiet and just watched, not wanting to interrupt them as they began putting together the pieces. And as each one got it, they turned to me and smiled a confirmation. The dead butterflies that normally stayed afloat resurrected, and a huge weight was lifted.

My wife stepped up and threw her arms around my waist. We kissed and then looked at the guys whose minds were now lit like Times Square!

CHAPTER 53

Safest Place on Earth

"Hey Rey, come in!" Porky said when I knocked on the door to his apartment. He seemed like the old Porky again with his big jolly smile. I stepped inside, my eyes taking in the immediate room with approval.

"This is nice." I said.

"Thanks." Pork replied, following my eyes around the room.

"So you've never been here before?" He asked, already knowing the answer.

"Stop rubbing it in." I replied, and we both laughed.

"I don't know why I thought he lived somewhere in Queens."

"Because that's what he told you. I remember." Porky replied as he gestured for me to give him my jacket to hang up.

"Man, I didn't think you were gonna be out so fast. I would've helped you."

"It wasn't a big deal. All my stuff I just threw in the backseat."

"What about all this?" I asked, referring to the furniture.

"It was all Sal's."

"Really? He sure had some weird taste didn't he?" Porky nodded. "Was this mother fucker colorblind?" We laughed.

"I don't think he cared much about matching. I think he just bought pieces he liked.

"What about your bed?" I asked Pork.

"Nah, I left it… You know, just in case."

"In case what? In case you decide to come back?"

"No. In case you have guess over." He corrected with a smile."

"Since when do we ever have guest over?" I asked as he plopped down in one of the chairs.

I took a seat in the modern couch with the antique cushions.

"Hmm, not bad," I said, snuggling a bit more into it.

"I know right!"

"Hey, I'm sorry, Wha'cha wanna drink?" Porky asked, about to get up. But I stopped him.

"I'm good, thanks." I said, shaking my head.

"Porky, look man, about Rosie…"

"She came to me yesterday when I was packing." Porky interrupted.

"She did?"

"Yeah, in fact, she helped me pack, and then gave me all the groceries she had just bought." He smiled. I was so relieved to hear this.

"She apologized, and then tried to convince me to stay."

"I didn't know this."

"I'm on my own now, Rey, and to be honest..."

"You like it!" I added. Porky smiled and nodded.

My emotions were all over the place at this point. Half of me was happy to see him now a man and on his own. The other half however, was sad to see him go.

He might've been twenty-four years old, six foot six, and three hundred and twenty something pounds, but no matter what...he was my kid!

"I wasn't ready for this Porky." I said to him, my face showing a bit of sadness.

"I wasn't either, but I think it's for the best. Look, I'm not even far from the Funky Junky. I can still pick up Dora from school, and I had promised Rosie, no guns!

"I'm sure Dora's happy about that."

"We both are."

"So you're staying with The Funky Junky, right?"

"Well, yeah, for now at least."

"Come on man, we need you! Everyone's getting fat over there, you seen Cuba lately?" I said, laughing hysterically.

"I told you to get rid of all those vending machines."

"Then I have people leaving the building every five minutes."

"At least they'll be exercising"

As our laughter began to simmer down, we sat there silent, both of us thinking with small burst of laughter still trying to escape.

As much as I wanted to just stay and hang out with him, I did have work to do, and had to get over to the office. Porky watched as I got up, I could tell he was feeling what I was feeling.

"I gotta get back." I said. Porky understood and nodded as he too got up from his seat, but before I could turn to the door he stopped me.

"Rey!" I turned to him.

"What's up?" He was quiet for a moment, looked down at his wooden floor, and then back up at me.

"Thank you, Rey." He said, his eyes dropping once again. I turned my entire body to him and subtly shook my head.

"For what?" I asked, a slight smile on my face.

"For everything!" A lump suddenly appeared in my throat and I had to force it down. "I never told you this before. But I owe my entire existence to you."

"No you don't, don't say that..."

"I do, Rey." I went quiet, and let him talk. "I remember everything Rey, like it was yesterday. I remember when I first saw you, you gave Junior money so that him and I can go eat some Pizza."

"Come on man, no big deal."

"It is when you haven't eaten in three days." I looked up

at him. "I was starving, Rey."

"I had no idea."

"I didn't either at that time, I thought it was normal. Junior used to feel the same way. You ever eat Sweet Peas right out the can?" Porky asked, but all I could do was shake my head. "They're not so sweet Rey, in fact, they're quite nasty, but when you're practically starving, you can't seem to get enough of them.

"Is that why you don't eat'em now?" I asked, and Porky nodded.

"That's why I never understood why I was always so fat. Junior use to say that sometimes he felt like eating me."

"Oh, God!" I replied, trying not to laugh.

"And I believed him."

I couldn't help it, and busted out laughing, though it was probably more so to hide the tears that I could feel rolling.

It was hard listening to everything he was telling me, and even though I used to give them money for Pizza every now and then. Never once did it cross might mind, that maybe, that was all they had to eat.

"When the truck hit us," Porky continued. "And I found out that Junior was killed, the only thing I was happy about was I knew he wouldn't be hungry anymore."

"Man, Porky, I had no idea."

"I know you didn't, Rey. You thought you were just giving a couple of kids some Pizza money. No, Rey, you were feeding us!

I just wanna say thank you. You saved my life. You fed me, gave me a place to call home. You gave me a grandmother, a mom, a little bratty sister, friends… and most of all, a Father!"

And as much as I tried to fight back those tears. I couldn't! Porky pulled me into those huge pythons of his and placed his head on top of mine. I could feel his body relax, as if I had just become the safest place on earth. I felt like a little old rag doll in his arms, and though mine could barely make it half way around his waist, I held him as tight, when suddenly, I felt him kiss me on the top of my head and then whisper… *I love you, Rey!*

CHAPTER 54

Mom and Pops

I sat in the studio listening to some more ideas, and no matter what they played or how good it was, it just wasn't moving me. I couldn't afford to go on a hunch, I needed a sure thing. The song had to be so special that the money would just climb out of my pockets and into the project. If I had to think about it even for a second, it was a no go.

I wasn't mad at anyone because everyone was working hard. Late nights and weekends were the norm at the Funky Junky. I would stay awake at night trying to figure out what was wrong, but I couldn't figure it out for shit.

It was a Sunday afternoon, and I was upset that we were going into yet another week without a project. Porky, Rosie, and Dora walked in which only meant the day was over. They had been walking around the City, doing a little shopping while we worked.

"How's it going?" Rosie asked. We all just sat there. Me swiveling back and forth in my chair looked at her and just shook my head.

Dora rushed over to Cuba and started hitting the keys on his keyboard.

"Dora, leave that alone." Rosie said. But Cuba just waved her off as it was fine. In fact he started showing her a few cool key strokes while we continued talking.

"You don't think you're just asking for too much?" Rosie asked as she went over and sat on the couch.

"I don't think I'm asking for much at all." I replied. Rosie looked at Red, and he looked away. Rosie and Porky laughed.

"You serious?" I asked him. Red got up from his chair. I could tell this shit was all getting to him.

"King, man, we're getting to the point now that as soon as we create something we're knocking it down before you even get a chance to listen to it. We're losing confidence in ourselves. We don't even wonder if the fans would like it anymore. We wonder if *you* would, because apparently that's all that matters.

My eyes glanced over at Cuba who I could tell was listening but occupied himself with Dora. I stared at the floor for a long moment, and then with all sincerity looked back up and said.

"I'm scared of failing!" I suddenly blurted out. Cuba stopped what he was playing but didn't look my way. Everyone else did!

"Remember what you told me, about how you were back in the beginning." Rosie began. "You didn't care who didn't like your Raps, you just rapped, and if they didn't like it, you moved on."

"That's how you got the deal, Rey." Red jumped in. "Had you not made those rounds and took those risk, you would never be where you are today."

"And that's a good thing?" I sarcastically asked.

"That's a great thing!" Rosie stated. Cuba had Dora playing some chords while he played a melody. Rosie continued. "Look at what you have, Rey. You've taken it beyond just being an artist. You've built an empire."

"I wouldn't exactly call it an empire." I replied.

"And maybe that's your problem!" She said. I looked at her waiting for her to explain. "You belittle your own self! It's bad enough we gotta deal with that from the critics, tabloids and fans, but to do it to yourself? Not to mention everyone who looks to you as a leader?"

"It's just that we have way too many obstacles in our way right now."

"Rey, when I was a little kid, and was in the hospital, you came to visit me." Porky joined in. "You told me that obstacles are not made to go around." I looked at him and squinted. I hadn't heard that saying in years. In fact, it was one Grams always told me. "You said, that they're made to go *through*, because once you do that, you've created your own path, and most people like to follow paths already created."

I remembered telling him that, and at that very moment, it made sense. I looked at Rosie, then over at Cuba and Dora as they both played the keyboard together. I looked at Red and he was nodding his head, and then back at Porky.

"They're just obstacles, Rey." Porky repeated, and at that

very moment, I heard something that sounded very familiar. I looked at Cuba who was showing Dora how to play this one particular melody. Red, Rosie and Porky also turned and looked their way.

I tilted my head a bit trying to place the song he was playing. Cuba looked at me with a big smile.

"I like that!" Nemesis said, Red agreed. I knew this song, but from where?

"Isn't that one of your old songs Rey?" Porky asked, and at that very moment, Cuba began to sing the old version of Yes Yes Y'all! My mouth opened wide, as if the dead had suddenly come to life.

"You told me about that song." Rosie said, nodding her head to it.

"It was because of this song that me and King met." Cuba said in between verses. "So you wrote that?" Nemesis asked, also bobbing his head to the rhythm.

"Yeah, but it didn't go quite like that." I replied, and then I started to rap it. Everyone smiled.

"Yo!" Nemesis said, "That's nice." Cuba stopped playing, and we all looked at each other as if a million light bulbs suddenly went off.

"Cuba, play it again from the beginning." He did as I said. I looked over at Red. He remembered the song. "Can you add a beat to that?" Red nodded, and pulled over his drum machine and started playing along. He immediately grabbed the perfect beat, and when he tried to change it, I stopped him and told him to go back to the other beat. He did. I looked at my daughter.

"Let's see what you got." I said, and she smiled. I would talk the line, and she would sing it. We did that a few times until suddenly she went off on her own and took it from there. I was confused. How did she know this song?

Come to find out, Cuba had taught it to her a while back, and they were going to surprise me one day, just as a joke, little did they know, they were seriously on to something.

I looked at Nem, and he smiled. He always knew Dora was it. In fact, they all did. I did too. I just never pushed the idea.

We spent another hour jamming out some ideas before calling it a night. I left there feeling as though this was it. The music was great. The lyrics were mine, and the artist... Well, she was special!

At the end we discussed the category it might fall under. Red kept saying it was Disco, but that scared me as that genre had been dead for several years.

Nem came up with Spanish Hip Hop, and Red changed that to Latin Hip Hop. Still it wasn't meshing with me. Though this music had within it, many different styles, which included some Disco, Hip Hop, Rock, Latin, there wasn't just one that would clearly define it.

"It sounds like Freestyle to me." Dora suddenly said. We all went silent. I turned and looked at her. "Freestyle?"

"Well, yeah, that's what everyone's listening to."

"I never even heard of that?" Nemesis said.

"That's because you're old!" Dora replied, and everyone

started laughing… except Nemesis.

"Hold up!" I jumped in. "Tell me about this Freestyle."

"Remember that group, Evolution that played in Miami when we were there?"

"At the restaurant?"

"Yeah."

"Well, that's the type of music they play. It's called Freestyle."

I looked at Rosie, her brows raised high. I then looked over at the fellas.

"Go hit up a few of the Mom and Pops. Bring back some of that Freestyle shit so we can check it out. The guys seemed excited and quickly got up and gathered their things.

I turned and looked at both my girls… and smiled!

It was as if the flood gates had just burst open. And though the format wasn't exactly new, it was still in its infancy, and therefore a huge opportunity was in place.

I knew this was it. I could feel it, and I would make sure that this time, nothing would get by.

Aside from the new songs we were working on, we also went back into our catalog to see if there was anything else we could possibly revamp with this new sound, and yes there were.

Focusing on this style made clear to us, who our main audience was, and surprisingly, it was the Urban Latino Youth. Basically me, fifteen years earlier!

The music appealed to all youth, due its running theme

about love, being in love, making love, lost a love or simply looking for love, an important subject for those young record buyers.

And for the first time ever, I felt as if I finally caught a wave, and I vowed to ride this mother fucker with all I had.

Red was so tuned into the latest dances, that figuring out beats that worked were a cinch, and Cuba was showing up every morning with melodies he claimed had come to him in dreams.

All that music that Mr. D had us producing, but that we hated, suddenly fit perfectly into what we were doing. Once again, confirming his brilliance. Even dead, this dude was coming up with hits.

After proving to the record company that we were back on track, Solar resigned us to their distribution, but this time, the ball was in *our* court. And though we probably could've asked for anything, all we really wanted was a constant green light, and so *that* we were granted.

Getting in stores was no longer an issue. Our records were everywhere, and now the only problem we were facing was supplying the demand.

In the beginning we were spitting out a new song just about every week, and the moment one of them would start bubbling, we'd get behind it and push hard.

But now we were at the point where we'd have several records, all popping at the same time.

Nemesis no longer had to go out looking for talent. They all now came to him! His job mostly consisted of developing talent rather than finding it, and that weekly release flow we finally had to simmer down.

We promoted Charlotte to her brother's assistant, and the two of them together worked wonders.

Vanessa's roster of dancers nearly tripled, and the wall between her room and the room next door was knocked down to make her place bigger.

We released solo artist, both male and female, as well as groups, duets, and trios. We exhausted every combination you can think of.

CHAPTER 55

A Bunch of Memories

Dora had a decent run, though the only song that popped for her was Yes Yes Y'all. Yeah, it became a Freestyle song, but after a couple of years on the road, she started to realize that this life just wasn't for her. Porky stayed on as her road manager, but the minute she hung up her mic, he was done! Had it not been for Dora I think he would've moved on sooner, but he would never have let her go on the road without him.

The minute the opportunity presented itself, Porky did what he always wanted to do, and joined the Army! He use to talk about it all the time, and I swore he was gonna go right after high school.

He was still young enough to enjoy a great career, I only wished he hadn't been stationed in Germany.

We only got to see him maybe once a year, but we were lucky, 'cause usually it was during the holidays.

We got a good five years in with Solar, but like all good things, it too ended. The Funky Junky was no longer the cool kid in town, but we did have an incredible catalog that kept us well padded.

Tragedy struck home when Rosie was diagnosed with cancer. I swear, had it not been for the people around me, I don't think I would've gotten through it. It was a short battle, and once she was ready to check out… She checked out!

I couldn't function for several months. Porky was able to take an extended leave, so he and Dora ran practically everything.

The studio was hired out, and Cuba and Red were the engineers. Licensing became our main bread and butter, but little by little we had to start letting people go.

Red was offered a great opportunity in Hollywood, and of course I gave him my blessing. Cuba was done! His arthritis made it impossible for him to play anymore. I offered to keep him on, to do basically anything he wanted, but he had a nest egg that he was ready to hatch, and so he moved back to Miami.

Nem and Charlotte had started their own independent label, working from one of the offices in my building. They focused mostly on compilations, licensing songs from The Funky Junky and other companies. They became very successful, and the leaders of that particular market.

They had become really close with Vanessa, and I was letting her run her dance school from the old spot at no charge, until I knew exactly what I was going to do. But the three of them set up a meeting with me one evening and made an offer to take over the building along with everything in it. And though I could've gotten a lot more money from someone else, I gladly took less knowing that it was for them.

And finally! The call I was praying for, when Solar Records made that generous offer to purchase my entire catalog. I wasted no time in closing.

The Funky Junky was now, nothing more than a bunch of memories, some bad, some good, but memories nonetheless.

I rented a small condo in Queens, and one day, Dora came over with her two kids, Rosie and Victor named after their grandmother and uncle.

"Got your mail." She said as she and the kids came over to hug and kiss me, after which the kids ran to the playroom and Dora took a seat in the chair across from me.

"How you doing daddy?"

"I'm good sweetie, a little bored, but good." I replied as I sat down and began sifting through my mail.

"Did you think about what you want to do?"

"Well, I'm too young to retire, so I gotta think of something." I came across a letter, and didn't recognize the name that sent it.

"What is it daddy?" Dora asked when she noticed my eyes begin to flood.

CHAPTER 56

Fades To Black

Dora and I walked into the huge church. At first I didn't recognize anyone, the reason being was because many years had passed, and many of us had changed, some a bit more than others.

All heads turned to us as we made our way down the long aisle towards the front where a row of seats were reserved for those closest to Cuba.

It was then that I began recognizing people, the first being my old buddy Red. He looked at me and smiled, his red hair now a weird orange that surrounded a rather large bald spot. He stood up and waited for me to get to my seat which was right beside his.

We looked at each other for a moment, he I'm sure exploring the lines on my face as well. And then we hugged!

"How you doing, Red?" I said into his ear.

"I'm good, King, how about you?"

"Heartbroken." I replied, my eyes flooding.

"Hey Uncle Red." Dora said, snapping me out of this sad trance I was about to fall into. I watched as they hugged, smiling.

"Oh my God!" He said, turning to me. "It's fucking Rosie, bro!"

"I know." I replied with a laugh and a nod. Suddenly realizing that the last time we saw each other, was at Rosie's funeral.

"Oh my God!" I said, Red and Dora following my gaze.

It was my old buddy, Vanessa. I spotted her huge teethy smile from the other side of the church. I guess she could feel me staring at her, because she suddenly looked my way.

That beautiful trademark smile of hers disappeared as she approached me. She grabbed me and threw her face into my neck, and cried hysterically.

I held her until she simmered down. She pulled back a bit and then pecked me on the lips.

"How you doing, Vee?" I asked, as we stood in front of each other holding hands.

"I don't know Rey, I'm happy, I'm sad… I guess I'm all fucked at the moment, and there it was again, that smile that got me through some really tough times. Dora, stepped up and handed Vee a tissue, and the minute she recognized her she lost it again and the two hugged.

Red stepped up and greeted her as well, and from there we all just started catching up with one another, when I spotted, entering the church, this tall gorgeous girl, I had to remind myself that I was in a church. Heads turned as she made her way down the aisle, and I wondered what her connection might've been with Cuba. Vee caught my eyes and turned to see what I was looking at just as the girl approached us.

"I had to park across the street." The girl said to Vee as the two threw their arms around each other.

"Baby, I want you to meet my family." Vee began as the girl stood in front of us with this huge smile.

Vee looked at me, and sort of laughed to herself. She got me good with that one, and all I could do was look down at the floor, and also laugh to myself.

"That's Red," Vee said pointing at each of us. "Dora and of course...

"King!" The girl herself blurted out!" We all laughed.

"Family, this is Sandra, my girlfriend!" We all practically cheered, embarrassing Vee more than she already was.

"Nice to meet you Sandra, and please, call me Rey." I said as we shook hands

"Sure Rey, and you can call me Sandy,"

"Deal!"

As the others greeted Sandy, I looked over at my homegirl and gave her a thumbs up and a smile, embarrassing her even more.

"I'm a huge fan." Sandra said to me, Vee nodding and pointing behind her.

"If it wasn't for the fact that you and I were friends." Vee said, "I don't think this would've ever happened." Vee joked, her finger pointing back and forth between her and her girl.

"That's not true!" Sandra confirmed, grabbing Vee in her arms.

I loved what I was seeing so far. Vee was a wonderful person, and it was great seeing her happy.

"I'm sorry, but I have to say it." Vee suddenly said interrupting our chit chat. "You are your mama's clone!" She said to Dora in a very serious tone.

Just then, someone grabbed me from behind, and squeezed. Immediately I knew who it was.

"Ah shit!" I said as I turned and looked at Nemesis.

"Sup King!" He said as our hands smacked into a tight shake, and then we hugged.

"Man, look at you!" I said, impressed of what he's turned into.

"Bro, straight up, this is all you!" He replied, his arms held out. "This dude," Nem continued, grabbing everyone's attention "went from being my mortal enemy, to my mother fuckin' savior!"

"Hello, we're in a church!" Said the voice coming up from behind him, and sure enough... It was Charlotte!

"Oh shit!" I suddenly said, before covering my mouth.

Charlotte was always fine. But the years did something unexplainable. She'd now become stunning, though a little money always helps.

"Hey Rey." She said in that soft voice and huge white smile. Dimples as crisp as ever, and her skin still flawless.

This was the first time I've ever hugged her, and God it felt good.

From that point on people kept coming over to say hi, and it was so good to see everyone, but I couldn't help it, my eyes kept shooting toward the entrance as there was one person missing, and I knew the service was about to begin, when suddenly, as if God had heard my prayer, in walked the only man I've ever loved. My son, brother, nephew, friend, whatever he was intended him to be to me, no longer mattered. He was my family, and I adored this guy!

"Porky!" Dora shouted out, and then took off running toward him. If I couldn't wait to see him, I could only imagine how she felt. Those two were like a couple of oddball Siamese twins, connected at the heart.

I watched as Dora jumped up on him, wrapping her arms and legs tightly around him, kissing him over and over all over the face. Porky loved it.

When he saw that she wasn't letting go, he continued walking toward us. We were all laughing as we watched him come down the aisle. He held his arms out to the sides to show us, he wasn't even holding her, but then wrapped them back around her.

Once they made it to us, Dora got down, her eyes still latched on to his, Vee held out one of the many boxes of tissues scattered throughout the church.

This was the first time I'd seen him since Rosie's funeral, and he looked great. Big and stronger than ever, his uniform, decorated with so many stripes and metals, this kid made me so proud!

"Hey Rey," He said, looking down at me, and the minute I heard that voice, that same voice that I remember ever since he was a little kid, laid up in the hospital... I lost it! and grabbed my boy with all I had!

"I'm so glad you're here." I whispered, between whimpers.

"I wouldn't have missed it," he replied, and I knew he was telling the truth, 'cause that's the type of guy he was. Though the circumstances could've been better, this had become such a beautiful reunion.

The lights in the church began to flash, indicating that the ceremony was about to begin. I sat in the middle with my kids on both sides of me and held both their hands.

"His name is Carlos Quinones." The Pastor, standing at the podium began," but to those who knew him well, we called him Cuba!" I looked around and it seemed like every one of the three hundred plus people seated, and standing nodded.

The Pastor, starting from Cuba's parents told us his story. Well, little did I know, the Pastor was his younger brother!

The Pastor then welcomed Red to the Podium. Red was the closest of us all, and stayed in touch with Cuba until his last days.

Red had moved away from music, and had gotten into film, and so was able to put together a nice little tribute video that played on a huge screen right above Cuba's closed casket.

The music that played in the background was clearly that of Cuba and Red as together they had such a signature sound.

The video was basically a visual version of the story just told by the Pastor. Cute baby pictures of Cuba in a nightie and bonnet, made the audience go aw!

The photos displayed were remarkable and you could tell that a lot of work was put into it.

At the end of the video the lights remained low until we can hear my old buddy's voice. The unfocused image began to clear, and there, propped up in bed, not looking bad at all, was Cuba.

"Now?" he asked the cameraman. "Okay... Hi everybody!" He said with one of those exaggerated Little Rascal waves. "Well, if you're watching this now, it can only mean one thing... I'm dead!"

And of course, no one was able to help it, everyone laughed!

The image on the screen became blurry as my eyes were flooding. I blinked hard, and could feel one of the tears break loose and roll down my cheek. I glanced to the side, and realized that Dora was watching me.

"There are probably only three of you in here, so I'm sorry to take up your time, and I'll try and make it quick." Again everyone laughed. "But this message is for one person in particular. You're sure he'll be there right?" Cuba again asked the cameraman.

"I promise." Replied the cameraman, confirming indeed that it was, Red. I looked over at him, and he smiled.

"King!" He began, "I told them to make sure you have a front row seat!" Everyone laughed.

"I do!" I yelled out, half laughing and half crying, waving at the screen. I swear, for a moment it seemed as if he looked right at me, and smirked.

"If anyone would've asked me before you and I met, how many more years did I expect to live, I would've told them, *not many!"* I looked down into my lap and wiped my eyes, then back up at the screen. "But you came to me, and blew some new life into me."

"Hey, I didn't blow anything!" I yelled out again at the screen. I realized that the Pastor caught that, and so I mouth to him the word, *sorry!*

"I just wanna say, thank you, hermano, thank you for everything you did for me."

"Thank *you*, Cuba!" I replied, this time low and to myself. Dora squeezed my hand and Porky placed his arm over my shoulder. I swear, I felt like a baby, cuddled by his parents.

"Now, I have a little something for you. I hope you like it. Unfortunately I am probably not going to be around to see how it turns out, so if it's great, it was all my idea. If it sucks, well then, it's Red's fault!" the laughter in this place, just wouldn't stop.

"I love you, King. And everyone else whose day I interrupted, thank you too for coming, God bless you, and until we meet again, I present to you, this…"

The screen fades to black, as colored spotlights begin to light up the stage, and a mob of little kids dressed in 80's Hip Hop apparel skip out to the original beat of Yes Yes Y'all.

Break Dancers, Graffiti Artists, and a kid that could easily play me in my own Docudrama. I couldn't believe what I was seeing and hearing as the entire house stood up and began dancing at their seats.

Suddenly, a little fat kid walks out who I could tell by the white bathrobe he wore that it was supposed to be Cuba. He got behind a keyboard followed by a little black kid with fiery red hair. It made so much sense, and everyone got it. He got behind a drum machine.

They began playing Yes Yes Ya'll in the Freestyle version, with a little girl singing it, we all laughed and looked at Dora who suddenly blushed. At that moment we realized that everyone on that stage represented someone in Cuba's life.

I looked around and saw people from the audience that I didn't even know point themselves out in the ensemble. This was an incredible production, and we all laughed when Porky walked out. For him, they used a grown up!

My heart melted when I noticed the tall skinny kid with the shades on, just sitting in the corner, reading the paper and drinking coffee. Then out stepped this cute little spunky girl, wearing jeans, sneakers, and a King tee-shirt, her hair up tight in a bun, with a phone wedged between her ear and shoulder while taking notes. I looked over at Red, and smiled. What an incredible tribute this was, not just to Cuba, but to us all, my eyes couldn't thank him enough. Then finally, it all faded to black.

THE END

Dear Reader

I just wanted to take a moment to personally thank you for reading Book 3 of Yes Yes Y'all, and though the dream of many authors is to one day have a Best Seller, and move a million copies, mine on the other hand is simply to move you!

Whether my stories make you laugh, cry, scream, or just allow you to share with my characters, their incredible journeys, I pray that you could find in them, something just for you. It could be the answering of a long grueling question, making you think about something you've never before giving thought, or just remind you to tell that special someone, that you love them.

Though none of the books so far are autobiographical, they do however run a parallel dimension to my own life, and therefore knowing them is in fact, knowing me!

I intend on writing until life's last page, when God finally says, The End! But until then, it would mean so much to me, if we could stay connected.

By logging on to Latifmercado.com, and subscribing to my mailing list,- you'll receive my Newsletter, alerts of anything new coming out of the La' Camp, Freestyle events headed your way, and of course exclusive gifts and offers just for you!

Thank you again, and I'll see you soon

Your friend

Latif

About The Author

Latif Mercado has been a part of the Freestyle Music scene for well over 25 years, and though his role in the beginning was minimal, the role he's been playing ever since, has been massive, and a major force behind the genre's continued success.

As a Booking Agent with a who's who roster of Freestyle Legends, as well as his managerial involvement with such industry icons as Lil' Suzy and The Cover Girls, rarely would you find a Freestyle event happening without Latif somewhere in the mix.

In an attempt to make people aware of the fact that Freestyle isn't just a music, but rather a culture, La' began writing books, in hopes of reaching fans through a medium they would never expect, and in 2011, his debut novel, FREESTYLE FOR LIFE, did just that!

Since then, Latif has released several books that, not only feature Freestyle as part of its overall theme, but also its main characters of Latin decent.

Though born and raised in New York, Latif currently resides in North Carolina with his wife, two grown children, four grandkids and a dog named Coco.

Latif loves hearing from his readers, answering questions, and sharing whatever advice he possibly can, whether it be on writing, or maybe something Freestyle related, so be sure to reach out, even if it's just to say hi.

For more information on Latif, or to connect with him on the various platforms, please go to LatifMercado.com

Books By LA'

FREESTYLE FOR LIFE

FEASTYLE

FREESTYLE PROMOTIONS
And the 7 Simple Steps To Getting Started

HOW TO BOOK A FREESTYLE ARTIST
IN 5 EASY STEPS

YES YES Y'ALL Book 1

YES YES Y'ALL Book 2

YES YES Y'ALL Book 3

COMING SOON

FRUITS & NUTS
A Novel by Latif Mercado

www.ingramcontent.com/pod-product-compliance
Lightning Source LLC
Chambersburg PA
CBHW070158260626
47160CB00002B/379